HOUND

MEASHA STONE

1

_____

Who knew gathering dirt on the rich and powerful could be so stressful? At least it was lucrative work.

Keagan rubbed the knot in the back of her neck while the driver rounded the last turn and took her up the drive. The night had been successful, but every muscle in her body ached. Working high-profile jobs always put her on edge.

She sighed and pulled her phone out of her purse.

Back in town.

The text put a smile on her lips. What better way to unwind than spending a no-strings-attached night with someone who understood what she needed?

Before she could type out a response, her car door was yanked open.

"Keagan, come quickly!" Sam, one of Elliot

Jansen's personal guards reached into the back of the car and held out his hand.

"What's wrong?" She let him lead her up the steps to the house. The night had been a success; she had several files on the flash drive tucked away in her purse to hand over. And she wasn't even late.

Sam cast a compassionate glance down at her and opened the main doors. She stepped into the house, expecting a whirlwind of activity, but the house was quiet.

"He's in the back room." Sam closed and bolted the front doors and went ahead of her down the long corridor to the back of the house.

Elliot Jansen stood at the fireplace, staring into the roaring, orange flames. The summer night was warm enough to need the central air, not a fire.

"Mr. Jansen? What's wrong?" She stepped down the single step into the family room.

Elliot Jansen turned toward her, not moving from the fireplace. His eyes were downcast, and a frown had settled on his lips. The thick-rimmed glasses he always wore had slipped down his nose.

"Keagan." He said her name as though it brought pain. He pulled his hand out of pocket and wiped it across his face. "Keagan, there's been a terrible accident."

Her heart screeched to a halt.

"What happened?" She hurried across the room toward him.

"Keagan—" His face paled slightly. "There was a plane crash, no survivors."

She gripped her handbag, her nails digging into the leather. Her mind raced, and names of associates she'd come to consider friends over the past years flashed through her mind. Working for Jansen, one of the most powerful families in Kassel, meant she could be sent to any number of places. Danger lurked everywhere, even for her.

"Katarina was on the plane." His words fell from his lips as easily as bombs tossed from a military jet. The reaction was the same.

An explosion of pain and confusion enveloped her. She stared at him, willing him to take it back. Say something else. Someone else's name.

Not her.

Not the foster mother who had raised her since she'd been a small child.

"No." Keagan stepped back, as though she could avoid the reality he'd just thrust at her.

"Keagan. I know...I know this is hard." He waved to Sam, who made his way over to her and helped her to the couch. She sank into the comfort of the cushions, but her mind continued to reel. Katarina was on a plane.

"I...I don't understand. She just arrived in Fairfax,

why would she be traveling again so soon?" She blinked. They must have the wrong person. Katarina was on vacation. She'd escaped Kassel for a month-long excursion overseas. She'd told Keagan she'd rented a house on the ocean for a month. She was looking to relax, not go anywhere.

Katarina had retired from Jansen's employment two years ago, making way for Keagan to step into her place. It was good money, and although Keagan had finished her degree in computer sciences, she had no plans to be tied down to a cubicle in the corporate world. Even while retired, Katarina had helped Keagan set up. But now that Keagan was fully emerged, Katarina could enjoy herself more.

She'd earned it.

"I'm not really sure." Elliot shrugged. "I'm told she decided to go on a safari. The plane went down just as they were arriving."

Safari?

Keagan blinked. Katarina didn't even like animals —she'd forbidden Keagan from having so much as a hamster growing up. Why would she be going on a safari?

"How do you know she was on the plane?" Keagan grabbed onto a slim thread of hope and pulled. "I mean, why didn't the airline call me?"

Jansen's eyes hardened. Being questioned, even in

a situation such as this one, wasn't something he took kindly to.

"I'm sorry." She shook her head. "I'm just...well...I don't understand."

"Of course. It's a lot to take in," he said, but his tone still suggested he wasn't as understanding. With him being the head of the family, she should just take the information he gave her and leave with it. But still, she sat there on his couch, staring at him as though he were something out of a horror movie.

Katarina had raised her to be respectful of Elliot Jansen. He was a powerful man, and he could help them a great deal, but he could also squash them if he wanted to. Not being his blood relation anyway, Katarina counted them lucky to have been given the opportunity to work for him without having to find a job in one of his night clubs or his underground businesses.

Keagan's phone vibrated in her purse, but she ignored it.

"What...uh..." She rose, brushed her hands over her skirt, then drew a deep breath. "What do I do now? I mean, who do I call to get her...to bring her home so I can arrange things?"

"I'm putting someone on that. You don't need to do anything. I'll let you know once it's been arranged." He gestured toward her. "Take some time. I know this was a bit of a shock."

She blinked. A tear slipped down her cheek, and she dashed it away with her fingertips.

"Before you go, did you get the drive?" he asked.

She paused a moment, having to force her brain back on the right track. His news had completely derailed her.

"Uh, oh, yes!" She reached into her purse and grabbed the slim drive. "I think you'll get what you need from what I was able to download."

He took the device and pocketed it. "Good. Once I have a look at it, a deposit will be made for you." He glanced at Sam. "Now isn't the time, but soon we should discuss your contract."

Keagan willed her mind to focus. The pain in her chest would have to wait. She would get through this without crumbling. She just needed that focus. Elliot Jansen's family room wasn't the place to break into a million pieces.

"Contract?" she asked.

He pushed his glasses further up his nose. "Well, like I said, we can talk another time, but...well...I never put you on a contract because you were Katarina's daughter. But now...with what's happened...I really will need something from you that tells me you won't run off on me if trouble happens."

He was questioning her loyalty?

"But we can talk another time." He waved a hand at her, his lips puckered with faux concern.

"Sure. Okay." She nodded numbly. Was saying no an option? Did she want the ability to walk away? Katarina hadn't talked about living outside the Jansen network, so she'd never considered it something she could do.

"Keagan, the car's still outside," Sam said softly from the doorway.

She looked over at him. His brow wrinkled, and his hands were firmly gripped in front of him.

"Oh, right." She drew a long breath. "Thank you, Mr. Jansen for letting me know."

"Of course. And my deepest condolences." He pressed a hand to his chest and gave her a sympathetic glance. "Go on home now, and I'll be in touch soon."

She gave a nod because it seemed the right thing to do, then followed Sam back out of the house. Every step felt as though she were dragging her feet through quicksand. By the time she made her way back into the car, she could barely breathe, so heavy was the weight of the pain.

"I really am sorry, Keagan," Sam said then closed the door. The driver pulled away instantly, whisking her off the Jansen estate toward her townhouse in the middle of downtown—the only place she'd called home in her life. But without Katarina it wasn't a home at all.

Her phone buzzed again, and out of habit, she pulled it out.

Meet up at ten, usual place?

She put her phone back in her purse and leaned her head into the window.

Jansen wanted to put her on contract. That was good, right? Being linked to him instead of just grabbing whatever crumbs he threw at her? Katarina would want that, right?

Her mind clouded with questions while her heart broke.

Katarina was gone.

Now what?

2

—————

Jackson Titon rolled over in the king-sized bed fitted with the softest sheets his bare skin had ever touched. He wasn't one for extreme luxury, but when it came to his sleep—he took it seriously.

"Hey, handsome." The soft voice of last night's pick reminded him he wasn't alone. And, this wasn't his bed.

Blinking his eyes open, he grinned into the emerald green eyes pinned on him. Her box-colored red hair was already brushed and swept into a high ponytail, and last night's makeup had been washed off and perfectly reapplied.

"Morning all ready?" He stretched his arms over his head. He hadn't meant to spend the night, but a few brandies after dinner, plus the few drinks he'd enjoyed at the Annex party had made the call of the siren's sweet bed all the more tempting. Plus, those sheets.

"Almost afternoon, actually." She laughed. "I'd let you keep sleeping, but Ash is looking for you." She scooted off the other side of the bed, fully dressed. When she turned, he caught sight of her ass. It had been a fun and very successful and satisfying night, but the sun had come up and with it, his responsibilities.

Jackson rolled off the bed and grabbed his clothes that had been randomly tossed about the room.

"You can shower if you want," Aubry said as she sat at the vanity. "There's a shower room attached to the suite." He'd contracted not only her, but an overnight suite in the Annex. The girls weren't allowed to take the clients up to their private apartments, so if a client wanted overnight accommodation, they needed to rent out the suite.

An excellent business model.

"Thanks, but I'll grab one in my room," he said, buttoning his jeans.

She paused and looked at him through the mirror. "Your room?"

"Yeah." He yanked his T-shirt over his head and tucked it into his jeans. Where was his belt? Glancing around the room, he found it dangling off the end of the bed.

That's right. It had been put to good use last night.

"In the main house. I'm staying with Ash for a few days until my shit is moved into my place."

She continued to stare at him.

"He's my cousin," Jackson offered.

She lowered her gaze. "You're Jackson Titon?" She turned in the chair with a surprised expression.

"I told you last night."

"You just said your name was Jackson, and you definitely didn't mention you were my boss' cousin." Her smile waned.

"Would you have taken my contract if you'd known?" He slid the thick leather belt through the loops of his jeans.

Her eyes wandered down to his movements. Clearly the memory of last night played in her mind.

"Probably not." She recovered her brilliant smile. "But I'm glad I did."

He chuckled. "Yeah, me too, babe."

"If you're going to go up to the main house and shower before you see Ash, you better hurry." She sauntered over to him and pressed a soft kiss to his cheek. "I'm meeting some friends for lunch, so I have to get changed out of this and into something more... well, brunch acceptable." She swept her hand over the light blue satin nightgown and sheer robe.

"I'd say you're pretty acceptable right now." He winked.

She shook her head with a laugh. "Don't start getting cheesy on me. Now hurry, or Ash is going to start pounding down the door for you," she warned before taking her leave.

JACKSON CHECKED his phone for messages one last time before leaving his room to meet with Ashland and Peter. The movers were going to arrive in a few hours, and he would have to get over to the house to make sure everything was taken care of. But first, his meeting with his cousins.

"There you are. He's been waiting." Peter met Jackson on the stairs as he was on his way down to the first floor of the house.

"I needed a shower." Jackson slapped his hand on Peter's shoulder. "It was for your benefit as much as mine."

Peter laughed. "Rough night?"

"Nothing I couldn't handle." Jackson followed Peter down the long hallway toward Ashland's office. He admired the artwork on his way. Many of the pieces were new to him, having been changed out from what his Uncle Samuel had used in his decor.

"These are all new," Jackson commented as they reached Ash's office.

"Yeah, most of them are Ellie's, but there're a few

pieces that belonged to Aunt Janet. Ellie found them up in the attic and had them brought out here." Peter opened the office door.

"Ellie's really talented." He leaned in to inspect the signature on the last painting. A gargoyle poised proudly on the highest tower of a castle overlooking a village. "Maybe she wouldn't mind letting me buy a few pieces for my place?"

"If you're done admiring my wife's work, can we get on with this?" Ashland's voice traveled from within his office.

"Get on with this?" Jackson repeated, passing Peter and entering the office. No matter Ash's wife's talent, the office had Ashland written all over it. It still held an ominous appeal, with the dark paintings, the deep purple draperies and the electrical sconces on the wall.

"I have a meeting this afternoon." Ash made a show of checking his watch.

Peter closed the office door. "What he means is, he's glad you're here, and we've missed you." Peter slapped Jackson's shoulder.

"I'm sure that's what he meant." Jackson laughed and took a seat in the armchair. "It's good to be back in Kassel, though. I will admit that."

Ash sank into his chair behind his desk and steepled his hands. "I am glad you're home, cousin, but, I do have a meeting to get to, so what's your business proposition?"

Jackson rolled back his shoulders. "Not so much a proposition as well, I don't want to go doing shit behind your back."

Ash's eyebrows rose.

"Elliot Jansen wants to do business with me. The liquor distribution I had set up in Hammelin is still working, I have men watching over it, and I'm overseeing it from here. But I want to expand into Kassel. Jansen's restaurants and dance club give me that opportunity, but I know you pulled the Titon family out of all dealings with the big families, so I wanted to bring this to you before I went ahead with anything."

"Jansen?" Peter sat in the second armchair and hooked his foot over his knee. "He came to you?"

Jackson cocked his head. "No. One of my guys knows a few of his crew; they worked together a long time ago. He made introductions."

"You don't fall under my authority," Ashland said. "This family isn't like what it used to be. My father kept everyone on tight leashes."

Jackson knew that fact well enough, his own father having been run out of town because he wanted too big of a piece of the Titon family. Second sons weren't important to Samuel Titon. Thankfully, his son saw things better.

"I don't want to go into business with anyone that's not clean with you, that's all," Jackson said.

"Like you said. I broke all ties with the families." Ash leaned forward. "But I don't want him thinking he's doing business with the Titon family. He's doing business with Jackson Titon only."

Jackson's jaw tightened. "Of course."

"Don't get pissed," Peter interjected. "It's not that we don't see you as a Titon, because you are. Blood is blood. But Jansen might see this as a way to get Ash or myself back in the game."

"There's one more thing." Jackson wanted to jump away from the subject of family ties. He was family, and Ash had never treated him other than that, but there was still a bitterness to it all. Samuel hadn't allowed Jackson's father to work in any of the Titon businesses as punishment for trying to strike out on his own, forcing him from Kassel.

Samuel's death had ended the coldness between the branches of the family, but by that time Jackson's own father had been on his deathbed. It had taken years for Jackson to feel ready to move his life back to Kassel.

"Okay, what is it?" Ash prompted.

"I want to buy in to the Annex." Jackson stared directly at Ash.

Peter shifted in his chair.

"Buy in?" Ash rose from his desk.

"Yeah. I don't want a partnership or anything like

that, but I want a piece of it. I'm willing to invest." Jackson leaned back in his chair.

"And how does that look to Jansen and other people you do business with?" Ash asked.

"It looks like nothing. My distribution business has nothing to do with Titon family business, like you said."

The door to the office opened, drawing everyone's attention.

"Daniel." Ash's jaw tensed. "What the hell?"

"Ash, I demand you take care of this right away." An older gentleman pushed Ash's man out of his way and barged into the office.

"Stanley." Ash waved Daniel away. "You don't just barge into my office."

"I understand," Stanley said, though he had no indications of actual remorse. "But one of your girls robbed me, and I demand you do something about it!" His voice boomed and his face reddened.

Ash raised his left eyebrow and stepped toward the intruder. As Peter stood from his chair, Jackson did the same. Whatever this fucker thought he was going to accomplish pushing his way into Ash's office, was probably not going to happen.

"First of all, lower your fucking voice. My kids are upstairs napping, and I won't let you wake them up." Ash's voice mellowed into a deep tenor. "Second of all, my girls don't need to rob anyone. So what the hell are you talking about?"

Ash's two toddler sons probably were taking a nap, but their rooms were too far away to hear anything happening in Ash's office. Considering the sorts of people he dealt with daily, he would never allow the boys to be in earshot of his conversations or other activities.

"Last month," Stanley started after a large huff, "I contracted one of your girls for the evening after meeting her at a catalogue party."

Ash maintained a bland expression, but Jackson could see the irritation in his eyes. Stanley needed to get to the heart of the issue quickly.

"Go on," Peter urged him.

"We met twice outside of the Annex, during which the last time she accessed my bank account and wiped clean one of my savings accounts." His voice rose toward the end of his explanation, but he clamped his mouth shut probably to stop himself from raging again.

"Who's the girl?" Peter stepped closer to them.

"Her name was Foxy Lady," Stanley explained. "She never gave me her real name."

"Foxy Lady?" Jackson asked with some levity. None of the girls he'd met the night before used stage names.

The scar over Peter's left eye stretched as he raised his brow. "We don't have any girls here by that name."

"That's the name she gave." Stanley dug out his phone from his inside pocket.

"The girls here don't use stage names, Stanley. And if they did, they wouldn't be so cheesy," Peter assured him.

"I have a photo." Stanley slipped his finger over the screen several times.

"How do you have a picture?" Ash demanded. "We don't allow pictures in the Annex. You know that. Your phone shouldn't have even been in there."

Stanley looked up from the screen, a slight panic danced in his eyes. "I know. I know. I didn't take the picture. She did with her phone, and then she sent it to me. So I would have her contact information." He explained, swiping faster through his phone.

"The girls aren't allowed camera phones when they're working and sure as hell not during a party." Peter stepped closer, his hand outstretched for the phone.

"Here." Stanley flipped the phone around to show them but held it back so Peter wouldn't take it.

A light ignited in Jackson's chest at the sight on the screen. Dark wavy hair framed her face. Burnt red lipstick covered her plump lips. She was smiling in the photo, with little crinkles around the edges of her deep brown eyes. It almost made him grin in return.

"She's not one of ours," Peter said firmly. "You met her here?"

"Yes. Here at the party three weeks ago," Stanley said.

"How much did she steal?" Ash asked.

"Two hundred grand, Ash." He gave Ashland a pointed look.

Ash stared at the phone for a long moment. "She's not one of mine, Stanley."

"I met her here. I don't give a fuck if she's contracted with you or not. I came here for a night of fun, and now I have a zeroed-out bank account."

"And you blame me?" Ash demanded with a hard tone.

"Like I said, I met her here." Stanley shoved the phone back into his jacket.

"Have you tried contacting her since you found your account empty?" Jackson asked.

"Of course." Stanley nodded. "The number is disconnected."

"Where did you meet her outside of here?" Jackson continued.

"At a motel downtown."

"How did she manage to get into your account?"

Stanley's cheeks reddened. "She went into the bank and closed it."

"She closed the account?"

"Yes. I had the account in my daughter's name as

primary holder – it was her college fund account. This...woman, walked in with my daughter's information and closed the account."

Jackson wiped his mouth to cover the grin playing on his lips. Sly little fox.

"What would you like us to do, Stanley? You obviously gave her access to things she needed in order to do such a thing."

"I want my money back," he demanded. "If this is the sort of thing that can happen to a man coming to the Annex for a good time, I'm not sure it's a safe place to play any longer."

Ash sighed. If word got around town that theft happened under his careful watch, it would hurt business. A lot. Right now, Ash was the only man in town who offered the sort of women he did with as much protection for the girls as the customer. If people began to suspect they could be victims of forgery and thievery while satisfying their thirst for the wicked, the waitlist to be invited to the parties would dry up.

"We'll find her," Jackson spoke up, causing Ash and Peter to whip their heads to the side to stare at him. "You'll get your money back."

Stanley's posture relaxed. "That's what I want to hear."

"We'll need some time, but we will track her down. If you could just send any photographs you have of her that would help." Jackson took a card from his wallet and handed it to him. "Just forward them to my phone."

"I'll do that right now." Stanley retrieved his phone and started tapping on his phone, swiping through the photographs. The rest of them watched as he repeated the process half a dozen times. Did they have a fucking photoshoot?

"I'll call you once we have something." Ashland gestured toward the door.

"I hope that's sooner rather than later. I don't want to have this conversation with my wife." He gave a curt nod then stalked out of the office, letting the door slam on his way out.

After a moment of silence, Ash turned his questioning stare on Jackson.

"I know her," Jackson said after letting several silent seconds tick by. "Knew her, actually."

"Oh?" Peter folded his arms over his chest.

"Her name is Keagan Foxx. I met her a few years ago."

"You dated this woman?" Ash's eyes widened.

Jackson laughed. "I wouldn't call what we did dating."

Ash's jaw tensed beneath his thick beard. With his shoulder-length hair and the jagged scar along his cheek, he looked as beastly as his reputation made him out to be, but Jackson hadn't been afraid of his older cousin since they were kids.

"She lives in Kassel?" Peter interjected before Ash could respond.

"She did when I knew her. On the north side, at the border."

"If I remember correctly, hunting is something you were good at," Ash muttered. For a time that Jackson worked directly for his father, he had the job of tracking down people who didn't want to be found. He hadn't let anyone get past him. Every man who needed hunting down had been found.

"Give me a few days." Jackson pulled his phone out and swiped it to life. Stanley's messages came through. "I'll find her and the money."

Ash gave a short nod. "You do that, and we'll talk about you buying in shares in the Annex." Ash offered his hand.

He'd get to hunt down Keagan Foxx, and he'd get everything he came home for. It was a win-win for him.

Jackson shook his cousin's hand.

"Consider it done."

3

K eagan snagged a glass of champagne from a passing tray and sank deeper into the room, away from the loud commotion of celebratory cheers. She found a comfortable spot near the patio doors where she could keep an eye on her mark, but blend into the background.

Apparently, a crash in a major stock brought cause for celebration to this particular group. The workers who lost jobs, health insurance, and any sort of financial security would probably disagree. She shoved the ire over the injustice of it down and drowned her irritation with the overly sweet champagne.

The past two years had taught her more than any book in school could have. Those who held small amounts of power were hungry for more, and they'd eat anything that had what they wanted. It was this level of gluttony that gave her such an easy way to earn a living.

Taking another small sip of her drink, she watched Mr. Potier throw his head back with another of his forced laughs. He slapped the arm of the man he was conversing with and shook his head while adding another quip to the conversation. Whatever they were talking about, Keagan wished they'd hurry up. She needed to get Herald Potier, owner of Potier Finer Brews, away from the crowd, and to a more private venue.

Although, she'd managed to have a short conversation with him earlier, she hadn't made any progress since. There wasn't need for concern yet, he would finish his circle around the room with his jokes and pleasantries, but then he'd be back at the bar. And that's when she would move closer to him.

"That's an awfully serious face for such a festive party." The deep voice sounded behind her.

Taking the interruption in stride, she plastered on a flirtatious smile and turned. Potier still had a short way to go before he made his way to the bar for his final drink of the night. She could placate this man then send him on his way. But when her gaze met with the man behind the voice, her throat clenched.

"Jackson." She breathed out his name and gripped the glass tighter as it began to slip from her grasp.

Jackson Titon, a faded memory from a previous life, stood before her.

He blended well into the scenery with his well-tailored suit, his dirty blonde hair slicked back stylishly from his face, and his confident posture. His grayish-blue eyes held her captive for a long moment.

"Keagan. I was right, it is you." He flashed a wide grin – the same one she had found mesmerizing when they first met. His deep dimple was buried beneath a thick beard now, but her reaction was the same.

She blinked a few times, breaking the spell. Mr. Potier would be headed her way soon, and the likes of Jackson would likely scare him away.

"What brings you here tonight?" She turned slightly to be able to keep Potier in her sideview. A few kind words, and she'd shoo Jackson away.

"I was just about to ask you the same question," he said, moving closer to her.

She sipped her drink, turning her attention back to the main crowd of the room.

"I don't remember you this quiet," he commented.

"I'm sorry, I was lost in a thought." She caught a glimpse of Potier moving toward another group, his glass nearing empty. He would be downing the rest soon then head toward the bar soon. At that point, she needed to be there to meet him.

"It was nice to see you again..." She took a step

toward the bar but was stilled when he placed his hand on her arm.

"Don't run off so fast." It wasn't a flirtatious request, but rather a deep-rooted demand.

"I really do need to go—" Her words dried on her tongue with the stern look he pinned on her.

"I just need a second, Foxy Lady."

She froze.

"Careful you don't spill your drink." His grin widened.

She tried to tug free of his grip, but he was holding her too firmly.

"Jackson, I don't know what you're thinking, but I really do need to go." She glanced at the bar where Potier was moving toward the bartender waving his empty glass in the air. If she didn't get there in time, she'd miss her chance. Without a direct introduction, the only way she would get close enough to him was a chance meeting. The exact sort she'd spent the better half of a month arranging to happen right now.

The bastard took his work seriously. He rarely socialized in public, and getting a meeting with him was damn impossible. Every angle she'd tried to get near him had failed. The party was her way in, and Jackson was ruining it.

"I'm sure you do," Jackson said.

Potier moved into her line of sight of the bar.

"Whatever you have planned for the evening isn't going to happen."

She shot her gaze up to his. "What do you want?" Better to get the conversation over with so she could make her move.

"For starters, I'm going to need the money you stole from Stanley McKinnley; then I'm going to need you to come back to Kassel with me." He brushed her hair from her shoulder and leaned into her ear. "I have some questions for you, and my cousin's interested as well."

She jerked away from him, spilling some of her champagne in the process.

"I have no idea what you're talking about. But I have to go." She spun around and headed toward the bar quickly, before he could grab hold of her again. But when she approached the bar, Potier was nowhere to be seen. She searched the crowded party and spotted his stark white hair just as he sauntered out of the room.

Fuck.

"Oh, did you miss your mark?" Jackson slid up beside her at the bar, resting his elbow on the edge and gazing at her with faux sympathy.

She tensed her jaw and slammed the champagne flute onto the bar.

"Can I get you something else?" the bartender

asked, picking up the glass and wiping away the spilled droplets.

"She'll have a glass of white wine," Jackson answered for her.

With her hands balled into fists, she turned her anger on him. "You bastard." She kept her voice low, but the couple walking past them glanced her way. "I don't know what you're really doing here or what you think you know about anything, but you just fucked up everything! I don't know when I'll get this chance again."

He grabbed her arm, pulling her toward him an inch and lowered his mouth until it was a scarce breath from her ear. "I know you stole two hundred grand from old Stanley, and you used my cousin's Annex party to do it," he said in a low growl that sent a familiar tingle down her spine.

Okay, so he knew what had happened between her and Stanley at the Annex, but that didn't give him the right to fuck up her job tonight. She could have gotten important information from Potier, and a few dollars if she'd played him right. Now she'd have to go back to square one and find a way to get to him again.

"How does that have anything to do with you?" she asked, attempting to tug free. The man had a grip like a damn hound dog.

"You used my cousin's business, snuck into his party, pretended to be one of his employees, and now one of his customers is threatening to warn others about attending the catalogue parties. That has everything to do with me," he explained, leveling her with a piercing glare. Those damn blueish-gray eyes still sent shivers through her body, even after all the years spreading out between their last tryst.

"What do you want? A refund?" She gave up on fighting his grip and curled her lips. If she got annoyed enough, maybe he'd just shove her away.

He gave a joyless chuckle. "First, you're going to give back the fucking money, and second, you're going to sit down with me and Ash and explain exactly how you got into his party."

That wasn't going to happen. She hadn't just waltzed into the catalogue party; Ash kept his security team tight. The party was basically a locked down event. It had taken planning and some help to get around the security. There was no fucking way she was turning on any member of the Jansen family. Snitches didn't merely get stitches when they turned on the family.

"We don't need to go all the way back to Kassel for that. I can tell you right now. I walked in." She smiled up at him, curling her toes in her too-high heels to brace against the pain of his fingers digging into her bare arm.

"You just walked in?" he asked in disbelief. Fooling him wouldn't be so easy. Jackson knew her as well as anyone could know her—they'd played around years ago. He'd see through any lie she told him, so going for half-truths would be the only way out of this. And she had, in fact, walked into the party.

"Yes. Now will you let go of my arm?"

"The money?" He pulled her toward him again.

"I don't have it anymore. So you're out of luck on that front." How else would she have funded her current investigation? Jansen paid well, but some wheels needed a lot more grease than she had on hand. Stanley McKinnley's contribution had been necessary to make tonight possible.

"Well, then I guess our business will have to take us back to Kassel." His full lips spread into a wide grin. She would have thought it playful years ago, but his fingertips went deeper into her arm. He wasn't playing.

She didn't have time for this. She had to get things back on track. Ashland Titon could deal with a little disgruntled client on his own. He'd give him a free pass at a few of the Annex girls, and he'd be happy.

"Jackson, just let me go. I'll be back in Kassel next month, and we can deal with it then. Right now, I really need to go." She put on a layer of charm that worked well enough to get her out of most jams.

"The only place you're going is with me," he said, straightening and looking toward the exit.

The bartender showed up and slid the glass of white wine Jackson had ordered for her.

"The lady's wine," he said and turned away. Jackass. Did he not see Jackson manhandling her, or was he so used to seeing the powerful men in this room being able to take whatever they wanted, that he was accustomed to turning a blind eye?

While Jackson continued to hold her left arm hostage, she grabbed the glass of wine off the bar with her right hand and threw the contents into Jackson's face.

"You bastard!" she yelled loud enough to assure she wouldn't be ignored by the crowd. "Keep your filthy hands off of me!"

Slightly distracted by the wine running into his eyes, Jackson softened his grip on her arm enough for her to yank herself free from his grasp.

"Ma'am?" A security guard dressed in a black suit and tie appeared. A coiled wire tethered from his ear was tucked into the back of his shirt.

"I'm fine." She took a step back. "But he's beyond rude and...handsy!" she cried, forcing tears to her eyes.

"Keagan, don't you—"

"Sir, you'll need to step back from the lady." The security guard put himself between Keagan and Jackson, distracting Jackson just enough that she was able to slink backward into the small crowd gathering to see the commotion.

"Excuse me, I have to leave," she muttered as she pushed through the people. They parted and let her through, seeming more than happy to hide her from the big brawny brute arguing with the security detail at the bar.

Not wasting a second of her gifted freedom, she rushed out of the main room of the house and headed outside. She made it down the steps and into a waiting cab without any further delay.

"Please hurry, my ex-husband is right behind me, and I don't want to see him," she pleaded with the driver.

He glanced at her through the rearview mirror then up the stone steps to the townhouse she'd run out of.

"Of course," he said with a curt nod and shifted the car into drive.

As they drove away, she looked out the back window. Jackson stood at the top of the stairs, searching for her up and down the street. She ducked down enough that she was certain he wouldn't be able to see her if his eyes landed on the cab.

"I don't blame you for rushing. Your ex-husband looks like a hound searching for his stolen bone."

She turned back toward the driver. "Yeah. That's a good description for him." She sank into the seat, letting her muscles soften. She'd gotten away.

For now.

4

Keagan stepped out of the bathroom in her pajama shorts and a tank top, more than ready for bed. It had been a long day, and a worse night. The luxurious hotel bed called to her like a siren to a pirate. Only, she was certain the mattress would definitely keep its end of the bargain and deliver a perfect night's rest.

But first, she needed to make a preliminary plan on how to get back on track.

Potier had been a solid contact. He'd been one of the last people to speak to Katarina before she'd embarked on her safari trip. If she could just have five minutes with him, she'd find out what Katarina had planned to do on her trip. There had to be another reason for her making that trip. Something made her get on that plane, and Potier had to have something of use.

Katarina wasn't a traveler. She was a 'lie on the beach and let the waves lull her to sleep' sort of vacationer. Why the sudden interest in the unseen world? And without mentioning it to Keagan? They'd talked every couple of days, but Katarina never once mentioned leaving the rental house to go on a safari.

While her laptop powered up, Keagan grabbed a bottle of water from the mini fridge and brought both to the bed. The night's boggle left her with few choices. Hunting him down during the work week was next to impossible. He didn't keep a regular schedule. There was a brewery awards ceremony coming up, but it would take some doing to get inside.

She never understood the appeal of beer. The taste reminded her of the time she'd rubbed the inside of her ear and then made the disgusting mistake of biting her fingernail. Ear wax and beer, similar tastes as far as she was concerned.

The soft glow of the side table lamp flickered briefly. She paused with her fingers hovering over the keyboard and listened to the room's silence. A woman laughed in the hallway, but then there was nothing. Not a peep. Maybe she should have gone home after her attempt to get Potier alone had failed. She'd only rented the room in order to have a private place to take him. But why let a room in the luxurious hotel go to waste?

Shaking her head at her overworked nerves, she opened her email and took a sip of her water while it loaded. She'd sent off another request for the death records that had Katarina's name listed, and she was expecting the rejection any time. She'd gone through the process three times already, but even with all the documentation of her adoption proving she was the next of kin, she was still getting the runaround.

She hadn't even been able to give Kat a proper burial. The small country the plane had crashed down in had handed over the passenger manifest, but unless kin could be proven, they didn't bother transporting the bodies. Keagan was one of five who hadn't been able to retrieve their loved ones. Even Jansen couldn't help her. Apparently, the Jansen family didn't hold much power in a country ten thousand miles away.

The lights flickered again, this time going out completely before stuttering to a low light again. No emails had come through, so she closed the laptop, and moved it to the bedside table. Maybe the heat was causing the air conditioner units to burn through the power in the city. A brownout wouldn't be unexpected, given the high heat index they'd been battling.

She fought back a yawn and decided to give up and get some sleep. She'd deal with Potier in the morning. Keagan swung her feet over the side of the bed, yanked off her socks and dropped them on the floor next to the bed. The light in the bathroom would stay on, since it was near the door. She left it on while she slept in case she needed to get up in the middle of the night. It also helped her sleep knowing if anyone walked in, she'd be able to see them clearly.

As she reached the light on the dresser, the power fluttered then died.

"Well, fuck." She tried the lamp, not expecting anything but being somewhat hopeful. Nothing.

She went over to the air vent and put her hand to it. Cool air still ran through the vent. Good, at least she wouldn't be baked alive while she slept. The lights must be on a different circuit than the air conditioner. She had no idea if that was really a thing, but it sounded plausible enough to put her at ease.

It was late anyway. She'd just go to bed and in the morning the power would be back on. She checked the door again, to be sure she'd bolted it and put the chain on, then felt her way back to the bed.

A shiver danced up her spine, making her freeze. She let her vision adjust to the darkness and surveyed the room. Nothing out of place; no one there but herself.

"You're losing it," she joked and made her way to her bed. A warm breeze blew in from the patio door.

Ice ran through her veins. She was on the seventh floor. And she'd locked that door before she left for the night. She was sure of it.

She forced her body to ease. Panic wouldn't get her out of whatever this was.

"Hello, Keagan." Jackson's dark voice pushed out any hope she had of getting to her purse in time.

She swallowed hard and closed her eyes briefly. Stay calm. If she had been able to get away from him once, she could do it again.

Clearing her throat, she slowly turned to face the patio. Her eyes adjusted so that she could make out his face well enough to send a bolt of fear through her chest.

She swallowed again, and her throat clenched.

"Jackson." She forced her voice to hold steady. It took every ounce of energy she possessed.

He stepped further into the room, and she held her ground. There weren't many choices for her. A quick dash to the door, and he'd be on her in a second. Jumping off the patio would lead to a broken neck.

"Jackson," she said when he kept silent. His eyes seared into hers. He didn't say a word, but she could sense every bit of his hatred, of his anger. "I know you're mad about the party, but—"

"Shut up," he said in a low, controlled tone. It was the sort of control that she'd been drawn to. Even when she was playing with him, she'd been attracted to him.

"Okay, I just—" Her words froze with his first step. By his third, she was pushed onto the bed. Kicking, she tried to shove him off of her, but he was too large —solid fucking muscle.

"Hold still," he ordered.

Like hell. She clawed at him and continued kicking.

He gripped her face in one hand and jerked her head to the side.

"No!" she screamed, but he slipped his palm over her mouth fast enough to keep it a mere muffle. Her fight continued, intensified, but he was too strong. He held her down and blew her hair away from her neck.

"Now-now, little fox. Don't fight so hard. You'll hurt yourself," he whispered just before a sharp prick hit her neck. Jackson brought his mouth to her ear. "Just relax, little fox. Just relax."

A fog formed, but she forced her mind to focus. She had to get away from him.

"Jackson, no, don't..." The words became jumbled, her tongue felt heavy, her eyelids even more so.

"Shhh, it's going to be all right." He brushed his hand over her head, petting her.

She jerked upward, one last ditch effort to get him off of her. But he was too heavy; she was too weak.

"I told you, you're coming back to Kassel. You have questions to answer." His words came from far away. They floated over her.

"What did you do?" she asked just before what little rays of light she could see faded away.

5

Heavy fog swirled through Keagan's mind as she slowly fluttered her eyes open. A slow drum beat inside her head, and her stomach rolled with nausea. Grabbing hold of her head, she gingerly pushed herself up into a seated position.

What happened, and more importantly where was she?

Slowly, her surroundings came into focus. A bedroom.

A scarcely decorated room, from the look of things. The faint scent of paint still lingered in the air, but there were no decorations on the walls or on the dresser. She sat on a king-sized bed, more comfortable than she'd had in her hotel room, and a white wardrobe stood in the corner of the room. Other than that, the room was empty. No night table, no lamps. The ceiling fan had a single bulb sconce dangling from it, but it wasn't on.

Enough sunlight poured through the windows on either side of the bed to illuminate the room well enough. She blinked a few times—the brightness increased the pounding in her head. Keagan slid off the bed and planted her bare feet on dark-stained hardwood flooring. No carpeting or throw rugs. She padded to the window and twisted the stick of the blinds to close the slats then went around the bed to do the same on the other side.

Somewhat more comfortable in the dim lighting, she took note of the three doors. Picking the closest one, she opened it to find an empty walk-in closet. She shut the door and pulled the next open, which revealed a full-size bathroom and a deep jacuzzi tub, as well as a stand-up shower. And it all appeared new.

The last door must lead out. She grabbed the handle and twisted, only to find it locked. Of course it was.

She yanked harder, hoping to break the bolt. When that didn't work, she kicked at the door, and threw her weight at it. But her feet were bare, and she didn't have much strength in her with whatever drug he'd given her still dancing through her veins.

Out of breath, and depleted of what little energy she'd had, she sank back from the door and leaned against the edge of the bed. He hadn't stripped her— she still had on her tank top and pajama shorts. Not that either of the items offered any protection or comfort at the moment.

The bolt of the door slid, and Jackson stood in the doorway, glaring at the door.

"I just had these put in," he complained, running his thumb over a small splintered piece. Apparently, she'd done some damage, just not enough to be of any use.

"Then you shouldn't have locked me in," she said, rubbing her temples. The throbbing had grown more intense with all her movements.

He raised his left brow and gave an amused chuckle. "You shouldn't have run from me at the party, then I wouldn't have had to go to all this trouble." He stepped inside and kicked the door shut behind him.

"What trouble? You've kidnapped me."

He grinned. "Yes, I did, but I wouldn't have had to if you hadn't run from me. That little trick at the party was a nice touch." He wagged a finger in the air, though he didn't look all that impressed.

"Jackson, what do you want? I already told you, I don't have the money."

"I know you did." He slid his hands into the front pockets of his jeans. As a younger man, he'd been attractive with his broad shoulders and narrow hips, but he'd grown over the years. He filled out every bit of his jeans and dark blue T-shirt, making him damn near mouthwatering. If he hadn't drugged her, kidnapped her, and wasn't keeping her hostage, she might have found his strong build, tattooed arms, and fierce expression arousing. But the situation being what it was, she couldn't allow his physical appearance to distract from what he had done, and what she would need to do.

Get away from him at any cost.

"So, what do you want? Why am I here?" She shoved off the bed and dropped her hands to her sides.

"You're here because you still need to answer how you got into Ash's party. And, you need to figure out how you're going to come up with the money you owe." He sounded so very matter of fact. Didn't he understand she had a much larger plan to work on and didn't have time for the piddly little shit like Ash's damn catalogue party?

"Fine. I'll find the money, and I'll send it to Ashland." She waved at the door. "Now, will you let me out and leave me be?"

His glare grew heated, and he narrowed his eyes. "You're not taking this seriously, Keagan. You can't just sneak into a catalogue party, pretend to be an Annex girl, steal from Ash's clients and then just wave it away. He's going to want to know how you got in. Who helped you?"

She stared at him. Telling him would create bigger problems than she had time or ability to deal with. The truth could potentially start a war between Ashland and Jansen. She would not be responsible for the bloodshed that would likely follow.

"You're his cousin. Just tell him the money will be returned soon, and to leave it at that," she argued.

He stared at her a long moment. "No."

"What?" She breathed a sigh of annoyance.

"I said no. I won't do either of those things. You're hiding something, and I want to know what it is."

"If I'm hiding something it's because it is none of your damn business, Jackson. Now either let me go or..." Her thoughts were all jumbled together.

"Or what?" Amusement had returned to his tone.

"Just let me go," she said without any strength. She was too tired for this conversation, too weak from the drugs to fight him. "I have to get home. I have something I need to do."

"What's that?" He folded his arms over his chest. Obviously, he was settled in to have a full conversation —one she wasn't in the mood, or the right mind to have.

"Jackson, please. I'm tired. My head hurts, and I don't find any of this amusing. Just let me the fuck out." Finding a burst of energy, she bolted for the door.

Her fingertips brushed the handle, before his strong arm wrapped around her middle and hoisted her from the floor. She struggled against him, kicking out at him and throwing her fists in every direction. He had her upside down, over his shoulder.

"Now, now, little fox. Don't be so quick to run out of here. You don't know what's on the other side of the door." He laughed and tossed her easily back onto the bed. She bounced once, before she scrambled to her knees, ready to throw herself at him. As though knowing her thoughts, he snatched her wrists and pinned them down to her hips.

"Jackson, this isn't funny. You can't keep me here!" she yelled at him. Her head would punish her later for this, but she was running out of options. She wouldn't just sit compliant while he kept her locked away.

"I'm not laughing," he said, pulling her toward him. "You're not leaving this room until you tell me what you're up to."

"Jackson, you wouldn't understand, and I don't have time to go through all of it."

Both of his dark eyebrows arched. "Really? Because as far as I can tell, my little fox, you have nothing but time here."

A thick lock of hair fell into her face, and she blew it away. She needed to keep him in her direct sight.

Would telling him really be so bad? It was not as though it would get her into any more trouble than she might already be in with his cousin. Though it could still drag Jansen into the mess. Jansen had given her a direct order to stop looking for answers that weren't there. He'd wanted her full focus on her work. She gave him a hundred percent of her energy when he put her on a job, but between projects she continued to dig. So long as nothing she did privately affected him, she was safe. But, thanks to Jackson, she was edging to a dangerous territory.

"What is it?" Jackson's brow softened.

She'd trusted him once, but that was years ago, and a lot happened between then and now. He wasn't the young boy she had fun playing bedroom games with anymore. He was a stronger, more powerful man who could take what he wanted whenever he wanted.

"Just let me go." She tugged her hands, but he only held firm.

"Ash is going to want to see you," he said, letting go of her wrists. "He's going to want to ask you a few questions."

"I don't want to see him." Keagan settled back on the bed.

He cast her an exasperated look. "You don't have much of a choice, little fox. Now, be a good girl and stop trying to break down my house. It's new, and I'd rather not have to start replacing everything because of your temper." He stalked to the door and yanked it open.

"A brand new house that just happened to come

with bolts on the outside of the guest door?" she shot at him from the bed.

He cocked a sly grin. "Not all the guest rooms have it. I had this one installed when I went to find you. I had a feeling you weren't going to be coming with me easily."

She tensed her jaw. "You planned to kidnap me?"

He shook his head. "I was hoping it wouldn't come to that, but I'll be honest." He stood in the doorway, leaning in toward her like he was about to tell her some great secret. "A small part of me was hoping that it would. It just makes the hunt so much more fun." He laughed.

"You asshole!" She smashed her fists into the bed.

"If I remember right, that was one of the last things you said to me years ago." He lost his smile a fraction. "But this time, you can't run away so easily." He tapped the dead bolt.

She jumped off the bed and rushed the door, but there was no getting around him.

"Jackson! Don't do this. Just let me go," she hated the repetition of her plea, but maybe if she said it enough, he'd listen.

"Tell me what I want to know." He lifted a shoulder as though it were just that simple.

"Fuck you!" She shoved at his chest, not expecting him to move, but needing to exert some force of her own will.

He grabbed her wrist and brought it up to his lips, brushing a warm kiss against the inside.

"Don't start acting like a wild animal, little fox. You won't like the treatment you get if you do."

Keagan jerked her hand from him and took a step back. "You're as arrogant as ever. If you think I'll be so easily scared, you're wrong." Though he'd been able to send tremors of unease through her body; they'd all been worth the reward of giving over to him. This wasn't the past, this was the present, and Jackson was in her way.

His smile widened. "Good. I think I'd be disappointed in you if you cowered too easily. But make no mistake here, Keagan. I will get what I want from you."

Rage built up inside of her, clawing and gnawing at her insides. Hitting him wouldn't get any reaction other than laughter, and she couldn't fight him anyway. Without thinking, without weighing out consequences, she spat at him. Her own eyes flew open as the wad of saliva hit his cheek and slid down into his beard.

She braced herself for retaliation, her muscles locking up while she waited for him to pounce.

He wiped his cheek. "Wild animal it is. Don't ever say, I didn't warn you, little fox."

He stepped into the hall and pulled the door quietly shut. She rushed to the door, pressing her hands against it. The deadbolt slid into place, locking her securely inside the room. She hadn't accomplished anything.

Well, anything other than pissing off Jackson. And her memories of his being angry didn't give her any reason to think the next time she saw him would bring her any warm, fuzzy feelings.

6

"What did she say?" Ashland asked after Jackson finished explaining the meeting with Keagan.

"She didn't say anything, yet," Jackson said through his phone as he walked around his kitchen, getting her lunch ready.

The feisty animal had an afternoon of lessons coming her way. Once she'd gone through her paces maybe she'd be more cooperative in answering his questions.

"When are you going to bring her here?" Ash pressed.

"Once I have all the answers. If she won't tell me, she sure as fuck isn't going to open up to you."

"Oh, I think I can be convincing." Ash sounded more confident than he had reason to be. He may know how to get his wife to tell him her secrets, and he could scare almost any man into spilling his guts, but he didn't know Keagan. If she wanted to keep something locked up tight—she would.

"Let me do this." Jackson grabbed the leftover roasted chicken from the fridge and placed it on the counter. He hadn't had time to get any staff into the house yet, so pre-made dinners were his lifeline.

"McKinnley's not going to wait much longer for his money. Does she at least have that?" Ash's patience waned.

"She doesn't," Jackson said.

"Okay, so how does she propose she fixes that? If Stanley starts talking about this, it's going to cost me business. Then it's not going to be just the two hundred grand she's going to owe."

Jackson spooned a few scoops of mashed potatoes onto the shredded chicken. "If I handle that, you'll agree to let me handle her my way?"

Silence stretched out.

"Ash. Stanley gets his money. I'll get the answers you need about her getting into your party. And I'll get five percent of the Annex." He leaned a hip against the counter.

"Five percent?"

"I'll throw in another one hundred grand," he said, offering half of what he'd originally planned to invest in the Annex when he'd brought it up to Ash to begin with.

"You're paying her debt?"

"I am," Jackson said with finality.

"And what will you do with her then?" Amusement played in Ash's tone.

"Whatever the fuck I want," Jackson answered.

Ash laughed on the other side of the phone. "I recall having those sentiments once, and you see how that worked out."

"Well, don't count on me falling for her and having my leg strapped to a ball and chain. I'll get your answers, get my shares, and let her go—probably."

Another chuckle. "Of course. Fine. Send the money over, all three hundred grand. Once you get the answers for me, I'll have the partnership papers drawn up."

"Great. I'll have Charlie bring it over in the morning," Jackson said.

"Well, good luck then."

Jackson popped the bowl of food into the microwave and hit the one-minute button.

"No luck needed." He watched the bowl spin on the other side of the door. "Once she gets what's coming her way, she'll start talking."

Jackson hung up while Ashland was still chuckling.

Just because Ash fell hard for his girl, didn't mean

Jackson would suffer the same fate. Keagan served a purpose, and once she didn't anymore, he'd send her on her way.

But first.

He took the bowl out of the microwave and shut the door.

It was time to feed his little fox.

JACKSON CARRIED the bowl with the shredded rotisserie chicken and mashed potatoes down the hall to the guest room where he'd put Keagan. He hadn't been lying when he told her he had the deadbolt installed just for her. After Ash gave him the task of tracking her down, he'd had the construction crew add the feature, along with a few other items before they wrapped the job.

It may have been a few years since he had Keagan Foxx in his clutches, but he remembered her vividly. She wouldn't hold out for too long with the information she clutched to her chest. And if he needed to give her incentive to talk, he had a damn good idea how to make that happen.

His cock thickened in his jeans just thinking about the fun they would have. He almost hoped she would keep holding out on him.

But in the meantime, she needed to eat. He'd

watched her at the party from the moment she stepped into the luxurious townhouse. She'd ignored every platter of appetizers that passed her, and she'd completely skipped the buffet. By his estimate she probably hadn't eaten anything in nearly twenty-four hours.

He had a few ways up his sleeve to make her uncomfortable enough to spill her secrets, but starvation wasn't one of them. That would be cruel, and he had much more pleasurable ways to show his cruelty.

Once he stopped outside her door, he listened. All quiet. Maybe she had fallen asleep? He hadn't exactly given her a welcome basket with anything to occupy her mind while she waited for him. Jackson pulled out the key and unlocked the deadbolt slowly. If she was sleeping, he'd leave her be. The drugs he'd injected could take a while to work themselves out of her system.

He reached for the doorknob but missed as the door was yanked open in front of him. A dresser drawer was shoved into his chest, which pushed him backward across the hall until he hit the wall. The bowl of food dropped to the floor and spilled onto the carpet. So much for her needing to sleep off the drugs.

Keagan threw her bare foot into his thigh and shoved the drawer harder at him before she dropped it and dashed down the hall. It took him a second to register the situation, then he kicked away the empty drawer and pelted after her.

Her feet were bare, and she had no idea where she was. It wouldn't be hard to catch up to her. He barreled down stairs to the first floor. The stairwell brought him to the back of the house. Listening for a moment, he heard the patter of her feet against the wooden flooring near the living room. There were two hallways she could take from the stairs, one led to the house's living area and the other to his office and playroom. He jogged down the hall, heading toward the sound of her running.

He found her at the front door, struggling with the locks. His line of business required a bit more security than a simple deadbolt on the front door. There was a keypad along with the regular locking system. She would need the combination to unlock the door even from the inside.

Casually, he sauntered the rest of the way down the hall to meet up with her while she continued to stab at the keypad. Frustrated, she grunted and started throwing her fist into the pad.

"If you break it, you're replacing it," he said smoothly. Her back muscles locked up at the sound of his voice. He moved to her side, staring down at her profile. A tear slipped down her cheek, surely from the frustration of a failed escape attempt. Well, she could keep the tears—she would need them in just a little while.

Slowly he sucked in air, calming his breathing from having to chase her through the house.

Her hands placed flat against the door, she pressed her forehead against it.

"Just let me leave, Jackson," she said quietly.

He hooked his finger around her hair and swooped it behind her shoulder. "That can't happen, Keagan."

With a burst of energy, she pushed away from the door, and turned to bolt down the hall again. But he was prepared this time and was on her within two strides. He wrapped his arm around her waist and hauled her off the floor.

"Let me go!" she screamed then kicked wildly, squirming in his grip.

"Not a chance, little fox." He moved quickly down the hall and back around to the room that better suited her current temperament.

She elbowed him in the chest, but he recovered quickly enough to open the door to the playroom. Once they were inside, he kicked shut the door and bolted it.

"Let me out of here!" She struggled even more. He'd had enough and dropped her to the floor. She landed in a heap, on her hands and knees. When she tried to scramble up, he placed his booted foot on her shoulder.

"No, little fox, you stay down there."

She tilted her head upward toward him and through the curtain of hair that had fallen over her face, the heat from her glare would probably scorch any other man. But he wasn't in his happy place either, she'd kicked him, hit him, and tried to bulldoze him. She had some lessons coming her way.

Her heavy breathing blew strands of hair away from her cheeks.

"You going to be a good girl, or do I need to keep my foot on you?" he asked.

Her jaw clenched.

"Your choice. I can pin you down if you need."

She shoved his foot off of her but stayed on her knees. Defiance raged in her blazing eyes, and her chest rose and fell quickly as she caught her breath.

"Now," he said going to the chest of drawers. "I was going to go about this all differently, civilized actually, but it seems you have other ideas." Jackson pulled open a drawer and dug around until he found a thin black leather collar. When he turned around back to her, her eyes widened. Her pupils fucking dilated.

Not much has changed then.

"You're not putting that on me, Jackson." She pointed at the leather collar dangling from his fingertips.

He smiled down at her as he stood over her. "I am putting it on you. And then I'm going to put you where you can relax and calm the fuck down." His gaze moved over to the metal crate in the corner of the room. Its bottom was lined with a plush cushion, making it a bit more comfortable. But it was still a cage, and if his memory served—not her favorite thing.

"The door's locked, and you already know you can't get out of the house. So, I really suggest you start behaving yourself. You've already earned a punishment for that little stunt upstairs."

"Punishment?" Her cheeks reddened. "Fuck you, Jackson. This isn't a game. I'm not that young naive girl you knew."

He squatted in front of her and captured her chin in his fingers. "I'm well aware of how much you've grown up, Keagan." He moved his gaze over her form. "You remember punishments, right?" he asked, while wrapping the collar around her neck. She started to pull away from him, but one hard glance at her, and she stilled. Good, she remembered.

"We were playing games then," she whispered.

He pushed her hair out of the way and worked the buckle closed at the base of her neck. Sliding a finger between the leather strap and her neck, he ran it along to her throat. It would be slightly uncomfortable at first, but she could breathe easily enough.

He lifted her chin until her eyes settled on his. "We're not playing games now, though." Jackson let go of her chin, rose to his full height and unbuckled his belt. Her gaze bolted to his hands, her cheeks flared red, and her eyes widened. "Take off your clothes and stand up."

"Jackson—"

"Take off your clothes and stand up." He enunciated each word slowly. "If you remember our time together, you'll remember I take punishments pretty damn seriously."

She had only earned two while they had been fooling around. They hadn't been serious about each other, so he hadn't kept her on a short leash, even though he suspected she'd thrive on one. But twice she'd pushed him until he delivered. He often suspected she had done it on purpose, wanting to feel his authority more than just when they were playing. He had never explored it with her, though.

He yanked his belt free of his jeans by the time she was on her feet. She turned away from him, swept her shirt over her head, then shoved out of her pajama shorts. Jackson stepped toward her, wrapped his arms around her, and pressed her back into his chest. Her body trembled as she drew a shaky breath.

"It's not so horrible," he promised her. "Have you been with anyone since me that delivered punishments when you've earned them?"

She stiffened, then shook her head. "No."

He'd go a little easier. Not much, or she wouldn't heed the warning never to try what she had done again.

"I want you to stand against the wall, with your hands flat against it. Stick your ass out for me, little fox," he whispered into her ear.

"I don't want this." She stiffened.

"I know, but you're going to do it anyway," he said quietly and released her. He wouldn't shove her against the wall. He'd give her a chance to go willingly. And she didn't disappoint.

Gracefully, she walked forward to the wall, pulled her hair forward to expose her entire back to him, then moved into position. He wouldn't strike her back —not with his belt—but she was remembering the flogger. His cock pressed against his zipper at her compliance, and the beauty that was Keagan.

He stepped to her left, folded the belt over into a loop, and palmed the buckle.

"Ass out," he instructed when she bent forward.

She arched her back, pushing her ass toward him. Fuck, if he could punish her with a good fucking, he'd much rather be doing that, but she'd earned a thrashing, not an orgasm.

"You're staying here with me until I decide otherwise. While you're here, you will never—" He brought the belt down across her ass. "Try to run away again." He lashed her again, and a red mark crisscrossed the first. He brought the belt down again on the bottom of her ass. She hissed and rose up to her toes.

"If you raise your hand to me again, you'll get much worse than this." He brought the belt down harshly across both cheeks, and she stumbled forward with a small yelp. She righted herself quickly, pushing her ass back out, ready for the next lash.

He drew a deep breath. Did she have any idea how fucking gorgeous she was when she submitted to him? Even when she hated it, when she didn't want to, she fell so easily beneath his authority. Nothing could be more beautiful.

Having brought his hand back once more, he delivered the hardest lash. She cried out again but remained in place.

While he slid his belt back into the loops of his pants, he watched her back tense and relax then tense again. Maybe she was warring with herself over her reaction, over her submission to the short whipping. She could take more than he'd given her, and if she attempted to escape again, he would bring down the full force of a punishment on her. But he wasn't entirely finished with her yet.

"Turn around and get back on your hands and knees," he ordered.

Her shoulders sagged, and her head fell forward.

He'd clearly touched a part of her she'd left ignored all these years.

"Now, Keagan."

With a heavy sigh, she sank to her knees, then moved down her hands. Her face remained down-turned. Not where he wanted it.

"Look at me, little fox," he said after he finished buckling his belt.

Slowly she lifted her chin, bringing her eyes to line up with his. A tear left a streak down her cheek. It couldn't have been from the spanking—he'd barely given her what used to be a warm-up for their play sessions. No, this reaction had to do with a hurt on the inside.

Did she not like this part of her? There would be plenty of time to explore it later, while he extracted answers from her.

"Since you made a mess with your lunch upstairs, I have to get you more. Go on into your crate." He pointed to the cage in the corner.

Her gaze swept across the room to the confinement waiting for her. "Jackson," she whispered, but didn't say anything more.

"Go on." He snapped his fingers. "I'm not going to wait all day. If I have to get the leash out and walk you there myself, there'll be another punishment."

Her jaw tightened, and her fingers curled into a tight ball on the floor. She hated the crate. Made her feel trapped. Well, she was completely trapped. Better she understand that sooner rather than later.

"Unless you want to spill all of your secrets?"

The muscles in her back tensed, her spine straightened, and one graceful movement after another, she crawled past him. He watched her regal motions as she crawled into the crate, her head held high. She would concede to the cage, but she would not give him what he wanted.

He shook his head and shut the door to the crate, working the sliding lock into place.

"What can be so bad that you would rather nap in a cage like the little fox you are instead of telling me?" he asked, without expecting an answer.

"I'll be back," he said, leaving her to curl up on the small mat inside her new room.

As he shut the door to the playroom, he flipped on the security camera. He'd be able to watch her from his phone, and an alert would be sent to him right away if the door to the crate or the playroom opened.

Technology was a wondrous thing.

7

Her ass hurt—nothing intolerable, more a dull ache—but the painful bruise on her ego was worse. She'd let him spank her.

Oh, she'd told him she didn't want it, but when he ordered her to get into position, she'd gone straight to the wall and obeyed. She could waste her time arguing that it was just habit. When they'd known each other, she had never disobeyed his commands. It was part of the fun, part of the game, but to lie to herself would waste precious time.

Jackson wouldn't be gone long, and in the time she had, she needed to come up with a new plan—a little more difficult to execute anything now that she was crated. This was a fact that brought heat to her cheeks and arousal to her sex. It shouldn't. What sort of crazy person could enjoy this sort of treatment?

He'd put a collar around her neck, and now he had her locked up in a crate. He was making her his little pet, and fuck it all to hell, her pussy was damp from the ordeal.

She rolled to her back and hooked her fingers around the bars on either side of her. Enough room for her to roll around with ease, and she could sit up with no issue. But still, she was naked, collared and locked up.

Couldn't she just tell him what was going on? She didn't have the money to pay Ashland, and that would be a problem. But maybe she could tell him how she'd gotten into the party. Maybe he'd understand the whole situation if she explained it all to him. Maybe he'd even be able to help with her search. He obviously had the funds.

And then he'd know she had ties to Jansen. The Titon family didn't work with the Jansens any longer, not since Ash's father died years ago. But just because they weren't in the business anymore didn't mean they were friendly with them. She'd used her connections with the Jansen family to get into that party. Telling Ash anything about it would pull him into her mess.

What a fucking disaster.

She flickered her fingers around the edge of the collar to the back of her neck where the buckle was secured. It would take only a few seconds to undo it and throw the damn strip of leather across the room.

And it would take Jackson all of a second to take offense to her deliberate disobedience.

Pressing her head back into the thick mattress of the crate, she groaned. So many easy options that came with not-so-easy consequences.

The door to the playroom opened, and Jackson sauntered back holding a metal bowl. Internally, she moaned. She'd seen that bowl before, or at least one just like it. They'd played with it once when he'd had her leashed and collared, and he'd fed her their dessert from it. Or rather, she'd licked up the vanilla custard from the bowl for his amusement, and later, her reward.

"I remember that look," he said with a grin, stopping just outside the crate. "You pretended to hate it so much that night, but your pussy had never been so wet for me."

She clenched her teeth. "I'm not playing anymore games with you, Jackson. You spanked me, you have me in this crate, and you have this damn collar on my neck. You get nothing else from me." She maneuvered herself to kneel, facing the door. "Let me out, let me get dressed, and let me go. People are going to look for me." At best, Jansen might notice her disappearance if he called her. He might send a few messages, and if she didn't respond, send someone to find her. He didn't like being ignored.

Jackson put the bowl down on the floor several feet

from the crate. The scent of cooked chicken and rice set her mouth watering and her stomach grumbling.

"You need to eat. I'm giving you a chance to eat. Take it or don't, but this is your only chance. If you want to be stubborn, you can wait until tomorrow, and we'll try again." He opened the crate door and went back to the bowl, nudging it with his foot. "But I'm warning you, you'll have to stay in the crate until it's time for another chance."

She swallowed. It was just food. Taking it wasn't conceding a victory to him over anything. And she would need her strength if she was going to outthink him. Because ousting him physically wasn't going to happen.

Determined to get through the ordeal with her pride fully intact, she crawled forward, out of the crate, and headed straight for the bowl. Eyes downcast, she wouldn't give him the satisfaction of seeing the blush blooming on her cheeks. Fuck him for wanting her humiliation, but worse yet, dammit, why was it making her cunt so damn wet? At this rate, he'd be able to see her arousal.

Once at the bowl, she tucked her ass inward and picked it up.

"No, no." He tapped the top of her head. "Little foxes don't eat like that, do they?"

She'd make him pay for this. And it would hurt. She'd make it painful.

Once she put the bowl back to the floor, she leaned forward, taking a chunk of chicken into her mouth. Mouthwatering. Jackson hated cooking, he either had a chef or he still ate from the ready-made meals at the grocer. She didn't really care at the moment; her belly was too empty for her to give it more thought. She dove into the food, using her fingers to scoop the rice and being slightly grateful he didn't stop her.

Jackson's hand rested on her back. With having to lean forward to get the food, her ass was up in the air slightly.

She tried to focus on chewing the last bit of chicken, but he slid his hand over her ass and then even lower. Her mind froze as his fingers swept through her folds, toying with her hungry sex.

"Just like last time." The arrogance in his tone made the situation even worse. "Such a wet little fox, aren't you?" he teased, sliding his middle finger into her pussy.

She curled her toes and forced the aroused moan back down her throat. It had been more than a year since anyone other than she had touched her pussy, and no one knew how to play with her better than Jackson.

"Jackson." She said his name on a low whisper, not trusting herself to speak any louder lest a plea for more of his attention escaped.

"Such a good fox. You ate all your food, and now

you're being so cooperative while I pet you." He slipped a second digit into her passage, and she leaned her head forward until her forehead pressed against the carpeted floor.

"Let's see how good you can be for me," he teased, sending a shiver up her spine with a flick of a finger across her clit.

She made a sound, something between a moan and a cry. It seemed her body was as confused as her mind.

"From what I could find on your computer, you've been searching for a Katarina Silverstone, even though she's been declared dead." He curled his fingers inside her, sending an electric current to her core. No one should feel so damn good while being questioned about their dead foster mother.

"I...fuck...Jackson, please. Stop." She tried to crawl forward, but a quick smack to her ass stilled her.

"I'm not done playing, little fox. Stay still." He pumped his fingers in and out of her pussy.

"What do you want?" She fisted her hands into the carpet. The pressure was already starting to build. The lack of attention over the past year had left her vulnerable, and Jackson always knew how to take advantage of her desires.

It had been one of the things she'd admired about him at the time. Now she would loathe him for it.

"Just tell me who she is, that's all. Trust me with

that much. Then you'll get what your body is really craving right now." He twisted his fingers and curled them again, striking the exact spot that could catapult her into the next realm.

"Harmless enough, right? Who is she to you?" he asked, flicking her clit harder with his pinkie finger while his other fingers pumped harder and harder into her, driving her to the very brink of existence.

He was right. It wouldn't hurt to tell him.

"Tell me, little fox. Tell me, and I'll let you go back upstairs to your room." He shifted his positioning behind her and pumped harder, further into her passage while spreading out his fingers to fill her completely.

She buried her hot face into the carpet, hiding from him or herself, she didn't know anymore.

Another touch to her clit, and sparks shot behind her closed eyelids. She wouldn't last much longer, and she knew Jackson would withhold his touch if she didn't give him what he wanted.

"Tell me and come for me. Give me what I want," he coaxed with that low, sultry tone he'd perfected over the years. "And you can have what you need."

"She's my foster mother," she answered, sucking in a long breath. She bucked backward, into his touch, craving more.

"Good girl!" he cheered, picking up speed with his

thrusts, and increased his play with her clit. "Come, sweet Keagan, come just like this for me."

Her hearing faded, the room went dark, all senses dulled aside from the electrical explosion inside of her. Wave after wave, her orgasm ripped the sound from her throat, stole the air from her lungs, and sent tears streaming down her cheeks.

Slowly, her body eased, and the sound of the room came back to life. He was still fucking her with his fingers, though he'd slowed. And he repeated the words *Good girl* over and over again.

Good girl. When was the last time that phrase could accurately describe her?

The fight went out of her body, and she crumbled forward. Jackson eased his fingers from her body and quickly scooped her up into his arms as he rose. She rolled her head into his chest, finding a small comfort in the fact that he hadn't changed his aftershave in all the years they'd been apart.

Something so simple from a time when she had been a normal girl. Before she contracted for regular work with a large crime family. Before she hunted down a dead mother, with the slightest hope she was still alive. She wrapped her arms around his neck, and nestled into him, wrapping herself with his familiar scent. The familiar sensation of security.

They weren't in the playroom for long. He carried her through the house and up the stairs. Jackson had always been a man of strong character. He'd said if she gave him what he wanted he'd let her go back to her room. And that's exactly where he took her.

Once inside the guest room, he laid her back on the bed. Her hands fell away from his neck and folded onto her stomach. With tired eyes, she stared up at his concerned face.

"You've been on your own for too long I think," he said, but the concern didn't wane. He wasn't talking about her livelihood. The man was focusing on her sex life. Which was so like him. She wanted to laugh at the absurdity of it, but she was too tired.

She reached up to the collar and ran her fingers to the back to the buckle. But Jackson pulled her hands away.

"That stays, Keagan. Get some sleep." He brushed her hair from her face. "I'll come back in a few hours, and we can talk."

She wanted to tell him to forget about it. That she wouldn't cave. She wouldn't tell him anything else he wanted to know.

But in the end, she only nodded, and let the darkness of sleep pull her away.

8

Elliot Jansen sat in front of Jackson's desk with his hands steepled before him. Jackson had agreed to this meeting last week, but with the development of Keagan, he'd nearly messed it up.

"I've thought about the terms of our agreement, and I think this is going to work to both of our benefits," Jansen said with a curve to his lips.

Jackson's chest relaxed, but he kept his face neutral.

"I'm glad you agree. We can start shipments as soon as you're ready for them," Jackson said, turning his attention to Charlie, his right-hand man. "Charlie here can set it all up. Just let me know who our contact is on your side." Jackson nodded at his long-time friend.

Jansen gestured toward his man standing near the

door, and he came forward. The overgrown oaf handed Jansen a business card.

"That's who you'll be dealing with from now on," Jansen explained. A first name, Sergio, and a phone number. It was a start.

"I have to say, I'm glad that we'll be working with the Titon family again. We did so well in the past with Samuel when he was alive."

The tension came back full blast.

"I need to be clear here. You're doing business with me. Jackson Titon, but not the Titon family. Ashland takes no exception to my working with you or any of the families that my uncle worked with in the past, but the Titon family is not involved."

Jansen frowned.

"It's too bad your cousin can't see the lucrative business he could be doing with us if he'd only stop being so stubborn." He dropped his hands to his knees. "But, in some ways, he is very much his father's son. Stubborn as a mule." He flashed half a smile.

"I can easily agree to that." Jackson laughed. "Can I talk you into a drink to celebrate the lucrative business venture you and I are embarking on?" His stomach soured at the forced pleasantries of doing business, but he wasn't about to thumb his nose at this deal. It meant doubling his distribution business and gave him solid footing in Kassel.

"I could use a brandy." Janson nodded, and Charlie went into motion.

Jackson glanced at the grandfather clock sitting in the corner of his office. It had been a gift from his grandfather to his father and had become Jackson's upon his father's death. The rumor in the family had been that Samuel Titon had wanted the clock, but their father had gifted it to Stephan instead. Probably just another reason Samuel treated his younger brother with such disrespect.

Jackson noted the time. He'd left Keagan up in her room for several hours. She had the full suite to roam around, but she had to be bored out of her mind by now.

"Am I keeping you from something?" Jansen asked, taking note of Jackson's long stare at the clock.

Jackson accepted the glass of brandy from Charlie and shook his head at Jansen. "No, not at all. I was just thinking I need to have the clock maintained."

Jansen looked behind him at the clock. "It looks rather old. I have a nephew that works with antique clockworks like that. I'll have him give you a call."

Of course. Spread the business around to the entire family. Jackson wouldn't blame him. It was how they all thrived. It was how he would thrive.

"That would be great. One less thing for me to worry about." Jackson smiled then took a drink of the brandy.

Jansen nodded and brought his own glass up to his lips, but as his eyes wandered over the desk, he froze. Jackson followed his gaze and found him staring at Keagan's laptop sitting on the corner of the desk. Jackson had brought it into his office to go through her hard drive. The woman was keeping such a tight seal on her lips, he'd hoped to find information on her computer.

He'd found some information, but without her explanations, none of it made much sense.

But why would Jansen recognize the computer?

Jansen took a long sip of his drink then placed the glass on the desk. He leaned forward, leaving Jackson with a hard stare.

"May I ask why you have that?" He pointed to the laptop.

"A friend was over yesterday, and she left it behind," Jackson answered without skipping a beat. Jansen knew Keagan, that much was now obvious, but why?

"And this friend...she just left the computer here?" There was more accusation in his tone than Jackson felt comfortable with. Whatever their connection to each other was, Jackson had a good sense that if Jansen found out Keagan was locked upstairs naked, he might take offense.

Well, hell.

"You seem concerned," Jackson said, downing the

last of his drink and depositing the glass on the desk. Charlie stiffened, but Jackson gave a subtle nod to relax him. Jackson hadn't had time to explain to Charlie about Keagan, but after he got Jansen out of the house, he'd have to.

"That computer belongs to a business associate of mine." Jansen leaned further toward it and pointing at a deep scratch in the case. "I inadvertently caused this damage to her computer."

"You know Keagan Foxx?" Jackson didn't bother playing games. If they were associates, that could explain how she managed to get into Ash's Annex Party unseen from his security team.

"I do."

"Interesting. We were friendly a few years back." Jackson veered away from taking the defensive side of the conversation and treated it as though they were simply discussing a mutual friend

"Hmm." Jansen sat back in his chair.

He couldn't outright ask him about helping her sneak into Ash's club without him thinking Jackson was helping Ash. And if he got wind of that, there could be trouble

No wonder Ash refused to work with these families. It was nothing but a fucking hassle and headache.

"I'm stopping at her house tomorrow. I could bring it for her if you'd like," Jansen offered, raising both brows.

Jackson's gaze held firm. Any sign of concern or surprise at his offer would make him suspicious.

"Thanks, but she's coming over in the morning, and I told her I'd have it for her. Not a problem." Jackson threw on a wide smile. This was nothing more than a coincidence—at least as far as he wanted Jansen to think.

"Ah. That's good." Janson gave a small nod, but his casual demeanor didn't quite reach his eyes.

"She's an associate?" Jackson hoped Jansen would be more forthcoming than he was sure Keagan would even attempt at being.

"Yes, I used to work with her mother years ago, but when she passed away, Keagan stepped up for me until I was able to replace her." Jansen made it sound like Keagan filed papers for him until he found a new secretary. Seeing as Keagan was gearing up to make a move toward the beer king just two nights ago, Jackson had some doubt about that.

"We just bumped into each other recently. Haven't had a chance to catch up fully," Jackson said when Jansen seemed to want more information.

"Friends are good to have," Jansen said as he rose. "I have another meeting in the city to get to, thanks for the drink." He gestured toward the empty glass then held out his hand to shake Jackson's.

"Of course. Charlie here will be in touch with

Sergio, and the deliveries will start flowing," Jackson assured him.

Charlie opened the door to the office and followed Jansen and his man out to walk them to the front of the house. Jackson sank back into his chair and stared at the computer

His little fox had a lot of explaining to do.

"Who is this Keagan woman?" Charlie asked as he bounded back into the office, gesturing at the computer.

"Relax." Jackson swiped his hand through the air. "She's an old friend, like I said."

"Right. And her computer sitting here has nothing to do with the new locking system you put on the guest bedroom or that you changed the security code to the front door?"

Charlie always had his eyes open wide. It was why he was Jackson's right-hand man—the person Jackson told almost everything to. Except about Keagan. He hadn't mentioned her. Or the deal he'd made with Ash.

"Oh, it has everything to do with all that. She's upstairs." Jackson pointed a finger toward the ceiling.

Charlie's blond eyebrows shot up. "What the hell? You have Jansen's business partner locked upstairs in your guest room?"

"Not partner. Associate. And I didn't know she

worked with Jansen when I... Well, when I brought her here."

"Fuck, Jackson. If he finds out..." He let his sentence die out. Always one with a bit of a dramatic flair.

"Look. I know what I'm doing. I do have history with Keagan, but the reason she's here is because she snuck into an Annex party and pretended to be one of the girls. Then she used that rouse to steal two hundred grand from one of the clients. I'm trying to find out how she managed to get into the party in the first place."

The color dropped from Charlie's face. "You mean the money I'm supposed to bring over to the Annex in the morning?" He flicked a thumb at the door.

"Yeah. That's the money."

"So, she still had it?"

"No. I'm paying it on her behalf for the time being. That way McKinnley gets off Ash's ass, and I have a little more time to figure out what the fuck she's gotten herself into." Jackson picked up his glass and sauntered over to the bar where he poured another drink. "Besides, once I get everything I need from her and hand it over to Ash, I'll have five percent of the Annex."

"No shit?" Charlie's grin washed away his frown. "He's really going to do it?"

"Yeah. The only thing left to do is get this last piece

of the puzzle settled for him. But"—Jackson threw back the brandy, welcoming the subtle burn as it slid down his throat—"first, I have to settle all this mess with her and Ash. And I need to find out why she's working with Jansen. As far as I knew, she had no connections to any of the families."

"Does it really matter? Just get the info and get your share of the Annex. You should have had some of it to begin with. Samuel had no right to toss your father out the way he did."

"That's the past. I'm not holding Ash hostage for what his father did." Jackson bore no ill will toward his cousin for his uncle's decisions. "Ash isn't like his father. Leave the past in the past," Jackson said. "Now." He rolled back his shoulders. "I need to have a talk with my guest. You can see yourself out." He brushed past Charlie.

His little fox had a few questions to answer.

The minutes crawled into hours, and the hours sloshed their way into a full day. She hadn't seen Jackson since the day before, when he'd tucked her into bed tired and wary from her experience with him in the playroom.

She had awoken from her nap to a plate of pasta and bread sitting on the nightstand. After she ate every bite, unabashedly wiping up every drop of the buttery sauce with the French bread, she had expected Jackson to waltz in and start questioning her more. But he never came. The sun eased out of the sky, and the moon shone bright through the window into her room, but he never came.

In the morning, she'd again woken to food on her nightstand. Bacon, slightly burnt, scrambled eggs on the runny side, and burnt toast. Though, she would give him credit—he had attempted to scrape off most of the burnt portion.

Apparently, breakfast was one meal he didn't have pre-made in his fridge or on speed dial.

With her stomach full, she'd made the bed. She took a shower with the towels left on the dresser. He still hadn't given her any clothing to wear, so she kept the towel wrapped around her.

She paced the room, her frustration growing with each step. How long did he think he could keep her locked away in this room? Sooner or later someone would notice her missing. The barista at the café she stopped at daily would eventually realize she hadn't been in, but would she bother looking into it?

Over the past few years, she'd made it clear she wanted no personal attachments, and she'd gotten exactly what she wanted. And now she was locked away, and no one would know. She hadn't seen Jansen in a while, and he might reach out soon. But if he didn't? Maybe when the money stopped flowing, he'd notice, but would he look for her or just assume she had run out on him?

A metallic click sounded from the door, and Keagan stopped her pacing. The door opened cautiously, like he didn't want to wake her if she was still sleeping. Half the day was gone already. How much sleep did he think she needed?

"Good, you're awake." Jackson smiled as he

stepped into the room, closing the door behind him.

She folded her arms over her chest and glared at him in silence.

"I have something for you." He raised his hand and brought a navy blue dress into view. Her navy blue dress.

"You went to my house?" She charged forward, intent on ripping it out of his hand.

He snatched the garment out of her reach.

"I did." His white teeth flashed with his arrogant grin. "I thought you might like some clothes, and since I have no idea what size you wear, I figured it'd be easier just to get your own clothes. There's more than this tucked away in my room. For when you earn them."

She fisted her hands but calmed her breathing. "Earn them?"

"Yes, when you're good, when you're honest, you'll get a piece of clothing." He touched the tip of his finger to her chin and pulled it up until he was looking down into her eyes. "Honest answers to my questions, and you'll get the dress."

She pulled away from his touch. "I'm fine just like this," she said, though they both knew she wanted real clothing. It wasn't that she didn't like being naked. She actually slept nude more nights than not, but to have her clothing taken from her, to be subjected to his rule on the matter, it put a humiliating lens over things.

"Hmm." He stepped up to her and in a flash grabbed the towel and yanked it from her body. The last trace of warmth it provided faded before her teeth could clench.

Fucking hell!

"You're such an asshole!" She stomped her foot. Realizing she wasn't exactly keeping her anger hidden from him, she became more flustered and leapt forward for the dress.

Again, he removed it from her reach and laughed. "No, no, little fox. Not until you've earned it."

"I'm not a little fox!" she screamed into his face, or as close as she could get considering he was maintaining distance between them.

"You are what I say you are," he answered simply and walked around her toward the bathroom. He tossed the towel into a basket.

"Fine." She gritted her teeth.

"Good." He leaned his ass on the footboard of the bed and dangled the dress from his middle finger. "How long have you been working for Elliot Jansen?"

Her throat dried. He couldn't know that. She'd been careful not to leave any trace of involvement with the Jansen family. If they went down for something, she wanted no part in it, and if she were ever to be caught, she wouldn't have any evidence involving them to cause them concern. She'd been smart.

"And before that pretty head of yours starts to

conjure up a lie, you should know I had a meeting with him yesterday afternoon."

Fucking hell!

"I've known Elliot Jansen most of my life. Katarina worked for him," she said, suddenly wishing she still had the towel on. Being interrogated naked had less appeal when she was trying to keep so much hidden.

"She worked for him?" he asked with an arched brow.

"Yes."

"Okay, so when did you start working for him? When did you turn into this petty little thief?" She could do without the judgment in his tone.

There was nothing petty about what she did. Identity theft, swindling the rich, it wasn't child's play. Unless you wanted to get caught.

"I don't work for him," she answered. She may kick back a small percentage of her dealings to keep his protection, but she didn't take orders from him. Well, mostly. When he had a job for her, she didn't have a choice, but she wasn't on his payroll. Not anymore. Not like some of the other men he employed to do his dirty work whenever he needed.

"Okay." Jackson rolled his eyes. "When did you work for him? And don't tell me you didn't, because you did. If you don't answer directly to him now, you did at one point."

She let her gaze slip toward the dress. As nice as it

would be to have something to wear, she couldn't give over so easily. A slip of fabric couldn't be enough to give Jackson a piece of the puzzle.

"We can finish this conversation downstairs if you'd rather?" he said, as though he were offering a choice between chocolate and strawberry ice cream.

"If I tell you how I got into Ash's party, you'll let me leave?" she asked him firmly.

He narrowed his eyes. "That's part of what I want to know, yeah."

"Fine. I paid one of his clients to bring me as a plus one. Once inside, he went his way and I went mine." She folded her arms over her stomach. "Okay?"

"Who was this person?" Suspicion pulled at his tone.

"I don't remember his name. I'd seen him coming out of a party the month before, and I approached him. I offered the money, he sent me a text to let me know when and where to meet him. Once I was inside, I gave him his cash." This was nearly the truth but far enough away from it that she'd have to keep track of her words.

He stared at her for a long moment, then sighed, letting his shoulders drop.

"I was really hoping you'd trust me with the truth," he said sadly.

"What makes you think I'm not?" she asked, noticing her own voice pitch a bit higher.

"Ash has security cameras on the entrance to the party. You aren't on the tape," he said with finality. Like she'd had a shot here, and she'd missed.

One of Jansen's men had told her the cameras didn't record. He'd told her they were just for security during the event, but Ash didn't keep recordings because of the anonymous nature of his clients. Jansen's man had been fucking wrong.

Or Jackson was lying to her.

She chewed the inside of her bottom lip. Which was it? Did she have bad intel or was Jackson trying to trick her?

"So, how did my sly little fox get into that party?" he asked.

She searched his features. "I already told you." All eggs in one basket. She knew Jansen's men. They'd never given her bad information before. Ever.

His mouth spread into a wide, satisfied grin. "I won't lie, a small part of me was hoping we'd get to play again soon." He hooked the hanger over his shoulder. "I'll be right back, little fox. We're going to have some fun."

And with a wink, he sauntered out of the room and locked her inside again.

He'd taken the dress with him, but the heat in her cheeks at his promise of what was to come kept her warm enough.

10

The woman just couldn't be straight with him. Fine.

Jackson tossed the dress onto the suitcase full of her clothing and picked up the other items he'd brought upstairs. As much as he would enjoy what he planned for her, he'd rather be administering it without her deception blocking him from her true submission.

She wanted to tell him. He could see the conflict in her eyes as she thought over what he had asked her. Whatever she'd been doing with Jansen over the years, had left her jaded. She didn't know if she could believe him.

If she had walked into the party on someone's arm, Ash would have already figured it out by now. No, she hadn't just sauntered in as a plus one. She was let in somewhere by someone, and he needed to find out who that person was.

Maybe she had paid someone to help her, and she didn't want to expose him, but it wasn't some schmuck off the street. No, he knew deep down it wasn't that simple. She wouldn't be so closed off if that was all it was.

When he reentered her room, she stood near the window. The blinds had been pulled down, probably so she could hide her nakedness from anyone who could see in. They were half an acre away from the Main Street. No one would be seeing anything in that window, but she didn't know that.

"What is that?" Keagan asked with a pointed finger and wide eyes at the item he held in his left hand.

"This?" He held up the fox tail by its tip. "This is your tail." He flicked the glass butt plug at the other end. "It's also a butt plug. You remember these." He winked.

He remembered vividly. He'd bought her a purple jeweled plug while they were playing with each other. She had resisted it at first, but once he'd had it in, she'd loved it. It would be the same here, though he hadn't had a tail attached to the plug before.

A soft blush blossomed into a deep red that reached her ears. He'd forgotten how arousing her embarrassment had been, but it came back to him in full force seeing it now. His cock lengthened in his jeans.

"I'll give you a choice here. You can either get on your hands and knees on the floor or you can bend over the bed." He gestured toward the neatly made bed.

Her throat worked, and her delicate pink tongue peeked out between her lips, wetting them and darting back into her mouth. Maybe she was having a hard time concentrating in order to make the call for herself.

"I can decide for you," he offered, being the generous asshole he was sure she remembered him being.

"No." She shook her head and whipped both hands behind her ass, like that would stop him. He chuckled at the cuteness of it, how innocent she presented at the moment. But he knew her, he remembered their playtime. She'd taken his middle finger past his second knuckle into her ass while he'd been sucking so hard on her clit, she burst into an orgasm right there. It had been fucking amazing. And if she would only give over, stop being so damn stubborn, he could give it all to her again.

"It's not a yes or no question," he said, stepping toward her. "It's an over-the-bed or on-the-floor question. What's your answer?"

Her gaze fixated on the tail in his hand.

"Don't," she whispered, and if he didn't know her better, he'd think she was going to break. But Keagan was made of strong stuff. She wouldn't crumble beneath him. He wouldn't allow it.

"Don't what?"

"Don't do this. Don't keep playing with me like... like you know me." She brought her gaze up to his. Vulnerability flashed in her eyes.

It was strong enough to give him pause, but not to stop. He had a job to do.

"I do know you, Keagan. At least I did, and I don't think too much has changed. I think your situation changed. Your path altered, but you, who you are on the inside, is the same. And I remember perfectly how much you liked that jeweled plug. Now." He cupped her chin and ran the pad of his thumb over her bottom lip. "Over the bed or on the floor?" he asked in a softer tone.

Her jaw firmed within his grasp.

"I think you don't want to remember who you were when we knew each other. Something happened after you faded away on me. What was it? Did Jansen get his claws in you right then? Is that why you ghosted?"

"I didn't ghost you. We weren't anything. We were just screwing around."

The dull pang in his chest caught him off guard, but he recovered quickly enough to squelch it. He hadn't been hurt then. Why would he feel any sort of remorse about it now? He had been curious about what had made her disappear so easily, but he hadn't chased her down to find out. He'd let her fade off into the past.

"Well, we're not just screwing around now," he said with more of a sinister tone. Maybe he had been a little irritated by the brush-off, and maybe seeing her now brought some of that back. But it wouldn't stop him from getting the information he wanted.

"No, we aren't screwing," she said with more conviction. Ah, so she was not as brittle as she wanted him to think. Maybe she could play her little tricks and games with men who were unsuspecting of her charms, but he wouldn't be played.

"Not yet, little fox, not until you're begging for my cock will you feel it again. And you won't even have the chance of begging until you've been truthful. So, I'll ask once more before I decide, floor or bed?" He released her chin. A small imprint of his thumb went white then reddened slightly on her skin.

"Bed." She dropped her answer between them.

With a raised chin, she went to the bed and gracefully laid herself over the edge, her ass high in the air as she rose on her toes.

Stubborn girl.

Gorgeous, beautiful, stubborn girl.

He pulled out the small tube of lubrication he'd

brought with him from his pocket and flicked off the cap with his thumb.

"Reach back and spread your ass cheeks for me," he directed while he squirted the cool gel onto the tip of the plug.

She sighed but moved into action.

"You can pretend you hate this, but I'm betting if I feel your pussy again, I'll find it as hot and wet for me as I did yesterday," he said, concentrating on getting the plug as lubed as possible. He didn't know how long it'd been since she had a plug inside her, and he wasn't looking to tear her. After all, he was somewhat of a gentleman.

"That was...a mistake," she muttered, keeping her face turned away from him. He moved closer to her, dropping the tube onto the nightstand beside the bed.

He took a moment to soak in the gorgeous woman before him. Her fingers were pressed hard into her ass cheeks, holding them wide apart for him. The dark ring of her muscle was ready for his intrusion, but there was no tension in her legs or her back.

It would make the insertion easier.

He placed a hand on the small of her back, and she started. "It's just my hand," he told her. "The plug is coming now. Deep breath and try not to clench."

"Right. Don't clench," she muttered sarcastically. "You're going to be shoving something up my ass, which is totally not normal, and I should just open up and take it. Don't clench. Maybe I should try shoving something up *your* ass and see how unclenched you can be."

He stared at the back of her head while she continued. Apparently, she had never realized how smart mouthed she got when she was overly nervous. Since she couldn't see him, he unleashed a grin.

"Are you done?" he asked when she finally paused to draw breath.

"Yeah." She nodded and pressed her forehead into the bed.

He pushed the rounded glass tip against her asshole.

"Easy," he said softly and pressed harder until it went forward. She hissed as it sank further and further into her and the wide part of the plug stretched her.

"Jackson," she whined.

"I know, sweet girl, just relax, try to push against it, and your ass will accept it easier," he instructed, running his hand in small circles on her back.

She groaned, but the plug eased into her more smoothly.

"Almost there," he said, as the widest part of the plug stretched her even more. She tensed, but once he started rubbing her back again, she softened. Finally, the widest part passed, through and the ring of muscle snapped shut around the narrow base.

"There," he said with some pride. She'd taken it well, without fighting him or trying to get away. He wouldn't be so stupid as to take it as a sign that she wanted him or thought this was anything more than him punishing her for not giving him the info he wanted. But he would still take the moment as a small victory. If she had fought him and made him pin her down to get it done—he would have. But that didn't mean he would have enjoyed it.

Well, maybe he would have, but her obedience, even when it was just common sense not to fight, still made his balls tighten.

Hell, he had better get a grip on himself before he was the one begging her instead of the other way around.

"There." He ran his hand over the tail, playing with it and making it wag. "It's cute." The red coloring of the tail faded into an off-white tip. Perfect for his little fox.

"Now what?" she asked, sounding as though she were talking to him through gritted teeth.

"Now, we go for a walk," he answered cheerfully as he pulled out the long leather lead he had coiled up in his back pocket and unraveled it.

"A walk?" She looked over her shoulder at him, then to the leash. Her eyes went wide, but her pupils were already dilated.

"Yes, I'm taking you down the hall to my room." He

reached over her back and found the metal ring on her collar. Hooking his finger through it, he pulled her off the bed to her feet. She pulled back a little, but it only took one hard tug before she settled down.

Once he had the leash clipped to the collar, he stepped away and raised his eyebrows.

"What?" She threw her hands in the air.

He laughed. "Such a naughty fox. Down." He pointed to the floor.

The command blessed him with another sweet red blush across her face.

When she didn't move, he gave the leash a tug toward the floor. Out of self-preservation, probably, she moved on her own to her hands and knees.

"Good," he said and snapped his fingers. "I've never had a pet fox before. I've had a puppy once, but never a fox." He then headed to the door, making sure to keep his strides small so she could easily keep up with him. The real trouble was going to start for her once he had her in his room. He'd grant her a small reprieve on the short walk there.

As they went down the hall, he slowed his pace. "Go a bit ahead of me. We're going to the second door on the left up there." He stepped to the side and pulled on the lead just enough for her to follow his directions.

She glanced up at him, promised vengeance raging in her eyes, but she kept silent. He took his place behind her, watching the tail swish back and forth with her hips as she moved. Her ass was as lush and sweet as he remembered, but it wasn't the physical beauty that made his dick so fucking hard. For all the annoyance her stubbornness caused, he admired her strength. He'd seen men cave and spill everything they knew with a mere show of a knife or a pair of brass knuckles being slipped on. He doubted Keagan would crumble so easily.

As they reached his bedroom, she sank back on her heels waiting for him.

"Good girl," he said, and for the first time since he'd brought her into his house, he wasn't trying to provoke her.

She must have understood the compliment to be sincere, as she lowered her gaze to the floor. Just like he had taught her. A small show of submissiveness to accept his praise. Fuck, his cock was going to burst from his pants if this went any further.

He threw open the door to his room and walked her inside in a hurry. With the door shut behind her, he snapped his fingers to get her attention and pointed to his bed. "Up on there, on your back, and spread your legs for me."

"No," she said, and yanked on the leash.

He froze. Her rejection wasn't the half-hearted denials she'd given him so far. This one was final.

Her eyebrows knitted together, and her lips pressed into a tight line.

His command had been given in a harsh tone out of his arousal being unmet. He'd probably scared her.

Crouching in front of her, he brushed away her hair from her eyes. Her dark eyes roamed over his face. Was she inspecting his reaction the same way he was doing to her?

"I told you, I won't fuck you until you answer all my questions, and you're begging," he assured her in a softer tone. As much as his cock was going to hurt like hell, he would not violate her.

"I can't tell you what you want to know," she said quietly.

"You can." He brushed his knuckles along her jaw. "I won't let anything happen to you, Keagan. I just want the truth."

She searched his gaze another moment, then broke the contact by looking away.

"I'll never beg you," she vowed, and just like that, the tenderness, as small as it was, was gone.

He shrugged. "Then you have nothing to fear. Now up on the bed." He shifted back to his feet. Bending, he unhooked the leash. He wouldn't drag her to the bed. She would go willingly.

And just like with the plug, she moved one step at a time until she was exactly where he'd told her to be. Such a contradiction, his little fox.

He went to the toy chest and opened the lid. He hadn't had a chance to fully unpack everything, but the toy chest had been the first thing he had worked on once he was able to move in. Having selected the vibrator he wanted, he pulled it out of the case. Brand new. The last one had broken when the girl he'd been playing with threw it across the room in a temper tantrum. She'd gotten her ass blistered for it, and within a week she was off finding a new playmate. He hadn't been sorry to see her go.

"What's that?" Keagan asked, narrowing her eyes trying to see it. He held it up for her take a better look, and her lips parted in surprise.

"Oh, don't worry, you're not going to like this part any better than you liked the plug going in." He reached between her legs, ignoring her legs tightening, and grabbed the tail, which he pulled from beneath her to lay it flat against the bed.

He put the vibrator on the bed, just a scant inch away from her pussy that was sweetly displayed with her legs spread so nicely for him. A thought came to him that gave him pause. Why let the vibrator have all the fun?

Jackson yanked off his shirt, climbed onto the massive bed and tossed the shirt to the floor. A king-sized bed might be excessive for a single person, but he liked the space it gave. And at the moment, the extra room was perfect.

He knelt between her legs and placed his hands on her knees.

"Keagan. I'm going to ask you again. When did you start working for Jansen?"

She clenched her jaw.

"Okay," he said and sank down on the bed until his mouth hovered over her pussy. Her arousal was evident, glistening pussy lips and the aroma—he took a deep breath. Fuck she smelled good.

With his thumbs, he pried apart her pussy lips. "Fuck, you're soaked, little fox," he said. Lowering himself down, he swiped the tip of his tongue through the folds of her pussy, gathering all of her sweet nectar.

He looked up the length of her body, past her stomach, over her breasts to her face. Her bottom lip was already tucked between her teeth, defiance set firmly in her gaze.

"Hands over your head, grab hold of the bars on the headboard and do not let go."

She didn't move.

He moved his right hand and spanked her pussy hard. "Did you hear me, little fox?"

She narrowed her eyes. "Fuck you."

"Oh...if you're a good girl, maybe." He laughed.

11

Keagan had no plan of escape here. Jackson was set on getting the answers he wanted, and if he touched her again like he had downstairs, she couldn't promise herself she wouldn't give in. Maybe if she got him angry enough, he'd just lay into her again with his belt.

"Fuck you," she tried to snap her legs closed, but he caught both her thighs in his powerful grip and pushed her thighs back down to the mattress. Years of yoga made the position easy to maintain, but his fingers were digging deep.

"We'll see." His words, while giving her no information at all, sounded very much like a promise.

Her body wasn't new to him, but it had been years. Surely the man had forgotten how quickly he could turn her into puddle of aroused goo.

The moment his tongue touched her clit, she curled her toes and sucked in a harsh breath.

He remembered.

Fucking hell.

What was it about the warmth of his tongue on her body that made her melt so damn easily?

He flicked the tip of his tongue over her clit. Electricity shot through her body, and she arched upward.

"Stay still," he growled against her sex. Stay still? Was he insane?

His tongue roamed over her clit, down her slit and danced at the entrance of her pussy. Her body clenched, which only reminded her of the fullness of her asshole. The plug was still there, never yielding. And when he made her body tighten, her ass hugged the glass plug, stretching her even more.

She let go of one of the bars and dropped her hand to her stomach, but he caught the move right away.

"Grab the headboard, now." Using his four fingers together, he smacked her pussy over and over until her hand was back where it was supposed to be. Now not only did a fire erupt from a simmering ember inside her core, but her pussy ached to be kissed and soothed.

She groaned, frustrated and annoyed with his barbaric measures. They worked too fucking well on her.

"The rule here is simple. You come only after

you've told me what I want to know. If you come before you do that, if you come without my okay, you'll be sleeping with a sore ass, and even sorer pussy. Do you get me?"

The gravely sound of his voice, sent a hot shiver through her. He meant it. This wasn't a game he was playing with her.

"Yeah, I get you." She turned her eyes up to the ceiling. She needed to find something else to think about, to focus on, because if she let herself delve into all the sensations he was giving her, she'd fall over the edge again. Too easily, just like she'd done downstairs.

As his tongue once again begin to lick, and his teeth scraped over her clit, her mind wandered to the moment he'd ripped off his shirt. He was all muscle and strength. Dark tattoos covered his chest and shoulders, all the way down to his wrists. He'd only had one tattoo across his back when they'd been playing together. She hadn't had time to see the new artwork, but she'd noted the way his muscles moved while he climbed onto the bed, like an animal stepping up to feast.

And now, she was the main course.

"Fuck!" She moaned, arching her body again to bring her pelvis upward toward his mouth.

The tight coil in her belly was getting harder and harder to ignore. Her thighs trembled while his mouth sent her entire body on fire. No matter how hard she gripped the headboard, she could not distract herself from the pleasure he was punishing her with.

She chanced a glance down at him, and found his silvery blue eyes focused on her while his tongue dragged along her sex—a man with his very own ice cream cone, but she wasn't chilled at all. How could she be, with this man touching her the way he was? Even with just looking into his eyes at that moment, being captivated by his glare, he could lock her down with just a look.

Out of nowhere, the pressure built to an unmanageable level, and she could feel the first wave of release ready to burst. She bit down on her lip, trying her damnedest not to give it away to him, but he knew her body. Even after all these years, he knew her.

"Are you going to tell me?" he asked, rolling his tongue around her clit. Just a tiny bit more pressure and she'd explode.

"No?" He took her clit into his mouth and sucked hard. She couldn't stop it. The rising tidal wave peaked, ready to fall.

And then he pulled back and hovered over her pussy, looking up at her while the wave receded.

"No!" She hit the mattress.

"Did you let go of the headboard?" he asked with a playful tilt of his head.

She grabbed hold of the bar quickly, not wanting

another volley of spanks. It would only serve to drag her right back to the edge he wouldn't let her fall over.

"If you want to come, you only have to answer the question," he reminded her then lowered his mouth over her sex again. She tried to push her legs closed, but his grip was still too hard.

She rolled her pelvis upward, but he stopped her movements by draping one arm over her hips. She was pinned. And while the restraint ramped up her arousal, his tongue dove in and out of her entrance. Her eyes rolled back, and her chest burned with each shallow breath.

The edge came into view, she could make out the cliff, and she wanted to run and jump over it headfirst. But as soon as she saw the sharp edge, he pulled away again.

"Fuck!" She yanked on the headboard.

"Want to answer?"

"Fuck you!" she yelled at him. This wasn't fair. None of this was fair. It didn't even concern him. It wasn't his club. The Annex wasn't his business.

"I'm really hoping for that, but you have to be a good girl first." He winked. Winked! And went back to torturing her with more pleasure than she could ever remember a man giving her.

He relented on holding her thigh. Sensing a reprieve, she relaxed, only to be dragged right up to the gates of heaven when he thrust three fingers into her pussy. He wiggled them, stretching her pussy while putting pressure on the plug in her ass.

"Jackson!" She couldn't hold out—it was coming too fast, and if she didn't get to take it she would surely lose her mind.

"Tell me, Keagan. Just tell me," he said, sucking on her clit while curling and pumping his fingers in and out of her.

"No." She would remain strong. She would not let him think he could control her in any way. Years had passed, and she wasn't the same girl she had been in college. He'd easily taken her under his control, had given her every reward for being his good girl, but this was not then. She had greater responsibilities now besides just having a fun time between classes.

"Okay, then," he said, mocking her with pretend disappointment.

A buzzing noise drew her eyes back down toward him. The vibrator he'd brought to the to bed was in his hands, and she watched with a mixture of panic and hope as he brought the rounded tip of it to her body. The intense vibrations rocked through her body and she arched, seeking out the very pleasure he held hostage.

Again, he brought down his heavy arm and locked her down. Drawing the vibrator over her clit in circles, he thrust his fingers harder into her pussy while pushing on the tail and activating the nerves in her ass at the same time.

How was she supposed to combat this? If she were stronger, less desperate… But as it stood, she wanted everything he dangled just outside of her grasp. Her fingers burned with the tightness of her grip around the bars of the headboard. Digging her teeth into her lip did nothing to help dissuade her body from obeying him.

"Just answer me, and you'll get everything your body is begging for," he said over the hum of the toy, between her gasps for air that would not satisfy her craving.

All sense flew away. It was a small thing he wanted, she could give it, she could give it and nothing else.

"Fine!" She cried out. "Right before I stopped seeing you." She huffed and sucked in a heavy breath. "Please, Jackson."

He stilled and looked up her length again. There was a lot more to this story, but he didn't look up to questioning her just yet.

"What is it you want, Keagan?" he asked.

She looked down at him, at his thick lips, his larger-than-life gaze. Her heart hurt to see him. Why? She hadn't done anything wrong walking away from him back then. She had missed him. But he was a member of the Titon family, and she couldn't work with Jansen and still see him. It could have been dangerous for them both.

"You, Jackson. I want you." She let go of the headboard and reached for him so she could touch his cheek. "Please."

His arched his left eyebrow. "Are you asking me to fuck you, little fox?" The teasing was gone.

"Yes." She nodded. More than the next heartbeat, she needed him to touch her, to cover her with his strength. Because once she told him everything there was to tell him, she was going to need some of it.

"You have to beg, sweet fox," he said, though he was already unbuckling his jeans and shoving them over his hips. It always amazed her how easily he could squirm out of his pants while lying in bed.

"I said please," she reminded him. "Don't push it."

He froze and turned a heated stare on her. She swallowed. Maybe she was the one who shouldn't push.

"Hmmm." He pressed his lips together. "Watch yourself," he said, a finger pointed at her. She scooted up the bed, when he shifted, reaching over her for the nightstand where he grabbed a condom. Quickly, he ripped open the package and rolled the condom over his cock.

She followed his fingers as he rolled the latex down his thick, long shaft. She couldn't help but lick her lips.

"Careful, you're going to get drool on my sheets," he teased her as he crawled up her body.

She blinked a few times. "I wasn't—" She shook her head.

He didn't give her a chance to say anything else. His mouth crashed over hers, and she wound her arms around his neck, letting him control the kiss. He nipped at her lip, and she found herself losing herself into the moment.

"Beg," he muttered against her lips as he reached between them to rub her clit. Instantly she was at the brink again. How magical was this man's fingers?

"Please, Jackson," she uttered, reaching up to kiss him again.

"We'll work on it," he promised, and with one powerful thrust was inside her. She cried out. The plug and his cock were too much, and her body stretched around both invasions.

"Hold still a second." He pinned her down to the bed with his hips. "Give it a second," he said, placing kisses to her cheeks. She was no virgin, but she'd never had the full force of his cock and a plug at the same time.

"It's...fuck, Jackson."

He started with shallow thrusts, but it was enough to drive her mind to another place. She pulled her knees up higher, and he growled.

"Fuck, woman." He nipped her earlobe. "Do that again," he ordered, and she moved again.

"Jackson." she clawed at his back, wanting to pull him in faster, further. No matter how full she felt, she wanted more, wanted all of him. And for the moment, she would give herself a reprieve as to why any of that was happening.

"Keagan." He thrust harder into her. "Fuck. Keagan, promise me. No more hiding things." He captured her face with his hands. "You're going to tell me everything."

She stared up at him, seeing the worry and concern in his eyes for the first time. He wasn't just acting on behalf of his cousin. Jackson wanted to know, because he wanted to help.

"Okay," she agreed.

He thrust again and again until she couldn't see straight anymore, and the dam wouldn't hold back.

"Jackson, please. Let me come, please, let me come," she begged, and didn't care how desperate she sounded.

"Fuck yes," he said and doubled his force. She pulled up her knees once more, and as his cock slammed into her, the dam burst, and her nerves flooded her with wave after wave of pleasure. The pulse of each orgasmic beat sucked air from her lungs, but she somehow still managed to scream out his name.

He captured her mouth again, taking her cries into his mouth as he rocked into her over and over again as the waves began to recede. He pulled back and plowed forward then stilled over her. A low growl emanated from his chest, and his hands tightened around her face as he found his own release.

With a shudder, his body went soft, and he dropped his forehead to hers.

"Fucking hell," she whispered.

His mouth split into a grin, and he laughed. "I forgot how much you love that phrase."

"It fits," she said, willing her body to slow down. Her heart still jackhammered against her ribs, and her lungs weren't keeping up with their workload.

He kissed her—a sound kiss from a man who was satisfied and happy. At least for the moment.

He rolled to her side, his cock gliding easily from her.

"The plug." She wiggled her ass against his bed.

He raised himself on his elbow and stared at her for a long moment. "No more lies or half-truths. All honesty from here on out." He touched her chin.

"I already said yeah." She rolled her yes.

He grabbed her chin. "Tell me again without my cock inside you."

She frowned. "I promise I'll tell you everything."

And once she did, he'd probably regret ever having found her again.

"I'm going to get this rubber off my cock, and then you and I are going to have a long talk."

"Okay, but first..." She wiggled again.

He sat up in the bed and shrugged. "What?"

"The tail?"

He swung his legs over the side of the bed. "Every fox needs a tail, Keagan."

She threw a pillow at his retreating form as he headed toward what she assumed was his bathroom. The pillow hit him in the back then fell to the floor.

He never even flinched.

12

J ackson placed a glass of water on the table in front of Keagan. After he'd given her a few minutes of rest, she'd gotten up from his bed. He'd taken her back to her room, leash free for the moment, and let her dress in the navy blue dress.

Now that they were sitting, both clothed and for the movement physically sated, he hoped she would be more clear-headed with her answers.

With her long dark hair brushed out and laid around her shoulders and the well-fitting blue sundress covering her curves, she took on the look of a professional woman. Someone who would fit right in with a board room of CEOs and investors. She held her head high, almost in a regal manner.

"Jansen said he's supposed to be seeing you this afternoon. Text him that you're not available," Jackson instructed and placed her iPhone beside the glass of water.

She looked from him to the phone, a plan already forming in that big brain of hers.

"If you call or text anyone apart from him, or say anything other than what I just told you to, you'll be spending the night in your crate." He leaned down, caging her in with his arms and bringing his face a scant breath away from hers. "And I mean all night."

She pinched her lips together and blew a huff out of her nostrils. It would have been cute—this pout of hers—except he got the feeling she was going to try for another power move soon. He needed to be on his toes around her.

Picking up her phone, she swiped it to life and punched in her key code. He stood over her as she found a message from Jansen telling her he wanted to see her. She quickly tapped out a response that she was visiting a friend all afternoon and she'd get a hold of him later.

"Good," he said and plucked it from her hand before she got any ideas that would get her in trouble.

"If he wants to see me, he's not going to be okay with waiting too long," she warned.

"I don't doubt that. So how about you come clean about everything so you can go back to your daily life and I can get on with mine." He put the phone on the table and sat in the chair across from her.

"I already told you, I started working for him right before I stopped meeting up with you," she explained.

"Yes, I know, but I want to know why you worked with him in the first place. And then you can get to the part where he helped you get into Ash's party."

Her eyes darted to meet his. She didn't think him that dumb, did she? He may not have majored in computer science and had taught himself to hack into any computer system currently available, but he had a solid head on his shoulders.

"Jackson. Isn't it enough to know that I'll never go back to one of those parties again?" she asked in a singsong voice that he didn't doubt had helped get her out of more than one jam. Some men were too easily persuaded by a woman's beauty and innocence. But she was no innocent.

"No," he said. "The fact that you're going to such great lengths to hide it tells me it's something that could cause trouble for Ash or Jansen. Mostly Jansen. So just explain it to me so I can help figure out a way to get Ash off your back and keep Jansen either out of it or see if I can keep Ash from going after him."

"Ashland doesn't want anything to do with the families, but he would attack Jansen?" she asked hesitantly, as if testing the waters.

"He doesn't want any dealings with them, no, but if Jansen did anything to jeopardize Ash's business, he'd have to act. I doubt he'd start a war, he's too much of a family man these days to risk it, but he'd find another way to deal with it."

Keagan sat back in her chair and cupped the water, playing with a drop of condensation as it rolled down the glass.

"What do you want to know?" Defeat deflated her confident posture a fraction. She had to realize if she wanted to keep Jansen and Ash from going after each other, she would have to trust him. At least a little.

"Start at the beginning. Why did you go to work for him?"

"Katarina died," she answered with a shrug. "She was already retired, and I was starting to take over for her with Jansen. But after she was gone, he put me on a contract."

"What kind of contract?"

"The kind that said I worked directly for him and agreed not to take any outside work. It's not really legally binding, considering some of the things he demands from his contractors, but if I were to go back on the contract... Well, different sort of contracts would be deployed," she said cryptically.

"I understand." He nodded. "How long of a contract was it?"

"Two years. It's over now, but I still work with him. I just have a little more freedom."

"Why let the contract expire?" he asked.

"I'm not sure, really. From what I understand, he

usually doesn't. Sort of a once you're here, you're here forever deal, but he didn't put a long-time limit on me, and then when it came due, he didn't force me. He still expects me to answer his calls and take a job if he offers it, though."

"So, he keeps you close but not too close?" Jackson asked.

"I don't get it, but yeah. He'd always been good to Katarina and me. When she died, he helped me get through all the legal stuff. I didn't have to deal with anything—he had it taken care of for me," she explained.

Jackson's teeth clicked as he clenched his jaw. Jansen didn't have a reputation for such generosity. "Okay, so he showed a little humanity. Where did you work?" He already sensed the dark cloud forming over his head.

"Nothing like you're thinking," she quickly said. "He knew I had gotten my degree in computers, and he asked if I could help him with a few projects. So at first that's what I did. I hacked into a few personal accounts to get dirt on a politician or cop. Eventually, he had me doing more detailed digs on people. Seeking them out, getting close to them to find real dirt on them." She lifted her eyes to his. "It wasn't exactly honest work, but I had nowhere else to go."

"You could have come to me," he said somberly.

Her eyes locked with his. "And say what? I'd been

groomed to work for this big crime family, but I didn't really want to anymore because my foster mom died. Except, I'm not sure she actually died. I was a hot fucking mess, and you and me said no strings. We didn't want anything like that. I wasn't about to bring my mess to your doorstep."

They had said no strings. Playtime and that was it. It had been enough. Or so he'd told himself.

"I would have helped. You knew my family had connections," he said with more heat.

"Yeah, I knew you were a Titon and your family had ties, but I didn't want to get any more involved in that world than I already was. So I did the projects, I learned how to hack the bank systems he wanted. I learned how to take over someone's identity. And within two years, I had finished my contract."

Jackson wanted to know more, but there was a lot of ground to cover here, so he moved on. "Okay, and then what? Why is he wanting to see you this afternoon?"

She shook her head. "I don't know. Every now and then he offers me a job. He pays well, and he's not a dick about it. Most of the time, I hear from Sergio, one of his guys and not him directly."

"And if you say no to a job?"

She scrunched up her lips and shrugged. "I never have."

"And if you get caught? You know he won't come

through with helping you if you get tossed in jail," Jackson pointed out. Foot soldiers didn't get the protection they thought they'd have if they got picked up by the cops. She'd probably get locked up and forgotten—unless she squealed. In which case she'd end up dead.

"I know. And I have taken every precaution I can so that I don't get caught, and if I do, I can't be linked to him."

He studied her silently for a long moment. "You said you're looking for Katarina You don't think she's dead?"

She let out a heavy sigh and took a long swig of her water. "I don't know what to think. Her body was never released, so I've never seen it. She's on the manifest for the plane that went down, but I don't even fully understand why she's on the list. She was supposed to be going on a Medieval castle tour, not a safari. The last person that I can track down that had seen her or spoke to her was Herald Potier, and you ruined my chance to talk to him."

Jackson kept his gaze firm. "You think he can tell you why she was going on a safari?"

"Yes," she said firmly, giving him a harsh glare.

"We'll get back to all that." He waved a hand. "Now, tell me how you got into Ash's party."

She darted her gaze away.

"The truth, Keagan, or we can go to the playroom

right now," he said with a jerk of this head toward the hallway.

With wide eyes she shook her head. "I don't want a fight between them."

He reached across the table and picked her hand, squeezing gently. "There won't be." It didn't suit anyone to have a war, and Jackson's first bit of business with the Annex shouldn't be too bring one to Ashland's doorstep.

"I reached out to his niece, well niece-in-law, I guess. She married Hunter, Jansen's nephew," she explained. "She'd worked as an Annex girl for a short time. She told me the security routes and where there was a door leading out to the gardens behind one of the bar set-ups. She did me a favor and reached out to a girl still working there who helped get the door open for me, and I slipped in. Getting into the garden wasn't hard since I blended in with the other guests arriving. But I didn't have an invitation to get into the party," she said, her cheeks reddening all the while. "Please, Jackson, you can't tell him that though. Not only will he think Jansen was involved, Jaelynn and the girl inside could get hurt."

Jackson gripped her fingers tighter when she started to pull away.

"Do you..." He closed his eyes for a moment and took a deep breath. "Does Hunter know his wife did this for you?"

She licked her lips. "No, of course not. He wouldn't let her. I've met him a few times over the years, he's... well...like you but all the time."

"What does that mean?" he asked more aggressively than he'd intended.

"I mean, well, you know...in charge," she whispered like it was some huge fucking secret.

"And by all the time, you mean?" He raised an eyebrow.

"I mean all the time, not just for sex, like for you," she said. How easily her cheeks deepened their blush when she talked about sex, and how quickly she would slip to her knees when provoked the right way.

He let go of her hand and sat back in his chair. "It's not a sex thing for me, either, Keagan. It may have been in the past—we were just fucking around—but it's an all-the-time thing for me."

She lowered her gaze. Had he embarrassed her by using her own wording?

"I didn't...I mean...I think we're getting off-topic here," she said bringing her eyes back to his.

"Not really. Because so long as you're here with me, you should understand that. It's not only when you're naked and on my leash that you'll be obedient and respectful, it's every moment of every day."

She swallowed hard at his statement and blinked rapidly in succession.

"I'm not here with you, Jackson. Now that I told you, I'm free to go, remember?"

He stared at her. He'd paid the money to Ash to keep her safe from Stanley McKinnley's retaliation. He could hold that over her head, but he wouldn't.

"Well, I guess that depends on you. Ash still needs these answers, and Jansen will find out his niece got his name put in front of Ash for the wrong reasons. You'll have two very pissed-off powerful men on your tail. You can go and deal with them both on your own, or you can stay, and I'll help you navigate the mess. And then we'll work together to figure out what happened to your mom."

A lightness bloomed in her eyes, and he wondered when the last time was that anyone offered her help.

"Why would you do that?" she asked softly with her head tilted in curiosity.

"I'm in between projects at the moment," he said with a grin. "But I'm not kidding around here, Keagan. While you're here, you're mine. In all ways."

Her lips dropped into a frown. "So, you'll help me in exchange for being your sex toy?"

He got up from his chair and moved around the table to her. Fisting her hair with his left hand, he dragged her head back until she was looking up at him.

"What I'm offering you is help, as a friend. You can say no, leave this house and go home. I'll still help you."

He hovered over her mouth, inhaling the sweet womanly scent of her. "But if you stay here, you'll have my protection, my help, and my full authority over you."

The tip of her tongue touched her upper lip. Fuck, he loved when she did that. His balls pulled up tight and his cock hardened. He would need to get more control over his own body if she was going to be staying with him.

"But just while I'm here," she clarified.

"Yes," he answered with a nod. "Just while you're here. When this is all resolved, we'll walk away." Just like they had years ago.

"And the only thing you gain from this is helping me?"

"I also keep my cousin from having a full-out battle with an old family he'd rather forget about," he answered.

Silence stretched out between them; her gaze wandered to his lips. Did she want his kiss as much as he wanted to give it to her? She'd have to give him an answer first.

"No more crate," she insisted.

He tugged her hair harder. "That's not up for debate, little fox."

"I don't like the crate."

"I know," his smile stretched wide. "That's why I love it so much."

"Then at least not a lot?" she asked softly, her pupils dilating and betraying her real thoughts on the matter.

"Only when you're naughty," he promised. "Now, give me your answer."

"Fine."

He tugged again.

"I mean, I'd really appreciate your help. I'll stay here with you."

"Good girl," he muttered against her lips then pressed harder, claiming her in a forceful kiss. Keagan touched his cheek as he deepened the kiss, sweeping his tongue through her mouth. She didn't push, or try to take control, but followed his lead.

When he pulled away, his heart beat against his ribs. Sharp tingles danced down his spine as he looked into her eyes.

"Now." He let go of her hair and stood straight. "I need the name of the girl at the Annex that helped you."

She blinked a few times, as though to switch her mind over to the new subject.

"Ash will fire her, Jackson. I can't do that."

He folded his arms over his chest. "Do we really need to go to the crate this soon?"

She opened her mouth, ready to shoot off an answer that would most likely give him reason to blister her ass, but clamped it shut before he had the opportunity.

"Can you promise me she won't lose her job?"

Ashland wouldn't let the girl get away with what she had done, but Jackson had confidence he wouldn't just turn her out if Jackson came up with a good reason. He just needed to find that reason.

"I'll do my damnedest to be sure she doesn't lose her job."

She huffed. "That's not the same thing."

"It's as good as you're getting, and considering you're the one who started this whole fucking mess, I really don't think you have a place right now to complain."

She thrust her chin upward at him, but still kept her cheek to herself. Smart girl.

"Her name is Aubry," she confessed.

Jackson's back tightened. The same woman he'd contracted for the night at Ash's. Maybe that could be reason enough to keep her employed.

Or it was reason enough to get rid of her.

"I'll call Ash and set up a meeting. We'll go over there tomorrow afternoon. In the meantime, let's go to my office and you can show me what you have so far on Katarina."

"You have my computer?" she asked as he took his phone out to get in touch with Ash.

He looked up from his phone and smiled. "You're not the only one who knows how to dig around."

"You hacked my computer," she accused.

"No. I just guessed your password." He started walking out of the kitchen. "You probably shouldn't use your safe word as your password." He laughed as he went down the hall. Obscenities were thrown at him from behind his back, but he let her have the moment.

She wouldn't have many reprieves now that she belonged to him.

13

The Titon estate invoked a stronger sinister chill as it came into view than it did when Keagan had last been there. Then she'd been confident in her abilities and skills. She'd had a task at hand. Get in and work the target.

This time was completely different. She was basically a condemned woman being hauled in front of the judge, who could switch hats to executioner within a blink of an eye.

"He's not going to hurt you," Jackson promised as he parked the near the front steps. "That's my job."

His joke didn't help.

"He could hurt Aubry. And Jaelynn could be hurt too. Not to mention Jansen getting pissed at me for involving her, and then ratting everyone out." And for what? An orgasm?

She bowed her head. That was a simplification of the situation. Jackson never would have let up if she hadn't told him everything. And now she had gained his help with Katarina. If she was alive, Jackson could help her. She wouldn't have to play the thief anymore to get the funds in order to keep her search going.

After he switched off the car, he reached over the console and squeezed her hand. "Trust me here, Keagan. I won't let anyone get hurt."

She leaned into his strength, knowing he had the means to help, but also that he might not have the power to make it happen. "Except Jaelynn. Odds are good she's going to have a serious talk coming her way once Hunter finds out, but that's not something I can do anything about."

She looked away from him, out the window to the beast of a house.

"Because if it was my wife who'd done what she did, you can bet your ass she'd have a hard time sitting for a long time." He chuckled.

"Your wife?" She jerked her attention back to him.

"I meant if I had a wife," he said quickly.

If not *when*. She gave a small nod. He'd been clear about what they were going to be—a temporary partnership. She would need to remember that while he maneuvered them through the shit storm she created here. He would help her, but his ultimate loyalty would land with his family. Not someone he was only hooking up with for the moment.

"We better get this over with," she said and reached for the handle. She climbed out of the car and stood at the bottom of the steps looking up at the parapets. "It's a very forceful house, isn't it?"

He chuckled as he came to stand beside her. "Ash isn't as scary as you think he is."

"If I can handle you, I can handle anyone," she said with as much forced bravery as she could muster and began ascending the steps.

"Maybe I've been too easy on you," he muttered, catching up to her as the front door opened. A man with a black patch over his left eye stood in the entrance. His hair was short and darker. This wasn't Ash.

"Peter." Jackson extended his hand.

Peter shook Jackson's hand and gave Keagan a curt nod. "I heard you over the speaker at the gate, and I told Ash I'd come get you. He's in the Annex office."

Jackson placed his hand on the small of Keagan's back and led her into the house. She was enthralled by the beauty of the artwork in the foyer and became even more so as they were led through a living room and another hallway.

"His wife does them," Jackson said to her quietly.

"They're fantastic," she responded.

"Right through here." Peter brought them to a door

hidden from the main view of the hallway. He punched a code into a keypad, and the door unlocked. "I assume it wasn't this door you came through?" he asked Keagan as she passed him and went into a new hallway.

"No, that wasn't it," she said, trying to keep her tone solid. This may not be like any other job she'd done, but it was still a job. Get in, tell them what they wanted to hear, get what she came for, and go.

"Leave her be, Peter," Jackson said firmly. "She'll tell you what you want to know. Just don't be an ass."

"An ass? Me?" Peter laughed. "If you think that was being an ass, I can't wait until you see how Ash is going to deal with this."

Jackson stopped walking and turned to Peter. "He's not going to scare her or touch her. If he does either of those things, I'll take her out of here."

Peter's eyebrows shot up. "You won't get what you came for either, then." Peter said.

Keagan looked at Jackson. What had he come for if not to help her?

Jackson eyed her quietly, shook his head, and moved forward, grabbing her hand and keeping her tightly at his side.

"The next door on the left," Peter announced from behind them. Keagan noticed the large double doors on the right and remembered them as leading to the room where the party had been held.

"You didn't use these doors either, I assume," Peter joked when he caught her staring at them

She looked up at him with a flat smile. "No."

"Come on." Jackson tugged her hand and pulled her into an office.

Ashland Titon stood in front of his desk, his hands pressed against the edge on either side of his body and his firm glare fixated on her as soon as she stepped inside. A foreboding cloud hovered in the air, and she stepped closer to Jackson. She'd seen Ashland that night at the party, but he'd looked less beastly then. His dark blond hair had been tied back, and he'd been wearing a suit. He had given the impression of a businessman. Now, standing in his office with his hair hanging loosely around his shoulders and his button-down shirt pulling tightly across his sculpted torso, he gave the appearance of an angry beast.

And she'd been the one to provoke him.

Jackson squeezed her hand gently and led her forward to her doom.

"Ash, this is Keagan Foxx. Keagan, I think you've seen Ash before," Jackson said.

"Keagan." Ash tipped his head in greeting, but no pleasantries fell from his lips, no smile to make her more comfortable or even an invitation to sit in one of the armchairs.

"Mr. Titon." She followed his manner and inclined her head.

"Jackson tells me you're ready to explain yourself." His dark demeanor carried over to his voice. He sounded as burly as Jackson when he was irritated, but unlike Jackson, she didn't trust Ash. He could hurt her. Not physically, Jackson wouldn't allow it, but he could ruin her search and her relationship with the Jansen family.

"You say it like I'm a little girl who had a temper tantrum at bedtime," she said lightly.

Jackson increased his grip. Apparently, now wasn't the time for humor. Or maybe Ashland Titon simply didn't have any.

"I'm sure Jackson wouldn't allow any such behavior," Ash told her with a twitch to his lips. "Tell me why you were here uninvited, and then tell me how you got inside."

Peter came into view, stepping behind the desk, assumedly to watch the events unfold.

"It wasn't through the main house door. I asked," Peter said with a playful grin. Did he find her nervousness funny?

She swallowed back a snarky comment meant for Peter. Insulting them wouldn't help her get through this any easier. Not that standing in a room with all three Titon men glaring at her was in any way easy to begin with. Did they have to be so damn formidable? Couldn't one of them at least look inviting?

Even Jackson, whom she trusted most in the room,

looked ready to pounce on her if she stepped out of line. She'd promised him she would tell Ash the truth, and if she went back on that vow, she knew what would be in store for her.

"Just let her tell you." Jackson gave Peter a pointed look. "Go on, Keagan." He shook her hand. A signal, she supposed, to get talking.

"It's a long and boring story. How about I just tell you I was able to get in through your garden doors and leave it at that?" She said with an airy tilt to her tone. She'd been good at this not too long ago. Figure out the personality that would most be suited to the person she was trying to scam and take on those characteristics. It worked every time. Tell them what they wanted to hear and how they wanted to be told.

But Ashland Titon wasn't a man easily read. His stone-cold expression remained locked on his face, with his firm jawline and his blue eyes fixated on her as though she might just poof into the air any second.

"Keagan." Jackson's warning rang loud and clear, his hard twist of her fingers emphasized his meaning as well.

"Summarize if you need, but I want to know how you got in and who helped you." Ashland kept his heavy stare on her.

She licked her lips. No way around it. Better just rush straight through.

"Fine. I've been tracking down information and to

do that I needed money. A large amount and quickly. I was here to...well...find an investor." She jerked her hand out of Jackson's before he could squeeze the blood out of her fingers. "I was able to get in through the glass doors you have leading from the garden into the main ballroom you use for the parties. It's behind one of the bars you have set up, so it wasn't hard to get inside behind the curtains pulled over them and then just sort of blend in."

"The back entrance into the gardens outside the Annex isn't locked on a party night because the guests enter through there," Peter said from his corner.

"Exactly, so it wasn't too hard. I just needed to step away from the crowd and make my way to that door." She shrugged and gestured with her hands. "It really wasn't hard."

"How did you know the door was there, and that it would be unlocked?" Ash asked—a logical question, and one for which she had an answer.

"Before I answer you, I'd like an answer first."

Ash's lips twitched again, something like a smile, but she didn't see any amusement in his eyes. So either he was fighting it, or he was attempting to hold back his anger.

"You have a question for me?" he asked with raised brows.

"Keagan, tread lightly," Jackson warned.

She hadn't discussed this with him, but he would

know her mind well enough to anticipate her. "If I tell you about any help I may have received from someone inside the party, what would happen to them?"

"A guest or an employee?" Peter stepped forward, becoming more interested.

She shrugged, forcing herself to play the diplomat. "Either."

"If it was a guest, they'd be banned from further parties," Ash stated instantly. "An employee would be terminated."

"As in fired?"

"Yes, fired," Peter shot at her.

She nodded. "I was just checking. He looks ready to tear apart my limbs at the moment, you can't blame me." She waved her hand up and down in front of Ash, who looked more likely to strangle her the longer she remained before him.

"Keagan." Jackson couldn't seem to say anything else besides her name. Maybe his irritation with her was clogging up his mind. "Tell him."

"I can't," she said, keeping her eyes entangled with Ash's while she said the two words that would send her straight to the damn crate when she got home.

"You can't?" Ash asked, his façade faltering with astonishment.

"No. If my telling you will cause that person to lose their position or their membership, I can't tell you. I swore I'd keep their identity safe."

"Keagan, I swear to you—"

"I'm not telling him, unless he promises me there won't be such harsh repercussions." She cut Jackson off before he could issue any further warnings or start issuing threats.

She tilted her gaze to the side to gauge Jackson's reaction. Her stomach dropped a good foot and half, and a heated shiver ran through her body. It would have been wiser to keep her gaze locked on the beast before her instead of the hound at her side.

"I'll assume it's one of the Annex girls, because I doubt you care that much about the clients of the Annex. So assuming that, I'll simply have them all brought before me, and I'll ask them." Ash pushed off from the desk, walking around it to his chair and plunking himself down.

"And if they don't come forward?" Keagan asked, starting to lose a touch of confidence in her plan.

"Then I'll fire them all and get a new staff. The list of applicants for a spot in the Annex is actually longer than you might think." Ash steepled his hands in front of him and stared up at her, waiting for her next move.

Fucking hell.

She hadn't thought he'd be so callous to all of his staff members.

"I'm also going to assume Jackson already knows which of the girls it is," Ash said, pointing his steepled fingers toward Jackson. "If he tells me, he'll get to keep his percentage. But if he doesn't, then it's forfeit. That was our deal, cousin, wasn't it?"

"What percentage?" She jerked her head toward him. "What is he talking about?"

Jackson frowned. "I'm buying into the Annex," he said, with a heated glare shot at Ashland. "But first I need to...resolve this issue."

A pang hit her chest. "You...so all of this, tracking me down, ruining my chances to get information from Potier was so you could buy into the Annex?"

"That's how it started, yes."

"And now? Once you get your shares, you'll just set me free on my own?" She shouldn't have been surprised. They weren't anything to each other, not truly. Why shouldn't he use her situation to his advantage? It was not like she hadn't done the exact same thing over and over again in her past.

"No." His low growl that suggested she calm herself down. "I meant what I said, I'm going to help you."

"Help with what?" Ash asked.

"None of your damn business," Keagan shot at him, too confused and angry to weigh the risk of yelling at Ashland Titon.

"Jackson." Ash turned his attention to him.

Jackson stared down at her, his nostrils flaring slightly and his lips pressing together so firmly they went white.

"Think of another punishment for the girl," Jackson said, turning his attention to Ashland. "She was acting on behalf of someone else. Promise she won't lose her position here, and I'll give you her name."

"Jackson, no. I don't want her punished at all," Keagan argued.

"Agree, Ash," Jackson said.

"No." Keagan rushed to the desk. "No discipline. No punishment. Do you understand? I won't be responsible for it!" Keagan shouted.

Ash's eyes wandered away from her to Jackson. "Breaking security protocol is a serious issue. There have to be consequences."

"Jackson. Don't." She whipped around toward him. "You said you'd let me handle this."

"I did." He nodded. "But you're not cooperating."

"You're just trying to save your shares. You're just thinking of your fucking wallet!" she yelled at him.

Jackson stared at her, his lips parted in surprise at her tone and words.

"I promised them," she whispered.

"What information did you need so badly from this person you needed to go through all of this mess?" Peter interjected.

"I'm trying to find someone," she said.

"Who?" Ash asked.

"My mother."

"That's what Jackson has promised to help you with?" Peter asked.

"Yes," Jackson responded.

"You said the girl here was acting on behalf of another, who is that?" Ash inquired.

Keagan lowered her gaze. She wouldn't betray them.

Jackson stepped toward the desk. "That's where things get more complicated. I need to talk to you about that."

Before Ash could respond, the door to the office flew open and a woman rushed inside.

"Ash, sorry to interrupt," she said with a bright smile. "Well, not really." She laughed. "I heard that Keagan Foxx was here with Jackson, and I'd like to talk with her.

"With me?" Keagan asked, confused.

The woman turned her brilliant smile on her and nodded. "Yes."

"Ellie. What are you up to?" Ash asked in the same no-nonsense tone Jackson used with her.

"Nothing." She looked over at Peter.

"Is my wife here?" Peter asked.

"She just got here. Now, can I borrow Keagan for a few minutes?" Ellie asked, stepping beside Keagan and slipping her hand into hers.

"I need to talk with you anyway, Ash," Jackson added.

Ash stared at both women for a long moment, his eyes narrowing on Ellie.

"Fine. Half hour then bring her back here and whatever you're up to, I'd think on it some more before you find yourself in a situation you can't talk your way out of," Ash warned.

Ellie squeezed Keagan's hand. "Half an hour. Plenty of time." She tugged on Keagan.

"Jackson. You promised," Keagan said to him as she was half dragged out of the office.

She never heard his response when the door closed and she was being towed down the hall by the strange woman.

———

14

"Where are you taking me?" Keagan demanded once she was inside the elevator with Ellie.

"Upstairs." The blonde turned to face Keagan. "We're going to figure a way to fix all of this," she said solemnly. "Ash will beat his chest for a while, but once we get to the bottom of everything, I think we can get him to see reason."

Keagan blinked back her confusion. "Who are you?" she asked as the elevator came to a stop and the door slid open.

"Sorry. I'm Ellie. Ash is my husband." She stepped off and waved Keagan forward.

"You're married to that man?" Keagan asked with some astonishment. She seemed so demure and sweet. "By choice?"

Ellie laughed. "I know he looks scary, but he's not that bad." She gave Keagan a sidelong glance. "No less scary than Jackson, I'm sure."

"Jackson's not scary at all," Keagan scoffed. "I mean, there's times he may look like it, but he's not... he's well...Jackson."

"You know him better than me, I think, but when I first saw him with all those tattoos and those cold eyes, I was a little taken aback."

"Your husband had a few tats on his arms that I could see," Keagan noted as they progressed further down a hall with several closed doors.

"He does," Ellie agreed, "but I'm used to him, I guess. Peter's not scary to me at all, but Jackson is almost as built as Ash. He just looks more...harsh than Peter."

"The three of them are cousins, right?" Keagan asked as Ellie brought her to a stop in front of a door.

Ellie knocked on the door and tucked a long lock of hair behind her ear.

"Yes. There's one more cousin that I haven't met yet, but Ash never talks of him, and Peter's only ever said his name once. I had heard of Jackson a few times before he came home, but they never hid him as much as the last cousin."

Keagan's curiosity was piqued, but the door opened before she could get out her question.

"Good, you got her out of there." A woman with

long blonde hair sighed and grabbed hold of Keagan's arm. "Come in."

Keagan stumbled forward into what looked like an apartment.

"What's going on?" Keagan demanded, yanking her arm free of the stranger's grip.

"Sorry, I didn't really explain anything." Ellie went past them down the short hallway. Keagan followed behind her to a well-lit living room.

"Aubry?" Keagan stopped cold when she noticed her pacing behind the couch, ringing her hands.

"Short explanation," The long-haired woman said as she maneuvered around the couch and stopped Aubry from walking around. "I'm Peter's wife, Azalea. That's Ellie, Ash's wife, and well, you know Aubry, obviously."

"Well, that explains who you are at least." Keagan folded her arms over her chest.

Azalea gave a weak smile.

"Aubry told us what happened," Ellie piped up.

Keagan's spine went straight as a board.

"It's okay. That's why we brought you up here," Azalea said.

"Jackson already knows," Keagan confessed.

"That's fine. Ash is going to find out. We just need to come up with a plan that we can offer as an alternative to whatever his plan is," Ellie explained, leaning against the arm of the couch.

"I was trying to get his promise that he wouldn't fire you," Keagan said. "I swear I wasn't going to give him your name unless I was sure you'd be safe."

"It's all right," Aubry said with a gentle smile. She rounded the couch and plopped down. "Ash won't be surprised when he hears it was me. It's not the first time I've done something stupid like this," she said with a hint of sadness.

"I shouldn't have gotten you or Jaelynn involved." Keagan closed her eyes for a moment. It had seemed so simple. Why had Stanley been such a cry baby about a few hundred thousand dollars? He had millions!

"Jackson knows about Jaelynn too?" Azalea asked.

"He does."

"Okay, well, Jaelynn will have to deal with Hunter. We can't do much to save her." Ellie pinched her bottom lip between two fingers while seemingly thinking out loud. "She can handle it—that's not an issue."

"Her connection to Jansen—"

"She hates Jansen." Keagan interjected. "Like with a passion hates him. She didn't help me because of him."

Ellie gave a curt nod. "You're right. I think we can leave Jaelynn alone for now, but we need to come up with something for Aubry."

"He's going to fire me, and I'll have to leave the

Annex," Aubry said softly, staring off into the empty space in front of her. "I'll have to go work in one of the slimy clubs down by the river."

"No, you won't," Azalea promised, though Keagan wasn't sure she shared her confidence.

"What would happen to you if it hadn't been something like this? What would he do?" Keagan asked.

Aubry blew out a long breath. "He'd send me to Dominick. He's in charge of the discipline for the girls now that Peter stopped." She gave Azalea a sidelong glance.

"Okay." Keagan warmed up to an idea. "Then can't we just offer to have this Dominick guy deal with it? Let him write her up or whatever?"

"Write me up?" Aubry laughed. "That's not how it works here."

Keagan blinked a few times. "Oh. He deals with the actual discipline, like physical punishment?"

"I know it sounds off putting, but it's not as bad as it sounds," Aubry was quick to say. "I would rather take a strap to my ass than lose my job when I mess up."

Keagan was in no position to judge. She'd found herself collared and caged by Jackson, and she hadn't hated it as much as her brain told her she should have. If the girls here found this arrangement to their liking, who the hell was she to judge it?

"I'm so sorry." Keagan sighed and sank into the loveseat. Then after a long beat, she asked, "Is this your apartment?" Light blues and grays gave the room a warm, inviting feel

"Yeah. I used to have a roommate, but this apartment opened up and Ash gave it to me." She leaned forward. "What if I offered to give it up, give it to one of the other girls, and I'd go back to one of the shared units?"

"You shouldn't have to give anything up because of me," Keagan said firmly.

"I could have said no," Aubry admitted.

"Did you get the information you were looking for?" Ellie asked when the room went silent. No one seemed to have much idea as to how to get them out of the mess.

"No." Keagan frowned. She'd put Aubry in danger all for nothing. "Jackson caught up with me before I could have my meeting."

"I'm just going to resign. Maybe Ash will still let me work at the clubs if I just walk in and take responsibility," Aubry offered as she rose from the couch.

"I don't want you to do that," Keagan argued following her down the hall.

Aubry grasped Keagan's hands and gave her a warm smile. "I could have said no to Jaelynn. I knew what would happen if we got caught. My decision isn't your fault."

"I put you in that position though."

"If you two are going down there, we're coming with. Strength in numbers," Ellie said hurrying toward them with Azalea right behind her. "Besides, maybe I can interfere if Ash gets too hot headed."

"I've yet to see you be successful at that." Azalea laughed as they made their way to the elevator.

"When it's not about me, I'm better at it," Ellie argued and jammed her finger into the call button.

Keagan listened while the three women shifted from concern to light-hearted jabs. They had a kinship Keagan had never felt before. Other than Katarina, she'd never been close to anyone. The longest relationship she'd ever had was with Jackson, and that wasn't even an actual connection. Fuck buddies at best.

"We won't let him bully you." Azalea slipped her hand into Keagan's as they made their way down the hall back to Ash's office.

These women were willing to have her back while she battled three Titon men, and it had been Keagan who'd been in the wrong. She didn't deserve their kindness or sacrifice.

And she wouldn't allow Aubry to take the fall.

15

"How long before they march in here on us?" Peter asked, pouring himself a drink and offering one to Jackson.

"I'm guessing we have a few more minutes," Ash grumbled from behind his desk. "If you would just fucking tell me, I wouldn't have to go through all of this." He pointed a straight finger at Jackson.

Jackson took the drink from Peter and threw it down his throat. Keagan had been gone for half an hour already, and whatever trouble she was causing would soon come barreling into the office. He'd need another drink before that happened.

"It's her information to give." He leveled a heated stare at his cousin. "You can't intimidate me, Ash."

"Even with your shares on the line?" Ash countered.

Jackson lifted his shoulder. "I'll get my five percent, but she'll be the one to tell you."

"You know I can't keep the girl employed. She broke a security rule. An important one." Ash drummed his fingers on the desk.

"Leave that for now." Peter waved his hand at Ash then sank into the chair beside Jackson. "There's something about Keagan you're not telling us. I want to know what it is."

Jackson rolled his eyes. "It's nothing that you need to know."

"Needs and wants are different things," Peter pointed out. "I want to know. So...tell me."

"It has nothing to do with this situation," Jackson argued, shoving out of his chair. He marched to the bar and poured himself a double helping of brandy.

"Then there's no reason to hide it," Ash said.

"Jackson. We're family. The three of us. If we're going to be in business together, and live in the same town again, we need to trust each other," Peter added.

Jackson sipped the brandy, going against his urge to gulp it down and pour another.

"She worked...and take note of the past tense there...she worked for Jansen." He took a large gulp of the brandy and melted into the sweet burn it left in his throat. Better than the throb starting in his head because of all this fucking drama. He was getting a better idea as to why Ash pulled the Titon business out from dealing with the other families.

Peter gently put his glass down on the desk and turned in his chair. "Past tense?"

"Past tense...mostly." Jackson nodded. "She still associates with him, utilizes connections and such, does an odd job here and there, but she is not on his payroll."

"And does he have anything to do with this?" Ash asked, his eyes already darkening with irritation.

"No. Not really. She did use her connection with him to get her way in here, but he had nothing to do with Stanley. She really is just looking for her mother."

"Who, if I remember right, was pronounced dead years ago," Ash added.

"She was," Jackson agreed, "but she believes that she may have survived, that maybe she wasn't on that flight. I've checked her computer files—she's been digging around for years. She targeted Stanley because he was a rich asshole whom she could manipulate easily."

"A weak mark," Peter said. "And does Jansen know that his associate is with you? Seeing as you're doing business with him now."

"He knows that we know each other, but no, he doesn't know she's staying with me."

Ash rubbed his temples. "This is what I didn't want."

"My business with Jansen doesn't touch you," Jackson argued before Ash could get his bluster in full swing.

"Not yet, no, but if this goes sideways with her? You think he's not going to come down on all of us? Cause trouble for Peter at the Tower? Start fucking with my clubs or the Annex? And then I have to get involved." Ash's voice hardened.

"What would you have me do?" Jackson asked, annoyed. This was his time to do business his way without the dark shadow of his father hanging over him. He had every right to earn his way in this town. It was his town too. Ashland Titon did not own Kassel.

"Nothing." Ash swiped his hand through the air. "Not yet. But there may come a time where you'll have to make a decision, and you won't like it." He fixed his gaze on Jackson. "So be ready."

"I'm—" Jackson didn't get to finish his thought before the door to the office banged open and four woman marched inside. Ellie led the pack, with Keagan, Azalea and Aubry filing in behind her. Jackson made eye contact with Aubry for a second before he found Keagan's gaze. A mixture of bravery and guilt of the condemned played in her eyes. She had her brow raised high, and her chin thrust forward, but she was wringing her hands tightly in front of her.

What was she up to?

"Ash. We want a word," Ellie declared, coming to stand before her husband's desk.

Peter stood up from his chair and moved behind the desk, lining up with Jackson and Ash. Apparently, a battle of the sexes was about to take place, and Ash's office was the chosen battlefield.

"Ellie, come here." Ash crooked his finger at his wife. She shoved her chin higher. "Ellie," Ash warned.

"No. You have to listen to us first. Then, if you still want a word in private, we can do that. But we have to speed this up because the boys will be up from their nap soon."

Jackson hid his grin by taking a long sip of his drink.

"Fine. Out with it." Ash stood at his desk with his arms folded firmly over his chest.

"Before you learn the full truth of what happened with the security issue, I want your word that you will not fire the person responsible." Ellie said.

Ash smirked. "Well, since Aubry is standing behind you there looking ready to lose her lunch, I think it's a safe bet to assume I know the culprit. So, no deal," he announced.

"Fucking hell," Keagan muttered.

"Ash." Ellie stepped forward. "You can't fire her. She was helping a friend."

"She allowed a stranger into the party who then

pretended to be one of my employees and stole a hefty amount of money from a client." Ash kept his firm tone.

"She had a damn good reason for needing to do it," Ellie proclaimed.

"Look, we aren't saying she can't be disciplined. Just not fired." Azalea stepped up to stand beside Ellie. Now they were protecting both Keagan and Aubry.

"You two don't have a say in this matter," Peter added for his wife's benefit.

"You aren't the disciplinarian here anymore, Peter," Azalea pointed out with a flick of her wrist. Peter's eyes widened at her tone, but she either chose to ignore it or hadn't noticed.

"Maybe not for the Annex, but I sure as hell am at home," he said. "A fact you'll be reminded of the second we get there."

Azalea's face flushed red.

Keagan groaned and shoved through the two women, putting herself in the front line.

"You owe me nothing. I know that, but please, don't fire Aubry. This wasn't her fault. I mean, this is all my fault. Sneaking into your party was wrong, and she shouldn't lose her job and the security that she obviously gets by being here because of me." She stepped further toward the desk. "Whatever punishment this Dominick guy would give her, I'll accept on her behalf."

Jackson's chest expanded.

"The hell you will," he said plunking his glass onto the desk.

"Keagan, no." Aubry stepped forward, but Ellie and Azalea wouldn't let her get any closer.

"I'm the one who started this whole thing. It's my fault." Keagan flattened her hands at her sides, no doubt awaiting her sentence.

"She knows the rules here," Ash said to her.

"I know she does, but I won't have her suffer because of me. I should have found another way to fund my search."

"Because stealing is wrong?" Peter asked with a trace of humor. The Titon family wasn't exactly living on the safest side of the law.

"No, because I had to involve people who had no business getting involved. I should have found another way to get it without needing them to help," she answered.

Ash stared at her a long moment.

"No one is touching her, Ash," Jackson said firmly moving to stand beside her. "If there are consequences to be meted out, I'm doing it."

Keagan whipped her head up to look at him, surprise in in her eyes, but he let it go unchecked. She had caused enough trouble to earn her a whipping, and if it would keep Aubry employed and Ash off his ass, he'd deliver it right there.

"Who is the other person?" Ash asked.

"No one here," Keagan answered.

"That's not what I asked," Ash pointed out with a tilt to his head. "If you want me to allow you to accept Aubry's punishment, you need to be completely honest. Who is the other person?"

Keagan's jaw clenched as she seemed to weigh her options. Jackson wouldn't give the name for her—she needed to do this herself.

"Jaelynn Bianucci. I knew she had friends here still," Keagan relented and looked miserable doing it. "But I'd rather you not act on that information."

Ash's lips twisted into a snide grin. "And waste an opportunity to fuck with Hunter? Not a chance. And I seriously doubt he'll accept your offer to take his wife's punishment for her, so don't bother with that."

Keagan's shoulders slumped.

"Aubry, come here," Ash commanded. "Ellie, get the hell out of the way, I'm not going to strangle the woman," he barked at his wife.

She narrowed her eyes but moved to the side to let Aubry through.

"Ash, I know, I know. I just keep getting into these messes." Aubry put out both her hands. "Maybe you could hold my pay for a week or two," she offered.

Ash frowned.

"I won't let you work for free." He glanced over at Peter then back. "I won't fire you, but I promise you the next time you disregard our security rules there won't be any more chances."

Aubry sighed with relief. "Thank. You."

"I wouldn't thank me just yet," Ash said with a tilt of his head toward Keagan. "Since you can't seem to remember the security rules around here, you'll start your training over from the beginning. Peter will take care of the details."

"You're demoting me?" she asked with tear-filled eyes.

Keagan looked ready to intervene, so Jackson grabbed her arm and yanked her to his side. He could save her from herself at least this once.

"Until you've gone through the training again, yes. Once you finish, I'll leave it up to Peter and Dominick if you're to be put back to your original position."

"My pay?"

"I won't change the base pay, but since you won't be taking private clients, you won't be earning as much," Ash explained.

"That's not fair," Keagan said before Jackson could stop her.

Ash flashed an angry glance at them. "What's not fair, Keagan, is I don't get the pleasure of seeing your ass striped red for all the trouble you caused. But I'm sure my cousin will see to your punishment as soon as he gets you out of my sight and back at his house."

Jackson slid his hand beneath her hair, gripped the back of her neck, and gave her a small squeeze.

Ash turned his heated gaze to Ellie. "Ellie, if the boys are up have Maria take them out back to the park. You wait in our room for me, I'll be up soon."

"Ash..." She lowered her gaze but kept standing firm.

"Azalea, we should get going too," Peter announced. "Aubry, go on upstairs. I'll have your new schedule for you in the morning." Peter rounded the desk toward his wife, and Aubry.

Ellie stepped back from Ash's desk, her cheeks red.

"Ellie." Ash's voice had softened. "Go on," he said with less heat.

As Aubry turned to leave the room, she locked eyes with Jackson and pinched her lips together. Like she wanted to say something to him but thought better of it.

"Let's go." Jackson pressed the back of Keagan's neck to get her walking. She must have finally realized it was finished, and she let him lead her out of the room without hesitation. She was smart enough not to say anything to Ash on the way out.

"Thank you, Jackson," she said to him as he climbed into the driver's seat of his car.

He paused in buckling his seat belt. "For what?" he asked curiously.

"For not letting that Dominick guy touch me, and

for getting me out of all that mess," she said and eased back into her seat, letting out a long breath.

She thought it was over. She actually thought she'd gotten away with all of it.

"I promised my cousin I'd handle the punishment, and I will," he said, clicking his buckle in place.

Her gaze snapped to his.

"You offered to take her punishment," he reminded her and started the car.

"Jackson, you already... I mean...haven't we already..."

"No, little fox. We didn't."

16

By the time Jackson pulled the car into his attached three-car garage, the sun had faded. Keagan glanced at the clock on the dash as Jackson killed the engine. Too early to plead exhaustion and beg for bed.

"What's on your mind?" Jackson reached over the console and picked up her hand, squeezing just enough for her to get the full warmth of the momentary tenderness.

"I'm really tired, and I was thinking maybe I'd go to bed?" She tried to yawn, but her body wouldn't go along with her deception.

His silence drew her attention, and she raised her eyes to meet his. Hard. It was the only way she could describe him at that moment. His jaw held tight and his stare was unrelenting. She found it difficult to breathe with him holding her gaze so intently.

"Are you afraid of me?" he asked, though he didn't sound concerned.

"No, of course not." She glanced away. "I know you'd never hurt me, I mean, not like that. Not...like maybe I deserve." She pulled her hand from his and rested her head back against the seat.

"You think you deserve to be hurt?" The leather upholstery creaked beneath him as he turned in his seat to face her. "Why?" He rested his elbow on the back of his seat, reached for a lock of her hair, and rubbed it between his fingers.

"Not hurt...I don't know. I shouldn't have involved those girls. I don't even know them. Now Aubry is losing pay and Jaelynn will have to face her husband. From what Ellie and Azalea said, it sounded like it wouldn't be easy." She looked back up at him. "Do any of your friends not solve their problems with spankings?"

His left eyebrow arched, and he huffed a soft laugh. "The spanking doesn't solve the problem, it just rights the ship."

Keagan rolled her eyes.

"When we were together, you got punished twice. Did you think it was so bad?"

"I thought it...well... I didn't like you being upset

with me. And once we were finished with it, it was like we were back to being us, or whatever we were."

"Exactly." He dropped her hair, touched the tip of his finger to her jawline, and ran it down to her chin. "How does it feel that you've caused some trouble for these other people?"

"Well, I don't care about Stanley if you mean him," she stated flatly. "He's a rich bastard who's a real asshole, so him losing some cash doesn't bother me in the least."

Jackson pressed his lips together, but it seemed like he was trying to suppress a laugh more than trying to look firm. Hell, the man didn't need to try when he wanted her to understand his disappointment. When he set his angry eyes on her, her skin lit on fire. And oddly enough, so did her core.

"Stanley aside. Aubry and Jaelynn."

"To be honest, I feel like shit. I wasn't thinking. I've never involved anyone on the outside in my jobs, at least not anyone that wouldn't know how to get out of a jam if they needed to. So I really am sorry they have to pay a price for helping me. They were trying to be kind, and look what it got them." She brushed his hand away from her chin. She'd been an ass involving them. "And Ellie and Azalea tried to stick up for me, which seems to have gotten Ash and Peter pissed off." She shoved her hands into her hair and rubbing her scalp.

"Don't worry about them. They can handle their husbands better than any man I've ever seen. They aren't in any danger." The left side of Jackson's lips ticked up in a half smile.

"Since I already feel like shit about everything, can we just let it go? I doubt Ash is really going to ask you if you went through with the whole thing," she said, patting his thigh.

What little of a smile he had fell instantly. "No."

"But—"

"You deserve consequences for what you did. Not for Stanley, I agree he's a prick, but you dragged Aubry and Jaelynn into something they had no business getting into. Your connection to Jansen makes it more dangerous for them. And you know that. You used them."

Keagan froze. She had used them. They had what she wanted. They'd been a means to an end.

She hadn't always been that person. She'd been thoughtful and warm and caring before Katarina disappeared. She never would have put anyone else in harm's way just to get something she wanted, but that's exactly what she'd done here.

"I could argue they're adults..." Keagan let the bullshit reasoning die on her lips. "They could have said no, but I used my connection to Jaelynn for my own benefit."

Jackson stared at her a long moment. "You've learned too much working for Jansen, I think."

"You wouldn't do the same? Don't you do the exact same thing with your distribution business?" She shot at him. She may have been acting selfishly, but she wouldn't allow him to lecture her on moral behavior. "I'm not dumb, Jackson. I know what you do, and I know you're salivating to get Jansen to use you for his clubs. I didn't realize the deal had already gone through though." She scrunched up her lips. Jansen would want to talk to her soon.

But that was a worry for another day.

"We aren't talking about me right now. I may use people, but I've never pulled someone outside the business into it without them knowing. What do you think Jansen will think when he finds out his nephew's wife was involved in sneaking you into Ash's party? Jansen has vowed to stay out of the Titon businesses. You getting his niece involved could have started more than just Hunter taking his belt to his wife's ass."

"Okay!" Keagan put her hand in the air. "I know you're right. I shouldn't have asked them. I know that."

"Good. Then there won't be any more trying to weasel out of your punishment." He reached over her to the glove department and popped it open. Jackson pulled out the collar he'd allowed her to take off for the trip to Ash's. "Put this back on."

"What are you going to do to me?" She accepted the leather strip from him.

"The last time I punished you, and not the other day, but when I really gave you a punishment, what did I do?" he asked while she worked the collar around her neck. She pushed the leather through the buckle but couldn't find the stupid hole to secure it. Jackson brushed her hair out of the way, took the leather from her hands and worked the buckle closed.

"So? Do you remember?" he asked once the collar was secured again.

"Yeah." She lowered her gaze, feeling the heat steal over her cheeks. "You used that damn cane." She huffed.

"And?"

He sounded like a man enjoying his appetizer while waiting impatiently for his supper.

"And you wouldn't let me have any fun the rest of the night," she summarized. It had been a moderate caning, but what had really driven his position home was how he fucked her all night without letting her come once. No matter how she'd begged, or bartered, he had kept her wanting.

"I think that's a good start." He winked and popped open his car door.

THE PLAYROOM WOULD HAVE BEEN an obvious choice for her punishment, but Jackson had never had trouble surprising her. After they left the garage, he grabbed her hand and led her upstairs to his bedroom, where he quickly stripped her and pushed her to the wall.

"Keep your nose to the wall. I don't want to see your face until I tell you to turn around." His voice was raw, his body tense as he pushed himself against her bare back.

She didn't give an answer, one wasn't required. Putting her hands on the wall, she pressed herself against it and closed her eyes. He planted one kiss to her naked shoulder and left her to stew while he moved around behind her. Drawers opened, a closet door swung open, then closed. Another door, a flush of a toilet, then a sink running.

She rolled her eyes and tried to let her mind wander. He could make her wait that way for an hour if he wanted to; she needed to find something to occupy her mind besides her guilt. She knew she deserved something, especially since everyone else involved was getting their comeuppance. But she didn't have to like the idea.

A sharp swish through the air behind her grabbed her attention. Keagan stood straighter and squeezed her fingers into fists. Whatever happened, she would not beg him for mercy. She would take whatever he gave her quietly.

"Tell me, my little fox, what brings your naked ass here to my room, waiting for my cane?" he asked almost playfully as he tapped the wooden rod to the bottom of her ass. Instinctively, she clenched.

"We already went over all of this— Ow!" She jumped up to her toes. The cane made contact a second time, driving another yelp from her. Dammit, she'd broken her own vow already.

"That's not what I asked. Now answer the question unless you'd like a few more?" He tapped the cane again, but lower this time, on her thighs.

She blew out a harsh breath. "I'm here because I involved strangers in my job."

A sharp smack to the top of her thighs made her cry out. She stepped back as the fire spread through her leg.

"Good. You also agreed to take on Aubry's punishment, isn't that right?" he asked, again lightly tapping her ass, but increasing the drumming while he waited for her answer.

"Yes," she whispered.

"Yes, what?" he asked, pausing his taps.

She blinked a few times. Finally, the word bloomed in her brain. "Sir! Yes, sir!" They never used titles when they played, but when he'd punished her, he had required it.

"Good," he said and delivered a forceful smack to her ass. She hissed and pounded the side of her fist into the wall.

He chuckled. "We haven't even started yet, little fox." He laid his hand on her shoulder. "Go over to the bed, bend over so your forearms are pressed into the mattress, and raise your ass up high for me. Once you're in position, you may ask me to begin your punishment."

He'd given the instruction in a low but stern voice that sent a warm current of arousal laced with dread down her spine. The object wasn't just to punish her, but to make her accept it. She would have to own up to what she'd done and ask him to wipe the slate clean for her.

With the damn cane.

Being in no true position to argue, she nodded and slid her hands off the wall. He stepped out of her way, and she strolled across the room to the bed. The last time he'd punished her with the cane, she'd had marks and tenderness for several days, but her heart had been lighter; her soul had been brighter.

She could only hope the same would be true now.

Once she draped herself over the side of the bed, she positioned her body as he wanted. She gathered her hair to one side and turned her face to him. His gaze was already leveled on her, and the seriousness of his eyes stole a beat of her heart, but she managed to get her mind in working order.

"Sir, will you please..." She swallowed. Pride had a bitter taste. "Will you please begin my punishment?"

He inclined his head. "You'll stay still. If your hands come back, we start at the beginning. If you bring them back a second time, I will bind you. If you kick out at me, you'll have your ankles bound together, and I'll plug your ass before I continue. Do you understand?" He stalked to the bed, holding the cane firmly at his side as he did so.

"Yes, sir," she said and turned to stare down at the comforter. Fisting it, she braced herself. Jackson wouldn't warm her up, not for this punishment. It wasn't only hers she was taking, but Aubry's as well. He would get straight to it.

No amount of preparation could prepare her for the first strike of the cane. She sucked in a gasp as electric fire coursed up her spine from the first blow. The second strike numbed her brain. All that would register was the utter pain of the cane landing again in the exact same spot. He kept the next strikes to the fleshiest part of her ass, but it helped only a little.

She screamed out on the fifth strike. Where was the reprieve between smacks?

He placed his hand on the small of her back, spreading his fingers out. He was probably just trying to stabilize her, to remind her to remain still, but she drew comfort from his warm touch. Even if it was to hold her steady while he continued his barbaric punishment.

The next blow shook her insides, and she fell forward onto the mattress. Her ass lowered, but he didn't stop to correct her. Instead he moved his hand from her back and slipped his arm beneath her hips. With them raised from the bed, he tossed the cane to the bed and spanked her with his hand.

A new inferno began to build. Each smack filled in the spaces the cane had not touched. There was not an inch of her ass left unbranded by his discipline. She tried to remain still, but the throbbing outgrew her ability to keep in one place. He responded by pressing her against his body for stability and lowered his spanks to her thighs.

She cried out and struck her fists into the bed.

"Enough! Jackson, enough!" she cried, tears streaming down her cheeks, and her body giving way to the temptation to fight off the assault of his hand.

He merely held tighter, spanked harder.

"I'm sorry!" she finally cried out, and with it, her body went slack over the bed. Remorse, true remorse poured from her chest, and she found herself sobbing lightly into his bedding.

The spanking stopped, but the burn of her ass would probably go on for days. Gently, he pulled his arm about from beneath her, and he sat on the bed beside her. Rubbing her back in small circles, he let her cry in silence. He didn't chide her or tease her, but simply let her have the time she needed to process everything bubbling out of her.

She hadn't cried so hard in so long she wasn't sure she could make herself stop. Everything, the pain of losing Katarina, the fear of dealing with Jansen, the guilt of all the horrible things she'd done beneath the guise of his employment, it all rolled right out of her with her tears.

"Okay, okay." He scooted further onto the bed and hauled her into his lap. She wrapped her arms around his neck and nuzzled into him. The musk of his after-shave reminded her of a simpler life she'd had once.

"I'm not who I used to be," she said softly when the sobs finally receded.

He tapped her chin with his knuckles until she peered up at him. With all the crying, she had to look a mess. Her eyes felt puffy and her cheeks were tight from drying tears. But his stare never wavered.

"No one is who they were years ago." He ran the pad of his thumb over her cheek, wiping away the last of her tears. "You haven't told me everything, but I get the feeling you weren't really given much choice. You were raised within an environment that taught you to become what was expected of you."

She sniffled. "I broke away from it, though." She

turned a teary gaze up at him. "I didn't extend my contract. I'm not tied down to him.

"YOU STILL USE him for your search and to make your money."

She sighed. "It's easy money, and I've been spending all my time trying to find Katarina."

"And now, you have me to help with that. No more jobs, Keagan. I don't want you to have anything to do with Jansen. You're more than what he made you."

"You work for him," she pointed out, but without any force. She was too tired to argue.

"I work with him, not for him. And that's different."

"Because you're a guy?" she scoffed.

"No. Because I can walk away from it any time without repercussion. I have work outside of him. You're still leaning on him. But now." He brushed his finger over her lips. "You can lean on me."

He pushed her chin further back. Warm emotion flashed in his eyes as he brought his mouth down over hers. She hardened herself at first, not sure what accepting his kiss could mean for her. Pressing her hands against his chest, she willed herself to shove away from him, but she softened against him, melting into his hold and his kiss. She surrendered beneath him, yielding to his kiss and parting her lips. Every part of her responded to his touch. His tongue brushed against hers, sending electricity through her nerve endings, and opened her entire being to him. She wasn't just accepting his kiss, his touch, his offer, but she was drawing him in, taking everything he had to offer.

She lost herself in his touch.

17

She tasted like butterscotch.

Jackson swept his tongue over her lips again and pulled back. Looking down at her wide dark eyes, he slid his hand up her back and into her hair, fisting it and yanking her head back.

"Your ass is going to hurt for a day or two." His cock twitched at the image replaying of her ass bouncing beneath the cane and his hand. Her ass would be red the rest of the night, and there'd be marks from the cane. Sweet, dark marks he might kiss in the morning if she was a good girl.

She stared down the length of her nose at him, and a wall started to build again, but he wouldn't allow it this time. He shifted on the bed, depositing her onto her back. Her little wince at the fabric brushing against her bruised ass only got his cock harder.

Maybe he was an asshole for enjoying her discomfort, but he wasn't going to waste time or energy exploring it.

He scooted off the bed, got to his feet.

"Lie flat, little fox, I want to see you. Really see you this time," he explained with his hands on his hips. He hadn't taken the time to explore her since bringing her back into his life. An error he'd rectify now.

"No, don't cover yourself. Put your hands over your head. Grab those rails again, like last time." He gestured toward the headboard. It had been an added expense to have the iron rings and bars added to the wooden frame, but it was money well spent.

She only hesitated a moment before reaching over her head and wrapping her slender fingers around the bars. Her knees, however, were still pressed together tightly.

"Open your legs, little fox. I want to look at all of you," he explained. The deep blush that exploded over her cheeks made his breath hitch. Fuck, she was gorgeous when she couldn't let her real emotions hide behind that wall.

He waited, clinging to the last bit of patience he had, watching her intently as she spread her legs open, giving him a glimpse at every part of her.

She was slender with shapely hips and thighs. The only blemish on her fair skin was a faded scar on her left side. Neat and small, probably from a surgery.

Nothing so vulgar as a knife or bullet. He clenched his teeth regardless. Something had hurt her.

Feeling the heat of her stare on him, he continued with his inspection. A small patch of brown curls led to her sex. Well trimmed, but he found himself wanting all the curls swept away, leaving behind nothing but a smooth surface so she couldn't hide any part of her cunt from him.

"Flatten your feet on the bed and drop your knees to the side," he ordered while pulling his shirt from his pants.

"Why?" she asked.

"Because I want to see," he answered. He pulled the shirt over his head, enjoying the way her gaze raked over his chest. He'd gotten heavy into ink after they had parted ways, and she hadn't seen all of the new designs and patterns tattooed on his skin.

His hand pausing on the buckle of his belt was enough for her to move swiftly into obeying him. She pulled her feet up toward her ass and spread her knees until she was even more on display. Her pussy lips parted with her movement, as though to open for him.

"You're already dripping your pussy juice on my blanket," he said, watching as her arousal did just that. He wet his lips.

"Jackson," she said quietly, when he continued to stare at her pussy.

"You have a pretty pussy, little fox," he said, yanking his belt from the buckle and working his jeans open. With a heavy shove, he pushed his jeans and boxers down to his ankles and kicked out of the cumbersome clothing.

Now, as naked as she was, he stared down at her, contemplating which part of her to devour first. She lifted her hips and moved across the bed an inch. Enough for him to see a dark welt on her ass. She'd taken the cane well enough. Thankfully he had no neighbors within screaming distance. She's shouted down the house, but she hadn't jumped away or tried to block him.

She'd been a good girl. A well-punished girl.

Climbing on the bed, he knelt between her thighs. She brought her eyes back to his. Dried tears had left a shimmering trail down her cheeks.

"You're gorgeous like this. Spread wide, open for me, bound by only your obedience." He trailed his fingertips from the top of her knee and down her thigh to her pussy.

He felt a tremor in her muscles as he reached her sex. Cupping her pussy, he pressed the heel of his hand into her clit and rubbed. He watched her eyes roll upward and her bottom lip disappear between her teeth.

"You're soaking wet, little fox," he teased, rubbing faster. She moved her left leg wider and moaned her response. "Don't you move your hands," he warned when her fingers loosened on the bars.

"Jackson," she moaned his name while raising her ass from the bed.

"You want this, Keagan. Your body responds easily to my words, my touches. You want me inside you." He locked his eyes on hers as she swallowed back her admission. Well, that wouldn't do.

"Admit it, tell me how much you want my cock in you. And not because you think you're in danger, not because there's anything to be gained except to have me fucking you." It was one thing to fuck a woman because he'd driven her to the brink so many times she would say or do anything to be allowed to dive over it. But it was entirely different when she wanted it because of the act itself. Because she wanted *him*.

She nodded, as though he would allow such a docile response. Silly fox.

"Words, Keagan." He stilled his hand on her sex. Her answer could not come from a deep pit of arousal, but of her own mind, her own heart.

She brought her eyes level with his. For a beat he thought she would deny him the truth.

"Yes, Jackson. I want you."

"What do you want exactly?" he asked, feeling playful again. Moving his hand, he spread his body over hers. The length of his shaft pressed against her clit.

Hungrily, he covered her mouth with his, diving his hands into her thick hair. She wouldn't be taken over so easily, though, and matched him, fighting him for the upper hand. He gave over, letting her deepen the kiss. He was consumed by his desire for her, to have her, to possess her.

She moved her hands from the bars, gripping his hair and submitting to him once more. He grabbed hold of one hand and pushed it over her head again, not to the bar, but down to the pillow. He did the same with her other hand, covering them both with his own and rising to stare down at her again.

Breathless, he found it hard to speak. Her lips were swollen, her pupils dilated beyond what he thought possible.

"I'm going to fuck you so hard, Keagan," he said, nipping her chin, her lips, then licking at her cheek. "So hard, you're going to scream, but I won't stop."

She nodded against his cheek. "Yes, Jackson. All of that." She bucked her hips, urging him to give her exactly what he promised.

And he'd never broken a promise.

He shifted his hips until the tip of his cock lined up with her pussy's hot wet entrance. Locking gazes once more, he thrust forward in one powerful movement until his balls hit her ass. She cried out, a wild and crazed sound.

He nibbled her earlobe and pulled back until he

almost left her completely, then drove forward. Again and again he did this, until the room filled with the mingling of her whimpers and the sounds of their flesh slamming into each other.

"Jackson!" she cried out, and he cupped her tit, rolling her nipple between his fingers.

He clenched his eyes, trying to find a measure of control or he would end this too soon. Pinching her nipple worsened his situation. Her cry tightened his balls to an unbearable point.

She moved her free hand to his back, digging her nails into his flesh as he pounded into her. Grinding his hips against her clit, he took her gasp of pleasure into his mouth and silenced her with a kiss.

Pulling up her legs even more, her already too-beautiful cunt gripped him, dragging him to the very brink of sanity. He stared blindly at the other side, knowing if he would just take a small step he could dive head first into a pleasure field. And she would deserve to be left behind. It had been his intention when they'd gotten back from Ash's house. To take from her and leave her wanting. A just punishment.

But he would find less joy if she were not taking the plunge with him.

Moving his hand from her breast to her cheek, he broke off the kiss.

"Come for me, my little fox. Come as hard and as loud as you can. I want to feel your cunt shutter around my cock," he ordered, barely able to find his voice. All energy had been diverted to keep himself in control, but fuck that.

"Jackson," she muttered while wiggling beneath his touch. Letting go of her pinned hand, he slithered his hand between their bodies, finding her swollen and wet clit.

"Fuck!" she screamed with the simple touch of his fingertip to the tightly bundled nerves.

He smiled down at her. Watching her lose her own grasp of control would be his undoing, but he didn't care anymore. Her eyes flew open, her body went taut like a guitar string waiting to be plucked in exactly the right way.

And he knew which chord to play.

"That's a good girl. Come for me. Do as you're told, little fox. Be my good pet. Do it," he ordered with what sound he could muster from his throat. She bit down hard on her lip, her fingers digging further into his shoulders.

Another flick of his finger and a powerful thrust of his cock and she came undone beneath him. Writhing and screaming, her body shuddered as her orgasm ripped her away from him. He drove his cock into her again and again, riding her release with her and chasing down his own.

She quieted slightly, and her body relaxed beneath him. The glassy look in her eyes gave him the permission he'd been waiting for and he plowed into her hot cunt again and again. The resounding flutters of her pussy around his cock as her orgasm faded, drew his own out of him. His balls tightened, and a white heat rolled down his spine.

"Yours," she whispered. A simple word. One syllable, and it unglued him. He thrust once more then a wave of pleasure and relief carried him away. Over and over again the waves crashed over him, as he spilled into her.

A scream brought his mind back together, and he realized it was him. He'd bellowed with his orgasm.

Once the last beat of his release vanished, he fell forward, pressing his forehead against hers. His short burst of breath met with hers while his heart tried to catch up with the rhythm of his lungs.

Gingerly, he slipped from her body, already missing her warmth, and rolled to her side. She scooted over to give him more room as he curled up against her. Turning over to her side, she stared at him, her arm folded beneath her head.

"You didn't use anything," she said quietly after several silent moments passed.

Understanding flooded him.

"I'm on the shot, but...well..." She lowered her gaze to his chin. He brushed her hair from her face.

"What?" he asked, half understanding her concern.

"It seemed like you and Aubry had...well, the way she looked at you, it seemed like there was something between you, or at least there had been at some point."

He pressed a finger to her lips. "Are you jealous that I fucked Aubry, or are you concerned that I wasn't careful when I did?"

Her eyes snapped up to his. Ah, a little of both. He didn't even try to hide his smile. She could think him arrogant; he didn't mind.

"I was always careful," he reassured her, letting his finger slip from her lips. He sat up on the bed and pulled the comforter down so he could get beneath it. She followed his example and climbed underneath.

He opened his arms for her and pulled her into his chest when she lay back down.

"So you and she...you were..."

"The last party she was at," he answered, pressing his mouth to her hair. When was the last time he'd held a woman to him like this? Definitely not the evening he spent with Aubry.

"Oh. You were a client," she said, but without any relief in her tone.

"What's on your mind, Keagan?" He reached over to the side lamp and clicked it off. The moonlight from outside cast a shadow over her features. He could still make her out, but maybe with the shroud of darkness she'd open up more to him.

"I was just wondering, that's all." But her body tensed.

"It was only the one time," he said, hugging her tighter.

"It's not really any of my business," she said, but the aloofness was forced.

"I guess not," he agreed. Though it brought up a question of who she'd been with recently. Jansen employed a large number of men— No, he would not let his mind go there, and he would not question her. Whatever happened before, was in the past.

"Jackson," she said softly when his eyes grew heavy and started to close.

"Yeah?"

"I don't hate that you found me," she whispered then quickly flipped over to face away from him.

He pressed his chest into her back and kissed her bare shoulder.

"I'm glad I found you too," he said into the quiet. An understatement, really, but there was still work to be done, and he wouldn't allow confused emotions to get in the way.

First things first.

18

J ackson sat at his desk while Keagan fiddled with her phone near the window overlooking the front yard.

"Are you sure he's reliable?" she asked, looking up from her phone.

"Yes, Keagan," he said with a harsh sigh. He'd told her this at least a dozen times.

"I don't see how he can get information that I haven't been able to get in all these years," she continued.

Jackson looked up at her from over the edge of his laptop.

"Because Jansen may have taught you who to swindle, he never taught you who has the information in this town. Charlie knows who to ask."

She muttered something under her breath and went back to her phone.

"Shit. Jansen wants a meeting," she said, unfolding her legs and climbing off the chair. "This afternoon."

"You said you told him yesterday you weren't interested in taking jobs from him anymore," he said casually, leaning back in his chair. It had been three days since they'd had that conversation, prior to her bending over his bed.

"I did." She thrust her phone forward. "Maybe he wants something else."

"Okay, have him come here," Jackson offered.

"I don't think that's a good idea. He might see that as me taking your side."

"My side of what? You were in business with him before. I am in business with him now. What side are you talking about?" He swiveled his chair to face her.

"I mean, I'm not working with him anymore, and then he finds out I'm staying here. He might think I ditched him for you," she said.

"So?" He shrugged. "You said you were free of your contract or whatever from him. Was that not true?"

"It's true. I just don't want to start anything. I'll just go into town and meet with him." She started tapping on her screen.

"What did I just say, Keagan?" He firmed his voice.

She finished her text then looked up at him. Did she think he was only playing at this? He'd promised to help her with Katarina, and he would, but he wouldn't let her go off rogue anymore. Not anymore.

"I understand what you said, Jackson, but I'm not a little girl. I've been dealing with Jansen on my own for years. I'm not going to hide behind you." She shoved her phone into the back pocket of her jeans and folded her arms over her chest.

"So, that's it, you're just going to make the call now?" He drummed his fingers on the desk.

She had the smarts to at least take a pause. "No, I'm just saying I'm not going to fall at your feet and be some damn rug for you to walk over. I can handle Jansen, and I will."

"I'm here!" Charlie burst into the room with one arm raised and the other covering his eyes. "Is everyone dressed?"

His first meeting with Keagan had been the day before when he sauntered into the kitchen early in the morning. She'd been on her knees, naked, eating a strawberry from Jackson's hand. Jackson didn't even try to stop her from running out of the kitchen to find some clothes, but he did talk to Charlie about not just bursting into the house so damn early anymore without announcing himself.

"Yes, Charlie." Keagan sounded irritated, but the blush on her cheeks relayed a different story.

Charlie dropped his arm and grinned. "Good."

"What do you want?" Jackson shoved from his chair.

"I wanted to give you a quick update on the delivery and also, to give you this." He pulled a folded-up paper from the inside pocket of his suit jacket and dropped it on Jackson's desk.

"What is it?" Jackson flattened it with his hands and quickly skimmed the document.

"The manifest of the plane Katarina Silverstone took when she left Kassel." Charlie pointed to the paper.

Keagan hurried over to the desk. Jackson firmly planted his hand on the edge of the paper when she tried to snap it up.

"I wasn't able to get this. The airline wouldn't give it to me, and I couldn't find anyone willing to get the information. Jansen was...well, that's when he told me to leave it alone."

"What do you mean he said to leave it alone?" Jackson asked.

"He said I needed to accept Katarina's death, mourn her, and move on. He didn't want me to wallow."

"Wallow?" Charlie huffed. "Go on, look at that list."

Jackson swept over the list. And there it was, second from the bottom.

Hunter Bianucci.

"What was he doing on a commercial flight?"

Jackson checked the seats. "In the seat beside Katarina?"

"Exactly." Charlie pointed at him.

"Hunter's been pulling away from Jansen business," Keagan said, leaning closer to the list.

"This was five years ago," Jackson said. "Before he met his wife and found his soul. Back then, he did what his uncle told him to do."

"I don't understand." Keagan's brow furrowed. "Why would Hunter or Jansen want my mom to go away?"

"That's a good question," Jackson said.

"Katarina said she was going on vacation. She never said anything about Hunter going with her."

"How well did you know them back then?" Charlie asked.

She shook her head. "Not that well. Katarina was getting ready to stop working for the family, so she had started introducing me more." She caught Jackson's glare and frowned. "She was training me to take her spot."

"Were you given a choice? I mean, was there some sort of arrangement that meant you had to take her spot?" Charlie asked, raising the tension in Jackson's chest. She'd had a hard-enough time over the past few years, and she didn't need Charlie's judgment.

"When Katarina took me in, it was the first time anyone had really made a spot for me. Like a real place. I'd seen plenty of dirty shit growing up in the system." She rolled back her shoulders. "The stuff Katarina did for Jansen wasn't that big of a deal. She basically stole from the rich, redistribution of wealth among the wealthy. And in the process, she was able to put a good roof over our heads. I never went hungry, I always had a meal to eat, and she took care of me. Following in her footsteps didn't seem like such a horrible idea."

"Financially, it wasn't. But it's Jansen, and that's where I'm concerned," Jackson said. "He doesn't have a solid track record of employing women for anything more than dancing in his clubs or running them underground."

"Yeah, but what easier way to get information than to send an attractive, seductive woman?" Keagan lips twitched.

"Are you saying you slept with men for intel?" Jackson's stomach clenched. He wouldn't judge her for it. He'd done worse to get information he needed for his own father or himself. But the idea of her selling herself for Elliot Jansen's benefit set a fire burning in his stomach.

"No. I never had to." She shrugged. "Men who want a quick fuck—they go to places like the Annex or the clubs in the city. The men I was dealing with, they just wanted to be listened to."

"Listened to?" Charlie asked, clearly confused.

"Yeah. Their wives didn't listen, they only had a list of demands. They wanted money or time or whatever else, but they wouldn't give their husbands a gentle ear. That's what most of them wanted, they just wanted to vent and be heard. I never had to so much as open my blouse."

"Seriously?" Charlie asked, disbelief clear in his tone.

"I know it's hard for you to believe, but women are capable of more than just spreading their legs," Keagan shot at Charlie.

Jackson laughed. "Don't be too hard on him. His main goal in life is to get his dick wet and swell his wallet."

Charlie pinched his lips together. A soft pink tint hit his cheeks.

"How about we get back to the topic at hand?" Charlie clapped his hands. "Do we still try to get that Potier to sit down with us, or do we go to Hunter?"

Jackson glanced at Keagan. This was her investigation. Jackson agreed to help, but he was trying not to overrun her decisions on this particular matter. Her meeting with Jansen alone in the city was an entirely different discussion they would have after Charlie left.

"Hunter might be an easier conversation. I know him, and as far as I know, he's never lied to me." Keagan frowned. "Maybe we should start with him."

Jackson nodded in agreement. "I'll get hold of him

and set up a meeting. Maybe this afternoon or tomorrow."

"I'm meeting with Jansen this afternoon," she said, stiffening her chin. Cute little fox thought with Charlie in the room, she would get to have the last say in the matter.

"Charlie. I need to have a...word...with my girl here. See yourself out," Jackson said, keeping his attention fixed on Keagan.

Relief flashed in his eyes. His escape had been granted. "Sure thing. I'll just text you the info on the delivery schedule for the Jansen clubs."

"That's fine." Jackson waved him off.

"Good luck," Charlie whispered as he stepped out of the room and closed the door behind him.

To whom exactly he was passing on his well wishes, Jackson didn't know.

19

Keagan made her way up the steps to Jansen's house clutching her purse at her side. Jackson grabbed hold of her hand, slipped it in his and gave her a squeeze.

She'd lost the argument about his accompanying her to the meeting, but at least she hadn't had to ask Jansen to go out of his way to meet her at Jackson's house. Going to Jansen at least might keep him from asking too many questions about what exactly was going on between them.

Which she would be grateful for since she hadn't the slightest idea what was going on between them. One minute she found herself laughing at something Jackson said, and enjoying the moment, the next she felt a dark shadow crawl over her because no matter the outcome of their search for Katarina, Jackson wasn't an ever-after deal.

He was short term.

"You should probably get a longer skirt if you're going to keep up with your stubbornness," Jackson muttered to her as he stepped up beside her at the front door. She let go of his hand and pulled at the hem of her skirt.

"Maybe if your answer to every disagreement wasn't to tip me over a piece of furniture, I wouldn't have so many marks," she whispered to him.

He only laughed. She couldn't muster any true anger at him. He hadn't stepped a toe outside the boundaries they seemed to be living within. It wasn't the disagreements that had gotten her ass tanned that morning, but her inability to keep her finger from popping up at him when she couldn't sway him to her way of thinking.

She'd never met a man she couldn't move, but Jackson seemed immune to her manipulations.

The front door opened, and the butler shuffled them inside with a warm greeting.

"How is he today?" Keagan asked Joshua as he led them down the hall.

Joshua, an older man with graying hair and slower gait, gave her a tight smile. "Agreeable."

Keagan relaxed. Over the past few years she'd

come to understand the importance of that one word when it came to Jansen.

"Good," she said.

Jackson walked behind her as they were escorted into the family room directly off the kitchen. Jansen sat on the couch reading a book, his glasses perched on his nose. Keagan smiled at Joshua as he left them with his employer.

Jackson started to step forward, but Keagan grabbed his hand. When Jansen was reading, he didn't like being disturbed. He'd finish, then he'd address them. And until that took place, Jackson would just have to wait.

After several minutes crawled by, Jansen snapped his book shut and pulled off his glasses. Why did men insist on so much show boating?

"Keagan." Jansen smiled and dropped the book on the coffee table as he rose from the couch. He groaned slightly as he arched his back. "And Jackson, good to see you again." He gave a curt nod.

"Good book?" Keagan asked, stepping further into the room toward him.

He glanced down at the book and shrugged. "An autobiography of a moonshiner. Interesting. Not as exciting as my own business, but I understand the appeal." He rubbed his hands together. "Come in, both of you, sit." He gestured toward the loveseat across from the couch.

"I'm glad you could come," he said, though his smile and his lighthearted tone came across as forced. Keagan sank into the comfortable cushions of the loveseat and folded her hands in her lap as Jackson took the spot behind her. His hands leaned into the back of the seat. She fought back the urge to pull him into the loveseat with her. He could hover over her if it made him feel better. She wasn't going to let him get in the way of her conversation. She'd been dealing with Jansen for years, and that didn't all just go away because Jackson had stepped into the picture.

"Of course. How have you been?" she asked casually.

His smile fell. "Not the best, I'm afraid. But—" He waved his hand through the air. "That's for another time. I have a job for you." He sat down on the couch again and tapped his knee. "Easy job, worth a few hundred thousand."

"I—"

"We talked about this the together day. I'm out of that business." Keagan raised her voice to speak over Jackson. She would handle this.

"Yeah. I know what you said, but I know you could use the cash. Something to tide you over until you get legit work, right?" He smiled again and waved his hand. He seemed so confident, so arrogantly sure of himself. Had his power gone so unchecked that he couldn't even take a simple no from her? She didn't make him a lot of money, nothing like the serious money the rest of his family and crew brought in. So why keep her tied to him?

"Well, thank you for the consideration, but I have to respectfully decline," she said, firmly planting her feet on the floor. She could not let him see even a crack in her demeanor or he would try to wiggle in there.

"What are you going to do, Keagan, live with this guy now?" Jansen threw his hand in the air toward Jackson. "I know you're staying with him."

Keagan drew in a slow breath. "You've been watching me?"

"I've been protecting you," he corrected her with a pointed finger. "Jackson Titon was tossed out of Kassel with his father a long time ago. I wanted to be sure you were safe with him."

"Whatever happened between Jackson's father and Samuel Titon had nothing to do with Jackson," she shot back at him. The cushion behind her back shifted as Jackson fisted the material. At least he wasn't flying off the handle.

Yet.

"Well, rest assured, I'm perfectly safe, and I still have my townhouse that's paid off. Financially, I'm fine. So, as much as I appreciate your concern and your offer, I'm afraid I do need to turn it down."

Jansen's lips pulled down into a tight line. He

didn't appreciate being told no, but Keagan would keep the answer the same. No matter what he offered.

"Are you working for him now?" He jerked his chin up toward Jackson.

"She doesn't work for anyone," Jackson answered in a tight voice.

"Why is it so important that I work for you still?" Keagan asked. She'd seen Jansen sever connections before without any ill will. The only loyalty he demanded was from his crew and family. Those whom he brought in here and there were free to jump from job to job, so long as they never brought any trouble down on the family.

"I just want to be sure you're settled. That you have what you need," Jansen said, forcing a softer tone. A chill ran through her.

"Why?"

"I should need a reason?" he scoffed.

"Yes. I mean, it's kind of you to have concern, but I'm not so young anymore. I'm twenty-five. I can, and have, taken care of myself for the past several years. Why take such an interest in me?"

Jansen's eyes turned cold, and his jaw tightened.

"Keagan." Jackson placed his hand on her shoulder. "Let's not question his motives."

"I'm sorry. I didn't mean to offend." She lowered her gaze briefly, which seemed to placate him enough that he relaxed. "I do need your help, if you're willing, though. I'm unable to get close enough to Potier to ask him some questions. He's a recluse most of the time, and I missed my opportunity the last time he was out in the public to speak with him," she said, wishing she could turn around and shoot a few eye daggers at Jackson.

"Ask him about what?" Jansen's eyes narrowed again.

"He's the last person to have contact with Katarina as far as I can tell, and I'd just like to ask him about her," she said.

"I've told you to let the matter drop, Keagan. For your own peace of mind. It does you no good to keep going over it again and again. How can you ever expect to fully heal if you keep opening the wound?" His fingers dug into his knee as he spoke. "I'm sure he doesn't even remember your mother."

"But I just want to talk to him, and I know you have dealt with him before. Maybe if you would call him he'd at least call you back?" She scooted up to the edge of the cushion.

His lips twitched. "I'm sorry, Keagan, but it's not good for you to keep this up." He pushed off the couch, again moaning with the movements. "If you change your mind about the job, call me. Jackson." He inclined his head toward him. "I understand our deliveries are getting underway. I'm glad things have gone so smoothly so far."

"I'm sure they'll continue to do so," Jackson said, still squeezing her shoulder.

Jansen gave Keagan one last glance. "I suppose I know where to find you if I need to," he said and walked out of the family room.

Keagan got up from the loveseat and pulled the strap of her purse over her shoulder.

"We've been dismissed," she said, annoyed at the abrupt conversation. They could have had it over the damn phone. She hadn't needed to drag herself across town to meet with him. "The king has left the room, so us peasants can leave," she muttered and stalked off through the kitchen back to the front door.

Jackson followed her, and before she made it halfway down the hall, he grabbed her hand and pulled her back to his side. Turning her to face him, he ran the back of his hand along her jaw.

"Don't let him get you rattled. He's an old man who likes to have his power displayed now and then. Let it go," he said quietly so they wouldn't be overheard.

She stared up into his eyes, wondering how he could tolerate such chest thumping without getting at least a little irked.

"Let it go. We have other things to do today," he said and winked.

"Like?" she asked as he tugged her to the entrance where Joshua was already waiting for them with the door open. She nodded her goodbye to him and let Jackson pull her down the steps to his car.

"Well, Hunter texted me back while you were talking." He showed her his phone and dropped it in the cup holder of the middle console. "He's busy today, so we can't interrogate him until tomorrow," he said with a slow grin spreading across his lips. "So we have all afternoon to...do whatever we want."

She eyed him. "And what do we want to do?"

"There's about an acre and a half of woods behind my house that I haven't explored yet," he said. After she climbed into her seat, he shut her door and made his way behind the wheel.

"Don't you need to work?" she teased, while he shifted into drive and pulled away from the Jansen house.

"I do." He nodded. "But that's why I have people who do most of the heavy lifting for me. I have to make a call later, and tomorrow night I have to go into the city for a meeting. But this afternoon, I can play."

The wicked smile that fell across his lips sent a shiver of excitement through her. Playtime with Jackson could mean so many things.

All of them panty melting.

20

K eagan stared at the items on the bathroom counter while nibbling on her fingernail. Jackson had left her with the instructions to get ready for some fun, and he fully expected her to obey. If she didn't, she doubted anything playful would happen. The man took his dominance much more seriously than he had when they were just playing around for a bit fun. Maybe because he wasn't the young boy anymore, but a man with ambitions and confidence.

The young man she'd known hadn't had many plans for his life other than working with his father—whatever that had meant. But the man with whom she'd reconnected knew what his path was and how he was going to get there.

She'd overheard his conversations with his men—

he treated them with respect and in turn they seemed as loyal as men in his world could be. Even when he was unhappy with a delay of a shipment, he hadn't berated the messenger. Jansen would have lost his head over such a small thing. Jackson was calm, collected...but if he was crossed, she had no doubt he would act with the same swift decisions as he had with her. Actions had consequences. He should have the words branded on his chest.

"Do you need help?" Jackson's amused voice came through the bathroom door clearly.

She scrunched up her face. It wasn't enough, apparently, that she enjoyed the games they played. He wanted her to be a more active participant.

Picking up the fox tail from the counter, she stared at the glass plug at the end. They'd played with plugs, but she'd never had to insert one herself.

"Keagan?" he asked, sounding more concerned than playful.

"I'm fine," she assured him.

"Then you have two minutes," he said.

Only two? How could she do this in just two minutes? Blowing out a harsh breath, she picked up the bottle of lubricant. She'd get the worst part out of the way, then she'd put the rest of the parts together.

The bathroom door opened as she squirted a generous glob of lubricant onto the tip of the plug.

"What are you doing in here? I said I'm fine." She glared at him in the mirror.

He shrugged. "I decided I wanted to watch." He leaned against the doorframe and folded his arms across his chest.

"Do you really need to?"

He raised his eyebrows and smiled, such playfulness that her stomach fluttered.

"I really do."

She rolled her eyes at him and decided to put her mind to the task at hand. If she could pretend he wasn't there, watching her plug her own ass with the damn fox tail, maybe her cheeks would stop burning so bright.

"Pull your ass cheeks apart, it's easier," he said from behind her. She tried to block him out and put one foot on the edge of the tub, contorting herself for the best angle.

"Rub the tip of the plug on your asshole to spread the lubrication," he instructed, and she tensed. Obviously, he enjoyed this just as much as he would once the damn thing was in.

"Bend over a bit more, I want to see your pussy as your slip that plug into your tight asshole," he said, his voice getting heavier.

She did as he said, if only to keep him from commenting on it again, but she found the new position also helped. Her asshole stretched around the widest part of the plug, and she paused, taking a gulping breath.

"Breath through it," he said softly. Encouraged by his presence now instead of embarrassed by it, she pushed the tail again, accepting the stretch and burn until the plug popped into place. She exhaled hard and let go of the plug. Her ass felt full and still stretched around the glass base, but the worst was over.

"Good girl," he said from the doorway. "Your little asshole took the tail nicely. I wonder if it will take my cock so easily when the time comes."

She twisted her neck to see him more clearly.

He laughed. "Don't worry. You'll need to take a larger plug first before we try that." He pointed to the other items on the counter. "Don't forget the rest."

She clamped her mouth shut. As much as she wanted to tell him to fuck off, her body was already responding to his behavior. Her pussy clenched, and her clit ached to be touched, but she could put the blame on the plug in her ass titillating her libido.

Keagan dropped her foot from the edge of the tub and chanced a glance at her backside in the full-length mirror. A purple stripe still decorated her left ass cheek from the caning days ago. It was fading, but slowly. Between her ass cheeks hung the reddish-brown tail with the white tip.

"Keagan," Jackson warned. He'd given her a time limit, and she was out of time.

She picked up the hair band on the counter and wove her hair into a tight ponytail at the base of her neck. The ears were next. Situated on a black head-band, the white-tipped ears matched the tail dangling between her legs. Once they were seated on her head, she glanced at the last item.

Keagan caught Jackson's gaze in the mirror. The allure of his shimmering blue eyes captured her for a beat. He was watching her, yes, but it was more. Like he wasn't only seeing her exterior. The superficial moments of movement while she wound the rubber band around her hair, sticking the headband on her head, he saw them, but now, in the mirror he really, truly, *saw* her.

"Let me." He stepped into the bathroom and picked up the thick leather collar lying on the counter-top. Keagan had already removed the thin play collar he'd made her put back on when they'd gotten home from Jansen's.

With her hair already out of the way, she kept her hands planted at her sides and watched, fixated on his hands, in the mirror as he wrapped the extra-wide collar around her neck. His eyes only left hers for a moment to find the buckle beneath her ponytail. Once it was secured, he curled his hand around the back of her neck, running it along the stiff leather to her throat where the thick metal ring hung. Hooking his thumb through the ring, he pulled her forward enough for the edge of the counter to dig into her hip.

With his free hand, he skimmed his fingertips up her hip, over her belly to her breasts. Her nipples were hard and peaked when he took one between his fingers.

"I have little bells that I want to hang from your tits, but that wouldn't be playing fair, and I don't want you to have any excuses," he said, tugging her nipple downward toward the counter.

She whimpered with the burn his fingers created then moaned when he pressed his hard cock against her ass, reminding her of the plug situated there.

"Excuses for what?" she asked before she lost all train of thought.

He moved backward and pulled her by the collar toward him. She whipped around, facing him.

"For our game." He winked. What's the point of having a little fox if I can't practice the hunt?" He dropped his hand from her collar.

He was going to hunt her? She followed him out of the bathroom, thinking he just wanted to have a little chase around the bedroom. It would feel a bit silly, but he'd never led her astray before when it came to new ideas in the playroom. But he wasn't anywhere near the bed.

"This way," he said from the doorway.

She froze.

"Jackson. Charlie could walk in. Anyone could," she covered her chest.

Jackson merely shrugged. "Charlie learned his lesson about unannounced visits, and my other men never just pop over. So..." He gestured again to the open door.

"Are we going down to the playroom?" she asked, stepping across the carpeting to the door.

He led her down the hall in silence. A thick black leash hung from one hand and the other carried a long, zippered bag.

"Not the playroom," he said as he started down the stairs. "I told you, I haven't explored the woods behind the house yet."

She stepped onto the tiled landing at the bottom of the stairs and froze.

"I'm not going outside like this." She turned to run back upstairs, but he'd been waiting for her because he snapped out a strong arm and grabbed her around the waist, hauling her off the ground. She kicked and squirmed, but he only laughed and held tighter.

"No one will see you, little fox." He carried her down the hallway to the back of the house.

"You don't know that," she huffed when he finally put her back on her feet at the back door.

He placed the bag on the table at the breakfast nook and unzipped it.

"What is all that?" she asked leaning toward him.

"Well, I was going to use to use rubber bullets, but I'm worried they would hurt you too much. They can leave a serious welt, and you'd be feeling it for days," he said, throwing a mischievous grin over his shoulder at her. "And not in the good way."

"You were going to shoot me?"

"How else do you catch a fox?" he asked playfully.

He shoved two items into the back pockets of his jeans but kept them palmed enough that she couldn't see what they were. When he turned back to her, he looked more like a grinning devil than a playful boy.

"You have a two-minute head start," he said glancing up at the clock mounted on the wall over the door.

"You expect me to run barefoot?" she asked, wiggling her toes.

He pointed to her shoes that were lined up at the door. "Put those on."

Of course he'd thought of everything. She slipped her feet into the ballet flats. They wouldn't offer much support, but at least she wouldn't be stepping on twigs with her bare feet.

"Ready?" He pointed at the clock again.

"Where am I supposed to go? And what happens if you catch me?" What exactly were the rules here?

"The back of the estate is fenced off, so you can go

anywhere within it. Hide if you want to, and when I catch you, well...you'll just have to see what happens."

"You're being vague on purpose," she accused. He knew she liked having things laid out for her before diving in. She didn't need to know every detail, but more than just *you'll see*.

His lips twisted into a satisfied grin. "I am. Two minutes."

"Wait, I'm—"

"One minute fifty-five seconds..."

She grunted and threw open the back door. Not knowing the full extent of what he had planned wouldn't keep her from letting him win so damn easily. If he thought she'd be easy to catch, he had another thing coming.

Thanks to her regular runs, she made it across the lawn in quick order. The ballet flats shielded her feet better than she had expected, making running off the obvious path easier. She dodged a bush then a low branch but kept moving further and further into the trees.

"Little fox!" Jackson's voice trailed behind her, but he was still in the distance. She couldn't stop yet—she needed to get further away and then she could find a place to hide. Once he caught up with her, she could double back to the house.

She leapt over a fallen tree, catching her shin on

the rough bark. Biting her tongue kept her from crying out. She'd have to check the wound later.

"Here, little fox!" he called out to her again, closer now. How could he have gained so much ground already?

Her lungs burned and her thighs where starting to get sore, but she climbed over another fallen tree and kept moving. The trees were fully budded out, so the canopy kept her in the shade, but it didn't keep the summer heat entirely from touching her. A thin layer of sweat began to build on her forehead as she pumped her legs and kept moving. The damn tail danced behind her, swinging between her legs now and again, and almost tripping her up.

She did her best not to take notice of the sensations the tail drove through her as the plug moved about inside her. Pausing to hear Jackson's location, she bent over and put her hands on her knees, gulping in breath. A crunch of sticks came from the left and she bolted to the right, trying to get far enough ahead of him that she would be able to find a place to burrow away.

His steps were closer. She chanced a glance over her shoulder and could already make out his form moving too quickly toward her. Cursing, she shoved her way through a brush, looking to find another way around.

She came to a boulder. Fucking hell. She couldn't

chance running back into the open with him so close. He'd see her right away.

Turning back around, she flattened herself to it, and tried to shimmy between the thick bushes and the rock, but the bushes were too thick. She couldn't get through. She'd trapped herself.

Freezing where she stood, she listened. Maybe he would run past her position, thinking she ran the other direction or around the formation.

"My little fox has herself pinned down, hasn't she?" His dark tone abolished any hope she grasped that she could get by him.

The bushes were pushed away from the boulder and Jackson came into view, with an arrogantly pleased smile. "You didn't hurt yourself did you, squirming in there?" he asked, though she doubted he was too concerned as he hadn't tried to help her out.

"I'm a little scratched," she admitted.

"You've lost your ears." He frowned, reaching into the brush to grab hold of her arm.

She felt on top of her head. He was right. They must have fallen off during the chase.

"Come out now, little fox." He lost his grip on her, and she slid further into the brush. Reaching outward to the left, she found a weak spot in the vegetation. The branches were lush but weak, so she could shove them far enough away from the boulder to squeeze through.

She smiled. "You haven't caught me yet, hound."

Keagan shoved at the branches, wiggled herself free and popped out into the open space a moment later. A few more steps and she could bolt back toward the house. What would the prize be for outfoxing him?

Out of nowhere, his thick, unyielding arm bolted out and wrapped around her stomach. The momentum of her run made her double over, knocking air from her lungs.

"I have now," he said and flung her to the forest floor. Before she could scramble up, he was on her, straddling her middle and staring down at her. She sucked in a breath and blinked until her vision stopped swirling. When it all settled, she was looking up at his firm eyes.

"You good?" he asked with worried eyes.

She drew an easy breath and nodded. "I'm good." She pressed her hands to his thighs. "But it's hard to move with you on me like this."

Amusement flashed in his eyes, and his jaw relaxed. He hooked two fingers through the loop of her collar and pulled her up slightly.

"No need to move just yet, little fox." With his free hand, he reached behind him, pushing between her legs until his fingers found her pussy. She jolted at the first touch of his warm fingers against her clit. Sweet tremors rushed through every muscle as he expertly played her body—plucking all the right strings. She mewled the melody he strummed out of her.

"There's my girl," his whispered, hovering over her face with his wild eyes fixed on her. His bottom lip tucked between his teeth, and he thrust two fingers into her pussy. The instant fullness of his fingers mixed with the plug in her ass, and she arched her body off the forest floor, whining with need.

"Can you come for me, little fox? Come so hard the trees shake?" He teased her, curling his fingers upward and finding the secret treasure inside her. She gripped his thighs, bucking up as best she could with his weight on her toward his fingers.

"Jackson," she moaned, closing her eyes and melting into the intense sensations he unleashed inside her. He leaned forward and his hard cock pressed into her stomach. She licked at her lips. She wanted him.

His thumb brushed her clit as he pumped his fingers in and out of her.

"Oh fuck!" she screamed. The pressure in her stomach built and built until the edges of her vision blurred into a tangled mess of oranges and greens.

"Come for me, little fox," he ordered and leaned back again, shoving his fingers further into her cunt. He slammed his palm hard into her clit as he fucked her with his hand.

"I...oh..." Her eyes flew open, finding him

instantly, and her mouth opened wide to unleash the scream bubbling out of her throat.

Another stroke of his fingers, and her entire body shuddered then exploded with sensations hitting her from all angles. She tried to scream, tried to unleash the fury of pleasure charging through her body, but no sound erupted. With her mouth opened, her eyes frozen on his, she shook and trembled beneath his weight as the ripples of her orgasm possessed her.

"That's my good fox, my good girl," he said softly as the last waves of pleasure eased away, leaving her body to sag back onto the leaves and twigs beneath her.

"Jackson," she said, licking her lips as her eyes dragged down the length of him to the bulge in his jeans.

"What do you want, little fox?" he asked with a canary-eating grin.

"You," she said and reached for his belt.

21

The way her gaze raked over his body down to where his cock pressed against his jeans, made him want to rip his clothes off and dive into her hot pussy. But he wouldn't rush this. Keagan wanted him, she was making this move, and he'd let his little pet have her way for the time being. But he would have her pussy clenching his cock before they were finished with their little game of hunt.

"You want my cock, little fox?" he asked, slipping his hand from her pussy. He kept her gaze trapped within his while he sucked and licked every bit of her juices from his flesh. Fuck she tasted like candy.

"Yes," she said, pulling at his belt.

"Don't be greedy," he said with a laugh and slapped away her hands. He yanked off his shirt as he climbed off her. Lying on the twigs was one thing, but having to press her knees into them was another. He wanted her full focus, and trying to ignore the annoying discomfort would only serve to distract her. He laid his shirt on the ground and rose to his feet.

She rolled over to her hands and knees.

"Here," he said, snapping his fingers and pointing to the shirt. With hunger burning in her eyes, she scrambled to the shirt and knelt on the fabric. It wouldn't offer too much comfort, but it was better than nothing. She pressed her hands onto her knees and looked up at him, waiting for him.

His belt jangled as he let it hang open and unzipped his jeans. If they had been back at the house, maybe he'd go slower, savor every second, but they weren't, and his cock ached too much for her touch. He shoved his jeans and boxers down and fisted his cock. She brought her eyes to where his hand slid up and down the length of his hard dick.

Her little tongue darted out and licked her lips. Did she realize she was showing her desires so easily, or was it completely beyond her control at the moment?

Stepping closer to her, he brought his cock toward her. "Put your hands behind your back," he instructed, squeezing his cock enough to relieve some of the pressure. It wasn't enough. It wouldn't be until he had her mouth wrapped around him.

She straightened, folded her arms behind her, and grabbed onto her wrists. Then she opened her mouth, sliding her tongue out for him. His heart stopped, and his chest expanded. Fuck, she was perfect.

"You remember the face fucking I gave you that first time?" he asked in a husky tone. It was taking too much control to keep from thrusting between those plump lips, to keep his voice steady.

She nodded, her lips twitching slightly, as though she wanted to smile but she didn't want to close her mouth yet.

"Good. Then you know not to touch or move. You just take what I give you." He touched the top of her head and led her forward to his cock. The warmth of her tongue touching the underside of the head of his cock, nearly undid him. He clenched his teeth and continued forward.

Her lips wrapped tightly around his shaft; her tongue ran along the underside of his dick. Taking a steady breath, he pushed forward and forward still until the tip of his cock touched the back of her throat. Instead of gagging and yanking away, she swallowed him down. The extra pressure around him sent a shiver down his spine.

"Fuck yes," he said and began to thrust in and out of her mouth, down her throat. She sputtered when he hit too hard, but he didn't slow his pace. Looking down, he caught sight of the spit pooling around her lips, saw the tears running down her eyes, and he could only grin down at her. She could pull back if she needed, he didn't force her forward, but she remained still.

"Fuck!" he growled when she sucked hard on his cock. Too much. Too fucking much. If he kept this up too long, he wouldn't get into her pussy, and he wanted that pretty pussy. He slid over her tongue again, then yanked free of her siren's mouth.

"Down." He snapped his fingers again and pointed to the ground. She wiped the back of her hand across her lips then fell forward as he demanded, then took it another step by pressing her face to the ground and wiggling her ass in the air.

Fuck.

He moved around her and fell to his knees. "This fucking tail." He flipped the tail up so he could lay it over her back. The tight ring of her asshole stretched around the plug. It would be even tighter with the plug in. He pulled her pussy lips apart and lined his dick up with her entrance.

"I want this pretty pussy. It's my pussy, isn't it, little fox? It belongs to me now, right?" He teased her with his cock.

"Yes, Jackson. Yours," she said and pushed back toward him, willing him to take her.

In one smooth thrust he was inside her, up to the hilt. His balls slapped against her clit as he slammed into her again and again. She moaned, clenching around his cock as he pounded her. The plug made her passage even tighter. She was so hot and wet and his.

Over and over again, he pulled her hips back toward him as he slammed into her. She threw her head back and cried out.

"You want to come again for me, little fox?" he asked, using one hand to twist the plug in her ass. "With your tail in? You want to shake your ass at me and find another orgasm?"

"Yes! Fucking yes," she called out and began to rock her body back at him while he plowed forward.

"Then do it!" He slapped her hip and thrust forward.

He reached around her waist and found her slippery clit. A simple pinch. That's all it took for her to lose herself beneath him for a second time. Her cunt pulsated around his cock as she flew away with her release.

He ground his teeth together, pumping into her once, twice, then he froze. His spine tightened, his balls pulled up, and with a roar he unleashed his come into her tight cunt. The intensity kept his back tense, his ass squeezed, and his cock embedded in her until the very last wave of his release faded away.

His throat burned and his mouth was dry as he slowly withdrew from her.

"Keagan?" He pressed a hand to her back and looked around her bent-over body.

She shifted, turning her face toward him, a weak smile dangling from her lips.

"I'm good, Jackson," she said softly.

His heart hammered, and he yanked up his boxers and pants, zipping up but leaving his belt undone. He grabbed his shirt and wiggled it from beneath her knees.

"C'mon." He helped her up to her feet and pulled his shirt over her head. She poked her arms through the sleeves and looked up at him with her dark eyes full of confusion.

"Just in case one of the guys came over while we were out here," he said and lifted her into his arms, carrying her the short way back to the house. It had felt further when he'd been chasing after her, but it only took a few minutes to get back into the yard.

"What did you have in your pockets?" she asked, half asleep already with her head tucked in the crook of his neck.

He paused a moment, then stepped up onto the deck. He'd forgotten all about the little vibrators he'd brought with him. The intent had been to tease her until she begged for mercy, but once he'd seen her, hiding in that bush, he lost all memory of his plans. The only thing he had known after that was that he wanted to be inside her.

"Toys," he said simply, maneuvering the back door open and carrying her through the kitchen and down the hall to the main set of stairs.

"You didn't want to play with them?" She yawned.

"Didn't need to. I had you," he said, carrying her down the hall to his room. He passed the guest room on the way but didn't even pause. She wasn't a guest anymore. She belonged in his bedroom. She belonged with him.

He brought her to the bed and carefully laid her on her side.

"I'm taking out the tail," he said softly.

She moaned, but her eyes were already closed. Since she couldn't see him, he didn't even try to hide his smile. The woman was so tired she would sleep through a butt-plug being dislodged from her ass.

He pulled her ass cheeks apart and carefully pulled the plug out of her ass. His cum leaked from her pussy, making a mess of her thigh, but he left it. Let her feel it when she moved, let it drip down her legs, and she would remember who marked her, who made her his.

Because no matter how impossible it was, she was his.

He pulled the quilt up over her and closed the blinds to the room.

"Aren't you coming to bed?" she asked, keeping her eyes closed.

"I have to make a few calls. You sleep." He pressed a kiss to her temple, grabbed the fox tail from the bed and left her to nap.

He'd neglected his work for the past week, and he needed to check in with his guys. If he wasn't heard from, they might start thinking they could figure out their own jobs.

His little fox would take her nap, and he'd do what he did best. He'd hunt down the profits, keep the dogs in line, and get the job done.

22

Keagan ran her hands over her stomach. Jackson's suggestion to go out for the evening had sounded like a good idea at the time. Hunter had called off their meeting, and after pacing around the house for over an hour, any reason to get out was welcome.

But that was before she stood in the swarm of the Tower. She'd put on a black dress. It was fitted and came to just below her ass. The neckline ran deep, showing off the swell of her breasts, and if she moved too quickly would be in danger of showing off more. When Jackson had taken her to her townhouse to find something suitable to wear for the evening, she'd felt playful. He'd spent so much time teasing and edging her, it was only fair she pay him in kind.

But now, standing in the club, waiting for him

to finish speaking with one of the managers, a flurry of nerves hit her stomach. His eyes had gone wide when she had walked out of her bedroom, ready to go for the evening. He'd looked ready to pounce on her, but he'd schooled his features and only beckoned her toward the front door.

Maybe she had misread him.

With her focus on the dance floor, she hadn't seen Jackson approach. He slid his arm around her waist, pulled her against him and pressed a firm kiss to the top of her head.

"Do you feel all of their eyes on you?" he asked, keeping close to her. With music playing overhead, he'd have to speak into her ear if he wanted to be heard clearly.

She gripped her handbag and surveyed the room. "No one's looking at me, Jackson."

"Oh, they are. How can they not with this damn dress you're wearing?" he growled.

She turned her face up toward him. "You don't like it?"

His lips worked into a fine line. "I should have gone with my gut and made you change," he said roughly, before tearing his gaze away from her.

"I wouldn't have," she assured him, lifting a shoulder. It was not a total lie. She would have argued, but she probably would have let him win.

"Peter's not here tonight, but we can take a table upstairs in the VIP section," he said.

She followed his pointed finger up to the second floor where tables had been set up along the balcony overlooking the club's main floor.

"You don't want to dance?" she teased.

His lips screwed up into a grimace. "Let's get something to drink first." He slid his hand back around her waist and down her arm so he could entangle his fingers with hers.

Jackson led her through the crowd to a glass-walled elevator. She'd been at the Tower once before, but she hadn't taken the time to enjoy the ambiance. It wasn't like other nightclubs. The dancers weren't grinding on each other or whooping and hollering for the next song. Instead of a DJ, there was a live band. No colored lights flashed all over the dance floor, but several chandeliers hung down, illuminating the space with a soft glow. Erotic paintings decorated the walls.

"On some nights there is live artwork," Jackson said once they were inside the elevator and she was still soaking up the club.

"What?"

"Live artwork. Like women bound with rope in various positions. It's kind of beautiful, actually, but doesn't look like tonight's one of the nights." Jackson pressed his chest against her and pointed at the alcoves along the second floor that allowed space for at least two people.

He'd trimmed his beard before they left the house, and the musky scent of his aftershave weaved around her. The edge of his beard tickled her shoulder.

She was supposed to be teasing him for the night, not the other way around. It wasn't fair. He wasn't even trying.

The elevator dinged and the doors behind them slid open. He grabbed her hand again and led her down the right side of the floor to a table where a bottle of wine had already been opened and left for them along with several plates of appetizers.

"You didn't eat much today." He escorted her through the roped entrance.

"Stuffed mushrooms." She grinned and dropped her purse on an empty chair. She reached for one. "I love these," she said then sank her teeth into one.

"I know. You had three orders of them at that hotel we stayed in that one weekend. I think it was at the lake."

He surprised her with his memory. She swallowed down the last bite. "You remember that?"

"I remember everything, Keagan." Light flickered in his eyes, sending another flutter through her core.

"Are you sure Hunter will be available tomorrow, or will he ditch out at the last second again?" she asked, turning the subject somewhere more comfortable.

Jackson poured the wine into her glass. "He'll be available." Jackson then waved over one of the waiters lined up against the back wall. Each section was assigned their own service for the evening. There would be no waving down a waitress trying to get someone to take their order.

Jackson asked for another bottle of wine to be brought up, then turned his attention back to Keagan.

"You just poured the first glass from this one," she said.

"They're big glasses," he said with a grin.

She laughed. "Are you trying to get me drunk?"

"I don't need such tricks with you."

"Samantha? Is that you? Yes, yes it is, Samantha!" A voice from the past interrupted them.

Keagan put a hand on Jackson's arm, keeping him in his chair, while she stood.

"Jared! What a surprise to see you here," she greeted the councilman with a bright smile. She didn't dare reach out to hug the man, for fear that Jackson wouldn't be able to hold himself back. The man was too protective and entirely too selfish to share.

"A night out on the town is needed now and again." The older man smiled. His soft eyes drifted from her to Jackson, then back again. "I don't mean to interrupt," he said quietly.

"Oh, not to worry. Jackson is an old friend. How are things?" She took a small step to the right to hide Jackson from view. He wouldn't stay in his chair long, and she needed to hurry up the reunion.

"Things are good, good." Jared nodded. Again, he looked over her shoulder at Jackson. "I'm actually on my way out, my—uh—friend, is downstairs already waiting for me. It was so good to see you again, Samantha." He gave her a warm smile, a quick incline of his head then off he went down the hall toward the elevator.

"You scared him," Keagan accused with levity as she sank back into her seat.

"I did nothing but keep quiet and watch your inter-action," he said with a raised eyebrow. "So, *Samantha*, how do you know the councilman?"

Heat touched her cheeks. "We had dinner together once, a long time ago." She popped another mush-room into her mouth.

"Hmmm," Jackson said, sipping his wine.

Their server arrived and placed the second bottle of wine on the table. "Would you like it opened now or would you prefer to wait?"

"Later is fine," Jackson answered, keeping his eyes fixed on Keagan.

She smiled up at the young man and reached for her glass of wine. Sweet and red. Jackson didn't forget anything from their time together.

"How many families were you with before Katarina?" Jackson threw her off with his question. They'd never spoken too much about their pasts. For a couple that was only in it for the bedtime fun, childhood memories didn't really belong.

"Seven, that I remember," she answered somberly. "When I was a baby, I'm sure there was at least one or two more."

Jackson stared at her in silence for a long beat. "Did any of them hurt you?" His question was given in such a low tenor, with such a steady calm, it made her pause. There was more to the question than what he asked. In truth, what he wanted to know was who did he have to hurt back.

"It was a long time ago, Jackson," she said, gulping down more wine.

"That wasn't my question." He hardened his stare.

"I will tell you this—living with Katarina was a dream come true for a girl in foster care. I never worried about anything with her. Ever." She placed a hand on his knee. "Let that be enough, all right?"

His eyes narrowed, and his lips tensed. Her younger years, life before Katarina, had been marred by violence and hunger.

"Jackson." She leaned closer to him. "I promise you I have no scars or nightmares from that time. It's the past. Let it stay there."

Jansen had told her the same thing when she'd

started her search into Katrina's death, but losing Katarina was different. It wasn't just the past, it was her present. It was everything to lose the one person who'd kept her safe and loved.

"I won't push it," he conceded. "For now."

She rolled her eyes and laughed. "Such a stubborn man." She chewed on another mushroom and sat back in her chair. "Now it's your turn."

"My turn for what?" Lines crinkled around his narrowed eyes.

"Why did you leave Kassel with your father? What happened between your dad and Ash's?" She draped her arms over the sides of the curved chair, waiting for his answer.

"It was a long time ago," he answered, throwing her own words back at her. Whatever happened had kept his family apart for years before Jackson felt comfortable enough to put his roots back down in Kassel. He might not want to rehash it.

"I guess that's fair." She shrugged, playing it off as though she didn't care one way or another.

"It is." He nodded. "It's also not a very exciting story. There were three sons, Samuel—the oldest; Vincent—Peter's father; then my own father, Stephan. Since Samuel was the oldest, he was groomed to take over the family businesses. Uncle Vincent worked well with Samuel, I suppose after my grandfather died, but my dad—he wanted more than what a third son should hope for. He wanted a branch of the family of his own. A full crew to run, but Samuel said no. My dad didn't take it seriously and formed his own business—one that didn't compete in any way with my uncle. But Samuel wouldn't allow it. He tried everything to destroy what my father was building."

"Tried?" she asked when he paused.

"He interfered with his distribution lines. Just fucked with him until he had almost nothing left. And then when my dad came to him, asking him to just leave him be, Samuel told him the only way he'd ever run his own business is if he left Kassel." Jackson took a sip of his wine. "So he did. We packed up and moved to Hammelin."

She eyed him. "When you came back here, did Ash have to give you permission? I know he's not working with Jansen or the Bertuccis anymore, but he's still head of the Titon family."

Jackson scratched beneath his beard. "No. I didn't ask him. I did let him know about me working with Jansen, but I don't answer to Ash."

"Well, now that you own part of the Annex, you sort of do." She tipped her glass toward him.

He chuckled. "Maybe a little, but I would hand back those shares if he ever became Samuel."

"Yeah. I've never heard anything good said about Samuel Titon, other than he did make a lot of people very rich," she said, popping the last mushroom on the platter into her mouth.

"Still don't want to dance?" she teased when the band struck up a slow melody.

His smile fell.

"You can't dance?" She laughed.

"Oh, I can, just not on the dance floor." He grabbed her hand and pulled her into his lap.

His hard length pushed into her ass.

"People can see," she said looking around for prying eyes. The other couples in their VIP sections were busy with each other, not paying them any attention.

"Let them spy if they want. Isn't that what made you put this on tonight?" He ran his hand up from her bare knee to toy with the hem of her dress. Another inch and he'd been able to touch her pussy. And then he'd feel how wet she was for him already. Even an evening talking about past secrets could set her ablaze for him. Merely having his eyes on her, showing his hunger for her, made her pussy wet for him.

"I wanted to tease you, but it hasn't worked, has it?" she asked, knowing full well she'd been beaten. He was never one for games, and she'd never been good at them either. But for once, she wanted the upper hand with him.

"I don't like men looking at you like they want you to be theirs, but it's a barbaric thought. Me wanting to brand you, to make you mine." He trailed his fingers along her bare neck, leaving a trickle of heat behind. She'd left the collar at home for the evening, but she didn't need it to feel its power.

She wet her lips. "Barbaric, yes, but I really don't expect anything less from you," she teased.

He paid her back by digging his nails into her thigh. She sucked in a harsh breath, letting the burn run through her body.

"I think, if I touch your pussy, I'll find you drenched for me, my little fox." He moved his hand up beneath her dress, so close, too close to touching her sex.

He brought his free hand to her face, swiping away her hair and tucking it behind her ear. She bit down hard on her lip, trying to tear her gaze away from his, but he had her locked. His fingers crept further and further up her skirt until he found her wet and wanting pussy.

"I was right," he whispered into her ear as he ran his finger through her slit.

She moaned. "Jackson." She grabbed hold of his arm. If her mind was trying to beg him to stop, her body pleaded for his attention. She parted her legs enough to give him easier access.

A smile cracked along his lips. Of course he wouldn't allow her to drive this carriage.

He slipped his hand out from beneath her dress

and captured her face with both hands. Bringing her to him, he slammed his mouth against hers.

This is what it felt like to be owned, to be so wanted by a man he would take what was his when he wanted. Without care for who saw or who commented.

Arousal pooled in her stomach, and she leaned into his kiss. He could have pushed her dress up and thrust his cock into her in that moment, and she would have been helpless to stop him. Lost in the haze his kiss put her in, it took a moment to realize he'd pulled back.

"Grab the bottle, Keagan." He slipped her off his lap and tugged down her dress.

"Why?" Her heart was still playing a desperate beat.

He tossed a pile of bills onto the table. "We're going home."

23

The house was dark when Jackson pulled Keagan up the stairs toward his bedroom. He didn't need the lights. What he needed was the fucking bed. Hell, even that was becoming optional the longer it took them to get there.

"Jackson, slow down." She stumbled behind him.

In one quick motion, he turned around and swooped her up, depositing her over his shoulder.

"You wanted to tease me with that dress, well this is what you get." He smacked her ass.

Instead of a gasp of pain, he received laughter. He smacked her again with more force just as they arrived at his bedroom. Maybe the playroom would be a better choice. He had more restraints in there.

No time.

He pushed open the door and barged forward into

the bedroom, depositing her onto her feet. The moon-light from outside shone in through the windows, casting a bluish light over her features.

"Leave it on," he commanded when she reached for the dress.

"You look like you're going to tear it apart," she said.

She wasn't wrong. He'd wanted to rip it off of her body since the moment she'd stepped out of her bedroom wearing the damn thing. He should have made her turn around and put on something else, but he sensed she had other motives for wearing it. She wanted to tease him, the way he'd done to her. Bring him to the brink of his ability to hold back and see if he would break.

She had dangled the treat in front of the hound, and now it was time to pay up.

He unbuttoned and shrugged out of his shirt, then tossed it to the floor. Her eyes darted to his belt. She deserved a few solid licks for thinking to play a game with him, but first things first.

He picked up her collar from the nightstand and crooked his finger at her. Dutifully, she approached him and swiped her hair up off her neck and offered herself to the collar.

Once it was wrapped around her slender throat and buckled, he cupped her shoulders and turned her to face him. Her eyes widened, but her pupils were already enlarged. With his hands still on her shoulders, he pushed her backward against the thick bed post.

"You hoped to tease me with this dress, make me mad with jealousy with other men looking at you. At what's mine?" With a single finger, he lifted the frail strap from her shoulder.

Her throat worked. Once ensnared, the little fox wasn't so cunning.

"Maybe I should mark you, brand you so no one would think to touch what's mine. They'd see the mark on you, and they'd turn away." He pulled the straps down her arms. She raised her chin defiantly, yet all the while lust filled her eyes, matching his own.

How had he let her disappear all those years ago without tracking her down? How had he just let her slip through his fingers?

He dragged the straps further down her arms until the cups of the dress fell forward. His gaze ran down from her face to her exposed breasts. She gasped when he took her nipple between his fingers and pulled gently toward him.

He kissed her, then whispered, "You would look so nice with those bells I mentioned."

Jackson released her nipples then watched, captivated, as her cheeks reddened and her breath picked up its pace. Her wet lips parted.

"No." He brushed her hands away when she

reached up to cover her breasts. The pinch hadn't been too hard but had been enough to leave a lasting burn once he let her go.

"Take off your panties," he instructed, standing back only a step. She reached beneath the skirt of the dress, wiggled the pair of black panties down her legs, then lightly kicked them away once they were at her ankles, along with her heels.

Advancing on her again, he captured her face with his hands, tilting her head back and crushing her with his lips.

Fuck, she tasted good. She wove her hands through his arms and grasped his neck, holding him to her, matching his own desire to be near her.

He broke off the kiss abruptly, nipped her lip then grinned.

"Grab the post, Keagan," he ordered while working his belt buckle open.

Confusion washed over her eyes.

"Lift your leg, put your foot on the chest." He nodded toward the hope chest pressed against the foot of the bed.

She raised her leg while reaching over her head for the post. He'd have to install a ring there later so she'd have something easier to hold onto, but for now she'd have to make do.

Unzipping his pants with one hand, he wrapped his arm around her waist and arched her body toward him. Holding her tightly, he thrust his cock into her, not taking the time to tease or toy with her, just taking what was his.

She gasped, but he didn't calm his movements. She was ready for him, waiting for his cock to impale her. Her pussy stretched around him, easily accepting him as he plowed into her again. Already soaked for him, she had no trouble taking the pounding he had planned.

She rolled her head to the side, exposing the length of her neck. Not one to miss an opportunity, he sank his teeth into the tender flesh just below the collar. She moaned, a sweet, needy sound that drove his cock further into her.

"Jackson," she whined as he ground his hips into hers.

"I know, baby, I know," he nipped her earlobe, then her neck again.

"Fuck!" She dropped her arms from the post and grabbed onto his shoulders, digging her fingernails into him.

The sharp burn ramped up his movements, sending him flying toward his orgasm.

"Should I let you come?" he mused between thrusts. She'd tried to tease him.

"Yes! Please, Jackson." She arched her body, lifting herself up and wrapping her free leg around his waist.

He held onto her, holding her to him while he

thrust up into her wet, tight passage. Pressing her against the post for leverage, he fucked her harder, with more determination.

"Oh, fuck!" Her nails went deeper.

"Don't hold back," he ordered, gripping her ass while driving into her.

She became unglued. Throwing her head to the side she cried out with her orgasm. She bucked her hips at him, trying desperately to ride out the waves overwhelming her. He wouldn't let her get off so easily.

"That's one. Now I want another," he whispered in her ear as she started to calm.

With wide eyes she stared at him.

"Oh, you'll give me another," he vowed, readjusting his body to press her ass against the post as well. Once he freed up his hand, he slipped it between them and pinched her clit.

She yelped.

"Come again for me. You can do it." He rubbed then ground upward into her while playing his thumb against her clit.

Anchoring her with one arm, he slid her down the pole enough to be able to hold her up while thrusting hard into her. Heat zipped down his spine. He wouldn't be able to hold much longer, but he wouldn't allow her to go without giving him what he wanted.

"Jackson...fuck...fuck...fuck!" She unleashed again, her second orgasm ripping through her body.

He pumped into her, riding her through it, driving her to the very end before he finally allowed his body to take its prize. The force of his own release froze him. Pressed against her, he clenched his jaw while his back arched, his cock emptying into her wet, ready pussy.

Haze slowly receded, and he blinked back to life enough to pick her up into both arms. His cock slipped from her, come dripped from her pussy down his hip, but he didn't care. She was exhausted, and he was beyond thought.

Carrying her to the bed, he deposited her in the middle. She sank back into the pillows and wiggled her delectable body from the dress. He took the scrap of material and flung it across the room, then shoved out of the rest of his own clothes.

"Jackson," she breathed his name once they were settled beneath the covers.

"Yeah?" He pressed a kiss to her forehead and pulled her into his embrace. This was right. Her body against his—this is what contentment felt like. No, fuck that, this is what love felt like.

His mind blanked, and his heart screeched to a stop.

"When we see Hunter tomorrow, you'll let me do the talking right? You won't interfere?"

Of course. Her mind was already back on track with her main objective.

He squeezed her to him. "Go to sleep, Keagan. We'll figure it all out in the morning."

"But—" She stopped with a pinch to her hip.

"Sleep."

With a yawn, she snuggled further into him, and within moments her breathing had settled into an even pattern.

Once she solved the mystery of her mother's disappearance, she'd be gone again from his life. He needed to prepare himself for that fact.

He would start in the morning.

24

Hunter's house was a hell of a lot more inviting than his uncle's. There was no half-in-the-grave doorman to walk them inside when Jackson and Keagan arrived. Hunter's wife had greeted them with a warm smile and hug for Keagan, and a narrow-eyed glare for Jackson. Hunter showed up and shuffled them all into his office to talk.

Jackson sat at the bar in Hunter's office cradling a beer in his hands while Hunter poured a glass of white wine for Keagan

"You saw my uncle yesterday?" Hunter asked after Keagan relayed where they'd come from.

"Yeah. He had a job offer." She accepted the wine glass. "That I declined."

Hunter's eyes snapped up to her. "And how did he take that?"

"About as you'd expect." She smiled and sipped her drink. "I told him I'm out, Hunter. Completely out."

Hunter put the bottle of wine down on the bar and stared at her silently for a long beat. "Are you?"

"Am I?"

"Out. Really out. Not going to do any job for him again?" he asked firmly.

Keagan glanced at Jackson then gave a firm nod. "I should have been out a while ago, but I was hoping his connections could help me."

Hunter folded his arms over his chest. "Help with what?"

Jackson took a pull of his beer. "We're trying to track down what exactly happened to Katarina Silverstone."

Hunter's jaw tightened.

"Sorry, I had to get the baby back to sleep." Jaelynn breezed into the room with a smile. Her hair was swept up into a neatly tied ponytail, and her simple pink dress gave her a youthful appearance.

"If I'd known it was her naptime I would have told Jackson we'd come later," Keagan explained.

"No, it's fine." Jaelynn waved a hand. "Can I have a glass?" She pointed to Keagan's wine.

"You can have juice," he said and pulled out a bottle of grape juice from beneath the bar and filled a wine glass with the white juice. Jaelynn rolled her eyes but took the glass and climbed onto the stool beside Keagan.

"I'm going to cut right to it," Keagan said, adjusting her seat on the stool. "You sat right beside her on the plane she took out of Kassel.

Hunter stared at her, but he made no attempt to deny it.

"I want to know why?" She took a larger gulp of her wine either for courage to be so demanding with a man like Hunter or for the courage to hear the answer.

"My uncle told me to." Hunter filled her glass again once she put it back on the bar empty. "He sent me to accompany her overseas. I did. The last time I saw your mother alive, she was happy for time away from Kassel."

Keagan's shoulders slumped.

"What did Jansen have to do with any of it, though? Katarina was mostly retired by then; Keagan was starting to fill in for her. She was just going on vacation, wasn't she?" Jackson asked.

Hunter twisted off the cap of a beer and took a long sip. "She was important to him."

"Important how? I mean, he was always kind to us —as kind as he could be, I guess. By important enough to give her an escort on a vacation?" Keagan pressed.

"She didn't work for Jansen in the same way he had you doing things. I mean, she did, but her main job was more...well, long term," Hunter explained while making everything more confusing.

"What does that mean?" Keagan asked.

"How old were you when you went to live with her?" Hunter asked his own question.

"Twelve," Keagan answered. "Why?"

"I didn't realize you were that old," Jackson said, leaning his elbow own the bar and twisting toward her. "I thought she adopted you when you were younger."

"No. My birth parents gave me up when I was a baby, but I floated in the system until I went to Katarina's house. She kept me." Keagan lowered her eyes, then took a long swig of her wine.

"She didn't adopt you?" Jackson asked. Why hadn't he bothered to learn more about her past before this? Shouldn't it have been something they talked about?

"No. She talked about it once, saw a lawyer, but it never happened." She pushed a plastic smile on her lips. "It was probably too expensive, and besides, I didn't need a piece of paper to tell me she was my mom." She lifted her shoulders. "She just was."

Her words said one thing, but the hurt in her eyes spoke an entirely different story. It wouldn't have been simply a piece of paper. It would have been a declaration.

"What does that have to do with why Jansen told you to take her overseas?" She turned her attention back to Hunter. He raised his brows then lowered them, as though he fought an internal battle.

"You know my uncle." He lifted his beer to his lips. "You don't ask too many questions."

"Or you could just not talk to him at all, like ever, cause he's an asshole," Jaelynn said into her glass as she drank her juice.

"Yes, you could avoid him completely," Hunter agreed. "And watch your language. Just because we have company doesn't change anything for you, little girl." His eyebrows shot up.

Jaelynn rolled her eyes.

"So you never asked or didn't know?" Keagan chose to ignore the building of tension between husband and wife. "Was she just on a fun adventure like she made it sound?"

Hunter pinned his lips together.

"Dammit." Jaelynn slapped her hand against the bar. "She's up again." She jumped off the chair. "She has your stubbornness, Hunter," she muttered. "Keagan, you want to come see her. It's been a while since you were over."

By the tension in her shoulders, Jackson could sense Keagan did not want to visit with the two-year-old. She wanted to stay and question Hunter some more. Jackson eyed Hunter, seeing hope rise up in his eyes and decided to give the man a hand.

"Go, Keagan. When you get back, we'll get this all sorted." Jackson patted her hip.

She narrowed her brown eyes at him.

"I'll be right back," she said and slid off the stool. She would be pissed that he helped Hunter get her out of the room, but he'd beg her forgiveness once he got her home.

Once the women were gone from the room, Jackson swiveled back to Hunter and pinned him with a hard stare. "Tell me."

"I don't think she wants to know," Hunter said quietly, probably because both his wife and Keagan could very well have been hiding around the corner. Keagan wouldn't stoop to eavesdropping, she'd just walk back in and demand her answers. But Jaelynn was somewhat more subtle.

"She thinks she does." Jackson leaned forward. "Is the truth that bad?"

Hunter frowned. "Do you think anything my uncle touches isn't that bad?" he answered.

"I've only worked with him recently, but from what Ash and Peter have told me over the years, I'd say you're probably right. But wanting to know and needing to know are different."

Hunter gave a small nod and pressed his hands against the edge of the bar. He looked conflicted still.

"Is she still alive?"

"Katarina?" Hunter asked with surprise.

"Keagan has hope that she wasn't on that last plane. She wants to talk to Herald Potier because supposedly he's the last person to have talked with her before she got on that plane."

Color fell from Hunters face.

Jackson sighed. "The last time you saw her alive..." he muttered more to himself. "You saw her after, when she was dead."

Hunter gave a slow nod. "Jackson, you don't want her involved in this."

"You have to tell me then. What is it?"

"Jansen ordered Katarina's death. I didn't do it, but Potier—he's not just a beer king, he's one of Jansen's henchmen. He works quietly and stays under the radar, so he's never been connected to anything Jansen's had him do."

"So he was the last person to see Katarina."

"Yeah, he was, but if Keagan gets him alone and asks him about it..." Hunter didn't need to finish the thought. Keagan's inquires were getting more dangerous.

"So Jansen hasn't been keeping her around because of her skill or because he gives a shit about her. He's keeping her around to be sure she's not snooping around?" Jackson wiped his palm over his mouth. "Why not just take care of her the way he did Katarina?"

Even thinking it sent his stomach into a whirlwind,

but it would have been the easiest solution to Jansen's problem.

"Keagan does have a connection to my uncle that's important to him. He's been protecting her since birth."

Jackson's brows snapped forward. "What the fuck does that mean?"

A resolved firmness took over Hunter's expression. "Keagan is my cousin," Hunter said in a low voice. "He got one of his girls pregnant but instead of making her get rid of the baby like he did the others, he let her have the baby. She died right after. He couldn't take her in. He was married, and his wife came from an even bigger family than his. Such disrespect would have brought the wrath of her father into Kassel."

Jackson's heart sank in his chest. "So he paid Katarina to raise her?"

"Once he found her again, yes. He hadn't been able to get to her in time before she'd been given to another couple, and then she was lost in the system for a time. He finally found her and gave her to Katarina. From what I understood, once Keagan was old enough, she'd be told about him. But then my aunt died, and Jansen didn't want to bring her into the family for whatever his reasons."

"How do you know all this, but no one else? As far as anyone knows, Jansen's heir is you."

Hunter huffed a laugh. "I'm not taking that hot mess when he goes, and he knows it."

"So he finally decided to tap Keagan?"

"Katarina wanted to keep Keagan safe from him. She didn't lie when she tried to adopt her, but Jansen put a stop to it. He blocked her in court as being her biological father."

"He killed Katarina to keep her quiet?"

Hunter stared at him a long moment. "Yeah. I didn't know until after I left her. I thought he paid her off to go away. It wasn't until he sent me to meet up with Potier with the money, and to get proof the job was done. I saw her." He licked at his lips. "I saw what he did to her."

"Well, that explains why Jansen won't let her meet him, but why keep her so close to him? He never told her about who he was. After Katarina was gone, he didn't come clean?"

Hunter scrunched up his lips. "That I don't get either."

Jackson leaned away from the bar. All he'd been tasked with was finding the girl who'd snuck into Ash's party, and now he found himself in the eye of the Jansen hurricane—a complete family shit show, and he was standing right in the fucking middle.

"You going to tell her all that?" Hunter took a swig of his beer.

"She needs to know Katarina is gone for good, and

if she knows how, maybe it will bring some sort of end for her," Jackson explained.

"I'll leave that up to you. She seems comfortable with you," Hunter said with a grin. "I haven't seen her like this since I've known her."

"We're not too different her and I."

"Yeah." Hunter took another swig of his beer. "I'm glad to see you're back in town, by the way."

"Thanks. I'm still not sure Ash is so thrilled with it. I get the feeling it's like looking at a ghost when I'm around."

"Maybe it is...you look just like him," Hunter said.

"Twins have that habit," Jackson said and turned toward the doorway. "Before they get back here, you haven't mentioned anything about Jaelynn's involvement with the Ash fiasco."

Hunter paused in bringing his beer to his lips. "What fiasco?" Concern flashed in his eyes.

"Nothing horrible," Jackson was quick to say. "He hasn't said anything to you?"

"I don't talk to Ash unless I have to, and since marrying Jaelynn and Serena's birth, I don't really have time for him." It was easy for Jackson to forget that they were all members of families that were long-time rivals. Sometimes they did business together, but they could cut each other's throats at a snap of a finger if needed.

"Oh. Well." Jackson smiled. "Since you gave me

some information, I'll give some to you. Keagan snuck into one of the Annex's catalogue parties to get in touch with one of the guys there that night so she could...well, so she could rob him when he wasn't looking. She was able to get inside undetected because Aubry, one of the girls there, helped her."

"Aubry," Hunter said the name with bitterness. "How is my wife involved?"

"Keagan used her to get to Aubry. I thought Ash would have called you about it for sure, he was pissed.

"I'm sure he was," Hunter said with a grin.

"You're not as upset as I thought you'd be," Jackson commented.

"Any disruption to Ashland Titon's day is fine by me. I'm just annoyed she didn't tell me about it. Ash could have taken it as an insult from Jansen."

"You know Ash wants nothing to do with the families," Jackson pointed out.

"Yeah, I know, but she shouldn't be meddling in the mess anyway."

"You might want to wipe off the grin before you talk to her about it."

"Oh, I'm not going to bring it up to her at all." Hunter laughed. "I'm going to have fun extracting her confession."

"She's finally asleep." Jaelynn entered the room with an impatient Keagan behind her. "What's so funny?" she asked Hunter.

"Keagan, I think it's time we go." Jackson slid off his barstool.

"But I still have questions." Keagan pointed to Hunter.

"Later." He hooked his hand through her arm. "We'll talk to you some other time." He inclined his head toward Hunter.

"Hunter." Keagan pulled away from him. "If you know something, you'd tell me right?"

Jackson looked over her shoulder to Hunter. The weight of her question crushed Jackson. She deserved to know; she needed to know.

"Keagan, if I could tell you something that would ease your suffering, I would," Hunter said in simple sincerity.

"Come on, Keagan, let's go home." He tugged on her arm and led her from the room.

She needed to be told.

He just needed to figure out how to tell her that her father was alive, and he'd killed the only mother she'd ever known.

25

J ackson kept the radio on the entire drive back to his house. Keagan tried to turn it down, but he'd brushed her hand away and turned it back up. She had taken the hint not to push him, but she wanted answers. No, she damn-well deserved answers.

Since she'd been swept out of the room with Hunter, Jackson had obviously found out something, and he was trying to keep it from her.

"Jackson," she said sharply as soon as he cut the engine.

"Not yet, Keagan," he said and climbed out of the car, heading straight for the house. She jumped out of the car and slammed the door before jogging after him.

"Jackson."

"One second, Keagan," he said and stalked down the hall toward the living room.

"No!" she yelled. "Goddamn it. This is exactly what I didn't want. This is exactly why I was doing this on my own."

He paused, his back still turned on her in the living room. "What?"

"Hunter told you something. He told you instead of me, and now you won't tell me," she said, heat rising in her chest. She wouldn't be played for an idiot. "This is about me. About my mother. Not you or him. But you two are being all *I'm the man* about this."

Jackson faced her, his eyes chilled. Her outburst probably wasn't the best way to go about getting what she wanted from him, but she'd been patient. She tried talking calmly in the car. She'd tried to ask Hunter her questions, but she'd been brushed off.

"I don't need the men in my life to fix things for me," she said softer, letting the tension ease from her shoulders.

"Keagan." He tilted his head. "I wanted to wait until we were home because I want to be able to talk without having to deal with driving at the same time."

She stared at him. "Oh."

"Sit." He pointed to the leather couch.

"Why?"

"Because I said to," he said, clearly exasperated with her.

Seeing as he had the information she wanted, she kept from arguing and sat down on the couch.

"It's that bad?" she asked, easing onto the cushion.

"It's...complicated."

"Complicated? Did he not know anything? At all? I mean he'd taken her there, why did he have to take her there? He had to have known something!" She started to rise again, but after a stern look from him, and she sank back down.

"Do you think you can stay calm and listen?" His eyebrows rose and he pinned her down with his serious demeanor.

"I'll listen." She folded her arms over her chest and scooted back on the couch. "But I think the question is will you tell me everything or are you going to filter out the information because you think it's not needed or that my feeble female mind can't handle it?"

He pointed a straight finger at her and stepped closer. "That's not fair. I've never treated you that way, Keagan." Hurt flashed in his eyes. The skin around his eyes crinkled as they narrowed.

She drew a long, steadying breath. He was right. He hadn't. He may have been overbearing and a down-right ass at times, but he had never treated her like she was a weak person.

"I'm sorry." She unfolded her arms and tried to relax. Jackson wasn't the enemy. He was on her side. "I just don't understand why Hunter couldn't tell me himself. This is about me, but I'm excluded."

Jackson pulled a chair closer to the couch and sat down, placing his hand on her knee. The warmth of his touch spread through her.

"He didn't exclude you on purpose. I don't think he told Jaelynn to take you from the room."

She tilted her head slightly. "He hadn't. She just wanted to ask about Aubry. She wasn't sure if Ash had gotten hold of Hunter or not. So, yeah, I don't think he had anything to do with that."

Jackson relaxed and squeezed her knee slightly.

"I will tell you everything he told me, and once I finish, we'll figure out what's next." His eyes warmed. "Together, got it?"

The crippling tension in her chest eased off. "Yeah, I got it."

"Okay," he said with a nod and unleashed every bit of information Hunter had given him.

She watched his lips moving as he went over everything that had happened. Her throat closed around the emotion bubbling up to the surface. At one point she moved her hand to her neck, searching for the collar, but it wasn't there. He hadn't given it back to her when they'd gotten home.

"He's my father?" Keagan said, dumbfounded, once Jackson finished. Again, she raised her fingers to look for the collar.

"It's a lot. I know." Jackson moved closer, his knee brushing against hers. He kept his attention focused on her, most likely searching for her reaction. But she had none. At least nothing that she could articulate.

Elliot Jansen was her father. Hunter her cousin. Katarina had taken her in because of the money. Had any of it been real?

"So I was just a job for Katarina?"

Jackson frowned. "I don't think so. When you were old enough, she wanted to tell you the truth about Jansen. That's what set him off."

"She wanted the job to be over." Keagan couldn't fight the sense of betrayal. It was everywhere. How could she ignore it?

"I don't think that's the case, Keagan."

It didn't matter. Katarina would never be able to tell her the truth.

"He had her killed so I wouldn't know I was his daughter? But then he took me in—well, pulled me in really." Keagan's mind whirled with questions.

"Hunter didn't understand that either. He said Jansen had a reason for not coming clean about being your father, but he didn't know what it was. I have a sense it has something to do with his wife's family."

"But she was dead. She died years and years ago," Keagan said. "What could a woman do to him from the grave? And why not just let me be? He didn't need to track me down in the system and put me somewhere where he could keep tabs on me. Why not just let me go?"

Jackson raised his shoulder. "That's what I want to know too. There's something more here. There's a reason behind this. He wanted you close but not too close, and that's what we need to find out."

"Then let's ask him," she said, ready to bound from the couch and march back over to Jansen's estate.

Jackson put his hand over her shoulder and kept her planted on the couch.

"We have to be careful, Keagan. You can't just barge into his house and demand answers."

Jackson made sense, her brain understood it, but the anger welling up in her chest wasn't ready to concede to the logic yet. "No. I'm done waiting. I want answers now." She tried to push off the couch again, but he shoved her back down.

"Keagan, calm down." He got to his feet and stood over her. "I'll crate your ass right now if you don't listen. I swear it."

She pinched her lips together, thinking of a million reasons to shove him aside and dart for the door. But there was one that stopped her. Jackson wouldn't let this go unresolved. He'd help her find out the answers and the full truth. She had to trust him.

"Back to the crate again, are we?" she asked, not caring that venom dripped from her words.

His grip on her shoulder tightened. "You'll be back

in the crate whenever I think you need time there." The conviction in his tone mirrored the seriousness of his glare. She'd given him this power, and if she really wanted to, she could snatch it back. She could push his arm away, and handle things in her own way, but playing how that looked in her mind didn't leave her with any victorious feelings. It left her feeling shallow and alone.

"Jackson." She sank back into the cushions. "I still want to talk to Potier."

He let her shoulder go and resumed his seat. Confusion swirled in his blue eyes. "Why?"

"He killed Katarina," she said flatly.

"You want to hurt him." He pointed a finger at her face with an arrogant lift of his chin. "And I'm not letting you near him. He'll kill you just for asking the question. No. Absolutely not. He's not the one we need. We have to get Jansen's reasoning behind all of this, and Herald Potier doesn't have those answers."

She gripped her knees. "If you won't take me to Jansen's to ask him, how do you suppose we figure that out?"

His left eyebrow arched in warning. "We'll figure it out." His phone sang from his pocket, and he took it out. "Fuck. I forgot. I have to get into the city for a meeting."

"Fine."

"Keagan." He tapped his response to the text and

dropped the phone on the couch beside her. "We will get to the bottom of everything. I promise." He paused for a beat. "Maybe you should come with me tonight. We're meeting at my cousin's club, Tower. I'll call Peter and see if Azalea will be around. You can hang with her while I have my meeting."

She shook her head. "I'm not in the mood for *hanging* with anyone."

He stared at her a long moment. "I'll see if we can meet here then."

"No." She laid her hand over his. "Don't do that. Go, have your meeting." Forcing a calmer demeanor, she continued, "I'm just going to order a pizza and probably go to bed early." She said this lightly.

If he suspected anything, he didn't show it. He tucked her hair behind her ear. "I don't want to leave you alone right now. You just found out some really heavy shit."

She smiled and leaned into his touch. "Deep down, I knew Katarina wasn't alive, but I still wanted to hope," she said, exposing herself to the truth she'd been hiding from herself. "And Jansen...well, I need time to process everything. I'll stay here. You do your business." She reached over to him and lightly tugged on his beard.

He grabbed her wrist and brought her hand up to his mouth, placing a warm kiss to her palm. The light brush of his lips over her hand cascaded warmth through her entire body.

"I'll order the pizza so it's here before I leave. Once I go, that door stays locked and closed. It doesn't open." He raised his brow. "I don't trust Jansen. He may have seemed to take the news of you turning down that job okay, but that doesn't mean he isn't pissed. He's wanted you close to him all this time, and now you're starting to take steps to get away. He's not going to take that well. Once we know why he's done all this, we'll have a better idea of what to do about it."

"Okay," she said with a short nod.

He got up from the chair, indecision still playing on his features. "What do you want on your pizza?"

"Mushrooms and onions." She gave him a warm smile.

"Okay. I have the menu in the kitchen. I'll put in the order."

"Jackson," she called over her shoulder to him when he reached the doorway.

He paused and turned back.

"Thank you," she said with all the sincerity in her heart. At first he'd been an adversary, but now he had her back. He was on her side and would fight alongside her.

If she would let him.

"No problem." He shrugged with a half-smile. Obviously, he didn't handle appreciation well. Men in his line of work probably didn't express their gratitude often.

Once he disappeared, she found her purse and dug out her phone. He would be gone in an hour or so.

I need to see you. Is eight o'clock okay? She sent the text.

A short moment later came the reply.

At the Flamingo Palace.

Jackson was right. They should have all the information before they acted.

So. She was going to get it.

26

J ackson took forever to get out of the house. Keagan watched from the master bedroom window as he drove down the long drive to the Main Street. Once his car was out of view, she checked the digital clock on his nightstand and cursed.

She wouldn't have much time, and she still needed to figure out how she was going to get into the city and down to the Flamingo Palace. In record speed, she changed out of the yoga pants and T-shirt she'd put on for Jackson's benefit and into the navy blue dress Jackson had packed for her. She'd be more comfortable in her black pant suit, but Jackson hadn't exactly thought of that when he'd tossed some of her things into a bag for her.

Her hair pulled into a bun at the back of her neck,

she swiped on a few more layers of mascara and was ready to go. Now, all she had to do was figure out how the hell to get there. She'd have to wait at least a half hour for a cab, and she didn't have that kind of time.

But first, how to get out of the house. The front door was still locked with the passcode, and he hadn't given it to her.

Well, it's good the house never got on fire!

She made her way into the garage and hit the button for the main door. To her surprise it opened immediately. A wind of hope blew through her. Jackson had three cars. She had no idea why he would need so many, especially since he always used the Dodge Challenger to drive them somewhere. But the why wasn't important right now. Right now it was the how she needed answered.

Keys.

She ran back into the kitchen. He had a junk drawer that he seemed to throw everything into. Yanking it open she started digging around. Menus for all his takeout meals, loose change, zip ties—she wondered about those for a second—but at the bottom she finally struck gold. A fob.

Fisting it, she ran down the long hall back to the garage and hit the button. The gray car beeped, and the doors unlocked.

"Thank god!" She shut the house door behind her and hurried across the garage to the car.

Once inside, she pressed the ignition button and had another minor victory as the engine roared to life. She tossed the fob into the cup holder and pulled out of the garage. There was no garage remote in the car. There was a panel outside the garage that probably closed it with the right code, which she didn't have.

Figuring Jackson would know she'd left once he was inside anyway, she decided to leave it and took off down the long drive. Thankfully, Jackson didn't live too far from the city, so she was able to find her way easily enough.

The Flamingo Palace was only half a block away from Tower, and that's where Jackson had said he'd be all night. She found a parking garage and pulled into it, hoping he wouldn't have used the same one and wouldn't see his own car sitting in the lot.

Leaving the car parked on the second level, she made her way to the stairs that would lead her into the club. Jansen had recently bought out the Flamingo Palace. What had once been a dirty corner bar had been revitalized into a trendy new night club.

Keagan breezed past Tony, the doorman, with a forced smile and wave of her hand. She'd met Jansen here numerous times, and she was recognized enough to not have to explain to them who she was there to see anymore.

The music pounded in her ears as soon as she stepped into the club's main room. Colorful lights swirled over the dancers, and Keagan remained on the edge of the room, sliding past clustered people until she made it to the stairs leading up to the VIP section.

Johnny stopped her, but once she looked at him, he nodded.

"Sorry, hon, didn't recognize you at first. It's been a while." He flashed a grin that used to make her knees weak. This time, it did nothing but ease her worry about getting up to where Jansen would be waiting for her.

"No problem, Johnny." She smiled at him then hurried up the stairs. The club's VIP section was an open floor with tables situated at the railing, over-looking the dancing and DJ stage. Larger, rounded couches were lined up along the back wall, offering a bit more privacy. And then there was Jansen's private room.

Another of his men stood outside the door, but he recognized her right away.

"Evening, Ms. Foxx." He gave a curt nod and pushed the door open for her.

"Hi, Sam." She touched his arm and entered the room. Jansen didn't know any of these men's names, she realized. He simply referred to them by their posi-tion. *The guy at the door. The one at the stairs. The front guard.*

Jackson didn't treat his men the same way. He knew all of them, took interest in them. She'd heard him on the phone the day before talking to Charlie about one of his guys in Hammelin who had just gotten engaged. Jackson had instructed Charlie to be sure they had a party planned, and he'd pick up the tab.

"Keagan." Elliot stood from his table with his arms open wide. He wore a gray smoking jacket over his blue silk button-down jacket. The top button was undone, showing off his silvery chest hair. She swallowed and forced a smile onto her lips.

"I'm glad you came to your senses," he said, stepping around the table and grasping her shoulders.

He wasn't alone. The guests he'd invited up to his private party room were either standing along the glass wall watching the dance floor or they were having their own fun on the couches.

"I didn't change my mind, Mr. Jansen." She kept her tone neutral while inside her body quaked. He'd gone to great lengths to keep his secret, and his reaction to discovering it wasn't hidden anymore could be explosive.

"Oh?" He dropped his hands from her shoulders and shoved them in his pockets. "Then what brings you here?"

"I have some questions," she hedged.

His eyes darkened.

"About what?"

"About my mother," she said, raising her chin.

Confidence. She needed to show him that she was not going to back down, and she was no longer afraid of him.

"What about her?" He grabbed a glass filled with a dark liquor from the table and downed it.

"I was able to track down the manifest for the plane she took when she left Kassel. There was something strange." She studied him for his reaction.

"Oh?"

"Yes. Hunter was on the list of passengers. In fact, he was seated with her. It's a curious coincidence." She tasted the question burning on her tongue. To come straight out and ask could set him off. Not to mention implicate Hunter in betraying his uncle.

"That is curious," he deadpanned. The times Jansen became unreadable were moments she feared the most.

"You did a good thing coming to work for me after Katarina died." He patted her cheek. "She trained you well, and you never failed me. Never gave me reason to doubt your loyalty."

Cold ran through her with his calculating glare pinning her down.

"And you could make yourself a lot more money if you kept working for me." He tilted his head to the right, like he was studying her reaction. "You're going to need money eventually, Keagan. You can't live off your nest egg forever."

He had a point, but she wasn't anywhere near ready to figure out a plan for her future.

"Why didn't you remarry?" she asked, letting the question pop out of her mouth. He unnerved her with his calmness, making her leap forward without calculating the costs of her line of questioning.

His frown deepened, and his eyes narrowed. "Why would you ask that?"

"Well, I mean, your wife passed away so long ago." Marielle Jansen was not spoken of in Elliot's presence. When she was younger, she'd thought it was because he still mourned her, but as she grew older, she'd realized the truth. Even from the grave, Marielle's family controlled Elliot. When brought face to face with that fact, Elliot would lose his temper. If she wanted the full truth from him, she'd need to maneuver around that trigger point.

"Did you love her that much?" she asked demurely as possible.

He burst into a loud shout of a laugh. "Love her that much?" He patted her cheek again. "Such a romantic you are. Let me get you a drink." He waved over a man from the small bar in the corner of the room. "White wine for Keagan here."

"Right away, sir," the bartender nodded then disappeared again.

"So why didn't you remarry?" she asked.

His lips thinned into a tight line. "One wife in a lifetime is more than enough."

Keagan took the glass of wine offered to her and thanked the bartender before turning back to Jansen.

"Did you come just to interrogate me more? What's done is done, Keagan. Your mother is gone. You have your whole life ahead of you, and if you'd let me, I could help you." He thought he was testing her in some way. Offering her a way back into his business, a way back under his rule?

She stepped closer to him, so close she could smell the lingering scent of his previous cigar still clinging to his smoking jacket. He wouldn't be baited into coming clean with her. She'd have to forge forward and brave the consequences. No matter how angry he became, she had to know the full truth. She needed to hear him tell her.

"I know, Elliot. I know you're my father, and I know you had Katarina killed to keep me from knowing it." She barely managed to keep the angry tremor from her voice. "I don't want to make a scene."

When she pulled away from him, she saw a cold rage in his eyes she'd never witnessed before. Was he panicked or just that angry that she could find out something he'd gone to great lengths to keep hidden?

"Out!" he yelled and slammed his glass onto the table. "Everyone out!" He waved his hands, and men worked quickly to herd the partygoers from the room.

Once Elliot Jansen has asked for a room to be cleared, no one stopped to ask why—they simply made their way out.

"I want to be alone with Keagan," Jansen snapped at Sam, who was standing inside the room now, blocking the door.

He glanced toward Keagan briefly, then gave a sharp nod and stepped out. No one would be coming inside now, not even if she screamed for help.

She took a sip of her wine, a lame attempt to look calm and collected. It would have worked better had her hand not trembled so damn much.

He eyed her as he returned to his seat. "So. You know." He grabbed the back of his chair, his knuckles white as he squeezed the leather.

"I do." She nodded. "And I don't care. It changes nothing for me. I want nothing from you other than help to see Herald Potier alone. After that, you'll never hear from me again."

He stared at her. The rhythm of the music being pumped into the room fell in line with her heartbeat. Or maybe it was the other way around. She couldn't tell which sense was what with him glaring at her with such heated anger.

"Do you know how much I sacrificed to keep you close? How much I risked by putting you with Katarina?" His tone dropped. "You are my only heir, Keagan.

I have no other children, because my wife, that cold bitch, wouldn't give me any."

"You have your nephews," she pointed out, trying to maintain her confidence. He was like a dog ready to attack. If she were to show weakness, show her fear, he'd be on her in an instant.

"That's not the fucking same! None of them even carry my last name." He hit the back of the chair with a fist. "I thought once Marielle had died it would be different. I'd bring you home, raise you right, bring you into the family business and you could take over the Jansen name. You'd marry, give me grandsons, it would all work out. But no. That bitch's family blocked me."

"Blocked what?" she asked, confused.

"Marielle's father owns a large chunk of Hammelin. He had solid connections here in Kassel years ago, and using those connections, I was able to build everything I have today. He's never let me forget his help, and with a few choice words, he could ruin me. He doted on his daughter like she was a fairy fucking princess. When we married, he made the stipulation that if he ever found out I had been unfaithful to her, he'd use the same connections to destroy me."

Keagan's chest ached. She was the proof Salvini could use to take back everything he'd helped Elliot build.

Slowly, she put the glass of wine down on the table

and cleared her throat. "So you wanted me only because I carried your blood in my veins and I would give you a grandson." She raised her chin a fraction. "But until Salvini dies, you can't publicly claim me."

Jansen nodded shamelessly. He didn't have a care in the world about her. It was all about his legacy, his family name, and what he wanted for his future.

"Wouldn't his sons take retribution on his behalf?" She didn't know much about the Salvini family, but Richard Salvini wasn't a man to be messed with, and his sons weren't any different.

He shook his head. "I doubt it. They never saw Marielle as the sweet innocent her father did. They won't stop me."

She blinked. He had never spoken so openly about his business dealings before. Not that she had any reservations about what he did, but he'd never been so plain about it.

"Okay." She drew a steady breath. What had she expected? A warm hun, blubbering apology for everything he'd done? This was Elliot Jansen—one of the four most powerful families in Kassel. He didn't apologize.

"Well, then this still works for us both. Set up the meeting for me, and I'll disappear. No one will ever have proof of your unfaithfulness to Marielle, and you'll get to keep your secrets."

"That's not enough, Keagan," Jansen said, a sinister gleam in his eye.

"I promise you, I don't care about any of this. I just want five minutes with Potier. That's all," she insisted louder, taking a step toward the door as he made a move toward her.

"I have sacrificed too much to just let you walk away now. I've spoiled you. Anyone who tried to leave me, tried to walk away from my employment like you did, and I would have had him shot in the head on the way out. But you. No. You, I let come and go as you please. I let you take the jobs that you want and disregard the rest. I've spoiled you, and this is what I get." He waved a hand in her direction. "Where's Jackson, by the way? Is he outside waiting for you like the Titon bitch he is?"

His snarl sent a shiver up her spine. She'd never witnessed him this angry before. Stories were spread all the time, and she believed he was capable of extreme cruelty, but she had never seen it firsthand.

"Jackson's not with me," she said and instantly chastised herself for her stupidity.

"Good then," he said. "Sam! Get in here!" he yelled.

Sam burst through the door looking for the danger. His eyes landed on Keagan, and his brow wrinkled.

"Take Keagan to the car. We'll be calling it a night early."

"No." Keagan stepped away from Sam. "I'm not going home with you." She switched her gaze from Sam to Jansen.

"Sam," Jansen said firmly and waited until Sam's gaze moved back to him. "Put her in the car."

Sam paused, but only briefly, then gave a curt nod. "Yes, sir." He reached for Keagan.

She bolted, running for the door, but this was Jansen's club. She had nowhere to go that one of his men weren't waiting to snatch her up. She barely made it out of the private room before Sam's arm wrapped around her middle and he hauled her off the floor.

"Don't fight, Keagan. I don't want to hurt you," Sam said into her ear as he carried her easily through the VIP floor to the stairs.

"Put me down, Sam. Please." She pushed at his arms. "I'll walk."

He hesitated, but then put her back on her feet. "Don't run," he warned then headed down the stairs ahead of her.

She surveyed the club as she made her way downstairs. Exits were blocked with security personnel. Maybe she could run through the kitchen and out to the alley.

As soon as her feet hit the floor, Sam's strong hand

was around her arm, and she was dragged to the side exit. She did the only thing she could think to do.

She screamed.

The music carried her voice away and squashed it before anyone could hear her.

She was out of options.

27

J ackson finished his drink and tapped the table with his fingers. He'd spent the past two hours listening to plan after plan for a new bar, a new restaurant, all sorts of new businesses along the river bank. He didn't give a flying fuck about any of them. He only wanted their assurances they'd be using his distribution line. But even the underworld had certain expectations when it came to manners, so he'd listened.

And finally, it was over. Armed with two more lines of distribution, he'd secured enough business to seal his permanent presence in Kassel.

"Well, I have to get home. The wife is going to be waiting up for me, and I still have to drop Stephania off at home." Thomas Jorsey chuckled and patted his girlfriend's knee under the table. She gave him a brilliant smile that matched the perfectly styled updo and painted-on makeup. Had he known the asshole was bringing his woman, Jackson might have pushed Keagan harder to join him.

"Not a problem," Jackson said, checking his watch. Nearly ten. Would Keagan be awake when he got home, or would he find her curled up in his bed sound asleep?

Jackson said his goodbyes, made the pleasant small talk to end the night, and watched Thomas usher his little plaything through the VIP hallway to the elevator to take him to the main level.

Exhausted, and frustrated by having to play the gentlemen for the past two hours, he sank back into his chair and reached for the bottle of bourbon sitting on the table.

"That bad?" Peter asked, his amusement doing little to lighten Jackson's mood.

"Expanding sounded better when I wasn't having to do all this fucking hand holding," Jackson said, pouring himself a drink. He'd have to hold off another one so he could head home soon. Keagan had a rough day, and he wanted to get back to her. Hell, he never should have left her to begin with, but he couldn't call off these two meetings at the last minute if he wanted to make sure the deals were finalized. Having the Titon name got him the meetings, but it was his job to see the job through.

Peter sank into the now-vacant chair across from Jackson and reached across for the bottle. A clean glass was placed before him. Jackson looked over his shoulder at the waiter standing nearby.

"They always do that?" Jackson jerked a thumb toward the man waiting patiently.

"If they want their next paycheck, yeah." Peter poured himself a drink and sat back, sipping the liquor. "It's been a long night."

"I can see that. Trouble in paradise?" Jackson teased, eyeing the glass elevator that would take his cousin up to the penthouse suite where his wife no doubt waited for him.

"Not at all. Azalea's working on a new account. She's locked herself away until she's finished the project," Peter explained, rolling his eyes.

"I thought you were all for her working?"

"I am, but I'm a greedy bastard and would much prefer having her in bed waiting for me at any given moment," Peter said with a grin as he downed the rest of his drink. "You know what I mean." He laughed.

"About what?" Jackson stretched his back. Sitting at this fucking table all night had left him stiff.

"Being a greedy bastard. I saw you with Keagan."

"I don't know what you thought you saw, but I'm just helping her with this mess about her mom." Maybe if he repeated it enough times, he could get his heart in line with his head.

Peter laughed. "Yeah. I'm pretty sure I said the same thing about Azalea. Just helping her with her mom trouble."

Jackson rolled his eyes. "We're friends."

"Friends?" Peter shook his head again. "If you ever were just that, you're not anymore, and I'm sure you know it. But you're in that denial phase. Ash went through it with Ellie, and I definitely went through it with Azalea, and now you're going through it."

"A family trait then?" Jackson asked bitterly.

"Us Titons, we're more stubborn I suppose." Peter blew out a long breath. "You get any further with the Jansen issue?"

"Ash won't like you asking."

"Don't care." Peter shrugged. "He just doesn't want to have the other families starting to knock on his door again, that's all. If it looks like he's involved with Jansen, they'll think he hasn't pulled out all the way, and they'll want to drag him back in."

"He doesn't have to worry, and by the time this mess with Jansen is over, I'm not sure I'll be working with him anymore." Jackson made a fist. "I won't be working with him anymore."

"What's happened?" Peter asked, dropping all amusement.

"We found out that Jansen ordered Katarina's killing. She was about to tell Keagan that Jansen is her biological father."

Peter put out his hand to stop him. "Wait. Her father?" He was silent for a beat. "That makes her his heir."

"I don't think she cares about that." Jackson hadn't thought about it in that context. He'd only been concerned for Keagan.

"She might not, but he will. If he didn't want her to know, there's a damn good reason. Where is she now?" Peter asked.

"She was exhausted, so she stayed home. She's safe, Peter. Jansen doesn't know she's aware of anything." Out of the corner of his sight, Jackson caught Charlie rushing from the elevators down the corridor toward him. His blood ran cold.

"What's wrong?" Jackson leapt from his chair.

"I saw her, Keagan, at the Flamingo Palace." Charlie paused to suck in a breath of air. "She was up in Jansen's private party room. I saw them through the glass."

"What the fuck is she doing there?" He clenched his teeth.

"I don't know. I was meeting with Sergio, checking out the delivery that arrived this morning, and then I saw her. By the time I got over to that side of the club, she was gone."

"Maybe she went home?" Peter interjected.

"I don't think so. Jansen came down from his room looking pissed then disappeared through the side exit.

When I went to the garage, I saw the mustang. She wasn't in it."

Jackson ripped his phone out of his pocket and hit her contact picture. The call went straight to voicemail. He hadn't received a single text message from her all night.

"I never should have fucking left her at home," Jackson growled, scrolling through his contacts for Jansen's direct number.

"Home isn't where she got in trouble," Peter said. "It sounds like she went looking for him."

"I told her to leave it until we could figure out how to approach him. She agreed. She fucking agreed!" Jackson hit the call button for Jansen and put the phone to his ear. "If that fucker puts one finger on her, just one, I'm cutting off his whole fucking hand." Jackson gripped his phone like it was going to fly away any second.

"Jackson, nice to hear from you." Jansen picked up the call on the fifth ring. "The deliveries have been going well, I hear. Sergio's happy with the product—"

"Where is she?" Jackson demanded.

A heavy sigh. "So, not a business call then? Shame," Jansen said. "She's here. With me. Safe."

"Let me talk to her." Jackson kept his tone even. Showing how distraught he was would only work in Jansen's favor and would do nothing to keep Keagan safe.

And he wanted her safe and sound so when he got her home he wouldn't have any guilt about stripping her ass bare and belting her until every inch of her ass was red.

"I think that can wait. Right now, all you need to know is she's safe and will remain that way so long as you don't get involved. I'll have her call you in the morning," Jansen said.

Heat ran through Jackson's veins, his lungs squeezed every bit of air from his chest, but he kept his outside demeanor calm. He had to. Her life could depend on it.

"The morning then. I'll come by, we can talk," Jackson offered.

"I think a call would be better."

"I'll be there, eight o'clock," Jackson pushed. "And if she's not there, or if she's hurt, well, then I'll have to get involved." Like he wasn't already. Jansen wasn't going to get away with taking Keagan.

"If you bring any of your men or your cousins with you, there will be trouble. Understand that."

"It will just be me and you. No one else needs to be involved." Peter's stare went dark at those words, but Jackson shook his head. They could argue about it later.

"Good to hear. We'll see what we can come up with in the morning. Sleep well." The call ended.

"Fuck!" Jackson roared as he stared at the screen.

"He has her and doesn't seem concerned in the least that anything will happen to him because of it."

"He wants to meet in the morning?" Peter asked.

"No. He wanted to have her call me in the morning. I insisted we meet."

"Jackson." Charlie tapped his own phone and tucked it away. "That was Ben. He said he went to the house and the garage door is wide open. No one's inside."

"She didn't know the code to close the damn door." Jackson pinched the bridge of his nose. "Why didn't she just stay the fuck home?"

Peter stepped up. "Is she the stay-home sort of girl? It didn't seem like it when I met her. She's been chasing after this information for years on her own. And from what I know of the work she did with Jansen, she's not unaccustomed to putting herself in dangerous situations."

Jackson shot a glare at Peter. Just because he was right didn't mean Jackson needed to hear it right then.

"I can't wait until morning. If he's taken her to hurt her, he's not going to wait," Jackson said.

"If he waits, it could be to lay a trap for you." Peter nodded. "I think you're right. Waiting until morning might not be a good idea."

"I'll call Ben and have him get Turner. Three of us. That's not exactly an army, but it's something," Charlie said.

Jackson sighed and ran his palm over his mouth. "If we all show up there, we could push him into hurting her."

"Let me call Ash. We'll get some men together as well. We won't all go in, but we'll be there, at the gates in case you need us."

"No, I don't want to cause Ash any more trouble with all this. It's my fault. I brought this down on us, I'll fix it." Jackson turned to Charlie. "Have Ben stay at the house and call Turner to meet us there. We'll go in the morning."

"What if he—"

"He won't." Jackson looked to Peter. "Ash isn't involved, but Jansen still won't want to piss him off by hurting someone close to me. It's a chain reaction. He hurts me, he hurts Ash, Ash hurts him. He won't touch her. He's going to use her to get something he wants. Or at least he's going to try."

"So what are you going to do?" Peter asked.

"I'm going to find out what it is he wants, and make sure I have in my possession before I see him. Then he can deal with me directly and leave her the fuck out of this."

"If she's his daughter—"

"She doesn't care about any of that." Jackson gave another order for Charlie. "I need you to do your magic. Find out exactly who his wife's father is. Hunter should know. I'm sure he's still alive and kicking. I think that's what's held him off from claiming Keagan all these years. I want a sit down with him before daybreak."

Charlie gave a curt nod. "I'm on it. I'll do that and head over to the house."

"Good." Jackson looked at the table littered with empty glasses and half-eaten appetizers. "Start me a tab?"

Peter frowned. "It's on the house. Go on. Do what you need to do. I know you don't want Ash involved, but I'm going to at least let him know what the fuck is going on."

"Fine, but that's as far as it goes." Jackson pointed to him. "I have to get going."

"Call me as soon as you know anything. If you need us, Jackson." Peter put his hand on his shoulder. "We're family. You just call. Got it?"

Jackson's chest lightened. He had back-up. He had a family.

"I got it." He darted off toward the elevators. He had a lot of information to uncover by morning and plenty of hours of worrying about Keagan to get in his way.

He never should have left her at home. She'd had a fucking shit show of a day, been dealt a stomach punch of information, and he'd just left her at home, sure she was okay to just chill while he went to work. He'd been a selfish prick.

It would be the last time. If he got her out of this fucking mess, he would never let her down again. He'd keep her protected, he'd keep her close, and he'd keep her right by his fucking side.

Forever.

But first, he had to get her back.

28

Keagan paced the bedroom she'd been thrown into the night before. How many times could a girl be kidnapped and locked away before she began to have a seriously cryptic view of the world?

Jansen hadn't said more than two words to her the entire drive back to his house. When he'd been on the phone with Jackson, he'd stared at her with a Cheshire cat grin planted on his old, wrinkly face. She'd wanted to lunge across the car at him and scratch out his eyes, but Sam was sitting next to her. Jansen sat across from them.

She twisted the rod on the blinds to open them. The sun was starting to rise. At least Jansen hadn't bothered her through the night. Not that she had been able to sleep.

Thoughts of all the horrible things Jansen could, might and probably do to her ran rampant through her mind. Trying to sleep had been a joke. She needed to be alert—just in case he didn't keep his word with Jackson and he decided to hurt her.

Why take her? If he wanted her silenced, he could have just handed her over to one of his men and made it happen. She was a nobody in Kassel. No one would even miss her. No one would call the cops to file a report. It was what made Jackson's job so easy in the beginning.

Keagan plunked down on the bed, staring through the thin slats of the blinds at the orange hue coming up over the tree line. She'd made such a mess of everything. If she'd just accepted Katarina's death and moved on, none of this would be happening.

But Katarina's death wasn't an accident. It had been a murder—a cold-blooded murder by someone who didn't even have any remorse over the matter. Jansen hadn't shown any regret or shame over what he had done. As he had relayed his sins to her, he appeared justified. As though he'd had no choice in the matter.

And all for what?

So after his father-in-law finally died, he could pass Keagan off to whatever asshole he deemed worthy of his family name, and she could give him a fucking grandson? The man was insane.

She checked the clock on the nightstand. Jackson wouldn't be arriving for another two hours. And what was he supposed to do? It wasn't like Jansen would just hand her back and ask them nicely to keep his secret quiet. He'd stolen her; Jackson wouldn't just let that slide.

The attributes she'd been so angry with, so annoyed by when he first taken her were now the very ones she counted on. Jackson wouldn't let anything happen to her. He was the only one allowed to cause her pain, and it was for her own pleasure as much as his own. If Jansen laid a finger on her, she knew deep in her heart Jackson would end him.

"Keagan." The door to the room unlocked then opened. A sheepish but still larger-than-life Sam stepped inside. The man could break her in half without exerting any effort.

"Sam." She slid off the bed and stood before him. He held a tray of food and put it down on the foot of the bed.

"I brought you something to eat." He brought his gaze up to hers. Shame rang through his expression. He worked for Jansen. Surely he'd done things worse than lock a woman up in a bedroom equipped with a warm bed and attached bathroom.

"Thanks," she said, folding her arms over her chest. "Did he say you could, or are you being a naughty boy?"

His eyes snapped up to hers. "He's expecting you downstairs after you eat." Sam didn't rise to her bait. This wasn't his doing, she knew it, but he was the one there.

"I'm not hungry," she said, eyeing the bowl of oatmeal on the tray. "What is his plan here, Sam?"

"I don't know. Honestly, I have no idea what he's up to, but I'll tell you this, I've never seen him so worried before either."

Of course Jansen was worried. She had uncovered his little secret, and if he didn't get rid of her, it could spread. But getting rid of her didn't fix the other warped problem he had. No heir. No direct heir. He seemed obsessed with having his bloodline continue.

"Is the door going to stay unlocked now or do you have to sit here and watch me eat?"

"If you're not going to eat, let's just go down." He opened the door and gestured her forward.

Still wearing her clothing from the night before, she walked down the hallway to the main staircase. Sam stepped in front of her and went down first. The house was quiet, and dead air filled the rooms as she followed behind Sam to the kitchen.

Elliot sat at the small table with a cup of coffee before him. He was already dressed in his day suit and he'd taken the time to slick back his gray hair and shave what little stubble he'd had before.

"Keagan," he said in a terse tone and waved at the empty chair. "Sit with me."

"I'd rather not." She looked around the kitchen counters. "I'd like my phone back so I can call Jackson." He'd taken her handbag when they'd arrived the night before.

"Jackson will be here soon enough. Don't worry about him." Elliot took a sip of his coffee. "You should be worrying about yourself."

"I'm not worried at all. You have two choices. You can kill me and end your line with me, or you can let me walk out of here and your bloodline survives."

Elliot chuckled while putting his cup down. "Those are my choices, are they? Letting you go and risk Richard Savini finding out you exist?

She went to the table, placed her palms firmly down on the top, and leaned over toward him. "I. Don't. Care. About. You. Or. Your. Business. I have no motive to tell anyone about our relationship. I only want one thing, and you can give that to me." She raised her chin.

"One-track mind." Elliot shook his head, mocking her with his disappointment. "I've already told you, I can't do that. It would only blow up in my face, and you'd get yourself killed."

She clenched her jaw. "Fine. Don't set up the meeting for me. Just let me go, and I'll find my own way into an introduction." She shoved off the table. "I will never tell anyone about what who you are to me. I don't care."

Hurt flashed briefly in his eyes.

"You want nothing to do with me either." His tone went dark. "Do you think you'd be sitting on all that money if it wasn't for me?"

A chill ran over her. "If it hadn't been for you, I would have led a normal life! But because of you, my mother is dead, and I've become a criminal." The full power of who she'd become since Katarina's death weighed her down.

"I don't think she wanted this for me," she whispered, tears blurring her vision. "All because of you." She flicked her fingers across her eyes. "I don't care who you are, or what you might be to me by blood, but I want nothing to do with you. And if that means you get away with everything you've done. I'm fine with that."

Elliot stared up at her from his seat, his jaw moving behind his closed lips. Maybe he was pretending to chew on her heart.

"Sir," Sam interrupted from behind Keagan. "Sorry, but it looks like Titon is here already."

Elliot's gaze swiftly moved to the clock. "He's early."

"He is," Sam agreed. "He's parked in front."

"Anyone with him?" Elliot planted his focus on Keagan.

"He seems to be alone."

"Let him in. Put him in the living room. We'll be there shortly." Elliot picked up his coffee cup and took a lengthy sip.

Keagan's heart kicked up into a gallop. What could Jackson do other than fight Jansen and his men? And if he hadn't brought anyone with him, there was little chance that would work. Sam may be the only man she'd seen so far, but that didn't mean Jansen didn't have more hiding all over the estate.

"What are you going to do?" she demanded. She couldn't let Jackson get hurt on her behalf. This wasn't his fight. It was hers.

Jansen wiped his mouth with a paper napkin and dropped it on his plate of untouched eggs and bacon. He groaned softly as he pushed himself up to his feet. In that moment he seemed feeble, too elderly to bring much fear.

But when he brought his gaze to meet hers, a terrified jolt ran through her spine.

"I'm going to kill him, and then I'm going to have you moved to one of my estates up north until I can find a suitable husband for you. Once you're married and pregnant, you can return to Kassel. And by then, Savini should finally have croaked and we can be the family we should have been all along."

He was beyond crazed. This plan—it was unbelievable. And if anyone else had laid it out for her, she would have laughed it off. But this was Elliot Jansen. He had the means and the men to do everything he just said.

If he killed Jackson, there'd be no one who cared to stop him.

And Jackson was just waiting for him in the living room.

She couldn't let it happen.

She had to save him.

29

Jansen's man, Sam, stood at the entrance to the living room with his hands folded in front of him. Jackson inspected the sterling silver picture frame on the mantel of the fireplace. Expensive frame to hold a picture of woman Jansen seemed to loathe. His late wife, in her younger years, smiled from beneath the glass of the frame.

Richard Savini might like the picture.

"Jackson!" Keagan's panicked scream came from the hallway. Jackson let go of the frame and jerked around toward the doorway.

Sam held out his hand.

"She's fine. Don't." He gave a small shake of his head. Something about the demeanor of the man gave Jackson confidence that he was right.

"How do I know she's fine if I can't see her?" Jackson took a meaningful step toward him.

"Because I promise you, he's not looking to hurt her," Sam said firmly.

Jansen popped into view a second later. Keagan, right behind him. Sam stopped her from rushing into the living room, while Jansen advanced on Jackson with his hand extended.

"Good to see you," Jansen said.

Jackson looked at the hand offered to him and slid his hands into his pockets. There would be no pleasantries or small talk.

"Keagan is coming home with me," Jackson said with finality. It was the truth. Jansen just needed a few moments to understand it.

Jansen laughed. "I don't see how that's possible given everything that's happened. No." He clapped his hands together. "She'll be going on a bit of a vacation, and you'll be...well...going to hell if your family's reputation is anything to go by."

Jackson heard the hammer of a gun cocked from behind him. There was a second entryway into the room. He'd expected more of Jansen's men to show up through there.

"Well, that might have to wait for a moment," Jackson said with a slight shrug.

"Sir!" Another of his men rushed past Sam. "Sir, Savini, is here! He's at the front door."

Jansen's face turned deep red. "Get rid of him."

"Get rid of me? I hardly think that's the way to greet your father-in-law." Richard Savini stepped into view behind Sam. Once Sam let go of Keagan, she hurried into the living room to Jackson. He kept his gaze off of her. If he saw her, saw the fear or the anger or the hurt lingering there, he'd have a harder time keeping his own anger in check.

"Richard. What are you doing here?" Jansen demanded. Apparently, his frustration at the situation outweighed his sensibility of manners for the most powerful man in Hammelin.

Richard stepped into the living room, slowly making his way toward Keagan. Jackson's body stiffened, but he kept himself from blocking her from him. An agreement had been reached, and he needed to trust in it.

Keagan held herself high while Richard looked her over. His eyes narrowed behind his thick-rimmed glasses as he inspected her features. For a man in his nineties, he showed no signs of mental decay.

"You look more like your mother, I think, but I see him in your eyes. You have the same chocolate eyes and your nose. Yes, I see it now." He turned back to Jansen, who looked more like a child waiting to speak to the principal than the head of one of the Kassel families.

"You know my mother?" Keagan asked softly, placing her hand on his arm.

He turned halfway back to her. "I did."

"I'm not sure what you're talking about—"

"Did you really think you could hide this from me, Elliot?" Richard stood straighter. He pointed a steady finger at Jansen. "Do you think I didn't know?"

Jansen's eyes went wide. "Know what?"

"Don't try to play me for a fool, you little asshole. I knew you knocked up Selena, but I couldn't find the baby afterward to have the paternity tested. And she disappeared. Probably your doing." He shoved his finger at him again.

"You have no proof of anything—"

"I will if this young lady will help me with a simple test. And once it's positive, you lose everything I ever gave you. You'll go back to being the small-time boss you were when I let you marry my daughter." He lowered his gaze. "She was right never to give you a child."

"She did it on purpose! I knew it."

"Of course she did, you idiot! She knew you were running around behind her back, but she couldn't prove it. And without the proof, I wouldn't let her walk out on you—a stupid decision on my part. But now, now I can take it all away, and you'll be the nothing you always were."

"I won't let that happen." Jansen's voice hardened.

The fear gave way to pure anger, and he gestured to the man in the corner of the room. "Do it! Him first!" He pointed at Richard.

Jackson shoved Keagan behind him, but before he could react further, a shot rang out in the room. The man in the corner crumpled to the floor.

Jackson followed the sound of the shot to Sam, still holding his gun ready to make another shot if needed.

"Sam?" Jansen asked, confused.

"Thank you, Sam," Richard stated with a nod. "If you'll just take Elliot here. We need to keep him safe while I finish my business with Keagan and Jackson."

"Of course, sir." Sam walked toward Jansen, gun still trained on him. Jansen fought back at first, but once Sam grabbed him, he settled down. If Sam was loyal to Richard, how many more of his men were as well?

"What the hell is going on?" Keagan asked from behind Jackson.

"Family bullshit," Jackson answered low enough that he was confident the old man hadn't heard.

Richard made his way over to them with a small smile.

"You've made this old man very happy," he said. "I've wanted to cut that bastard out for the longest time."

"Then why didn't you?" Keagan asked, coming out

from behind Jackson. She wouldn't stay hidden for long, Jackson knew that.

"He had the backing of several powerful families here in Kassel. If I were to go against our agreements when he married my daughter, it could cause war between the Kassel families and those in my area. No one wants that sort of war. I just needed the proof."

"And I can give that to you," Keagan said.

"Keagan," Jackson gave a warning. If she was going to manipulate this man after he just helped save them all from a gun fight, Jackson would have to intervene.

"You want something in return?"

Keagan licked her lips. "Yes. I want a meeting with Potier."

Richard looked to Jackson with a puzzled expression.

"He killed my mother—my foster mother—and I want a word with him."

"Keagan, I don't think—"

"I will see what I can do." Richard nodded. "Also, technically, you are Elliot's only direct heir, which means, once he's stripped of everything, whatever is left will be yours."

"I don't want anything from him," Keagan said firmly.

Richard Savini smiled. "I don't blame you, but still, wait until it arrives and decide before you throw it away. Jackson, thank you for taking my call last night.

I'm sure you were pre-occupied with other concerns, but I'm glad we were able to help each other with this situation." He turned to Keagan with a soft smile. "And I'm glad Elliot wasn't stupid enough to hurt you in any way."

"What is going to happen to him?" Keagan asked, looking toward the door Jansen had been manhandled out of.

"Don't worry about him." Richard looked around the room. "He must not have trusted more of his men. I expected to have at least a small army running to protect him."

"My men took care of that," Jackson explained. Charlie, Turner, and Ben rounded up enough men to quickly squash the security Jansen had at the house.

"Excellent. I'm going to get home. I haven't even had my breakfast yet, and I don't want to deal with my son-in-law on an empty stomach." He patted his stomach then filed out of the front door where Sam had dragged Jansen.

"Can we go now, too?" Keagan asked, once Savini was gone from the room.

Jackson looked over at the body on the floor. Blood pooled around him, soaking into the carpeting.

"Yeah. Charlie and Turner can clean this mess up."

"What about the other men? You said they took care of Jansen's security? What does that mean exactly?" Keagan asked as he led her to the front door.

"Don't worry." He kissed the top of her head.

"I need to find my bag. He took my phone." Keagan started to pull away to head back down the hall toward the kitchen.

Jackson wasn't letting her get away just yet. "Charlie can find it and bring it home. I want out of this fucking house."

She hesitated a moment but didn't give him any more trouble. As it was, her ass was about to be ignited when they got home. Even if she didn't realize it yet.

Charlie passed them as they made their way to Jackson's car, where Jackson waited until Keagan was settled in the passenger seat before explaining to Charlie and Turner what was to be done in the house.

"You got it," Turner said, and followed Charlie up the stairs.

"Done commanding your officers?" Keagan joked when he climbed into the car and snapped the seat-belt in place.

He sighed, picked up her hand, and kissed the inside of her wrist. Jackson inhaled her scent long enough to reassure him she was safe. She hadn't gotten hurt and that her snap decision to take on Jansen by herself hadn't gotten her killed.

But it was about to get her punished.

"You are in so much trouble, little fox," he muttered against her wrist.

"Trouble?" She had the audacity to sound surprised.

He let go of her wrist and pushed the ignition button on the car.

"So much trouble."

30

Jackson's house swarmed with men by the time they arrived home. Apparently, there was more to a family takeover than simply annihilating the family head.

"Take her up to my room and don't let her out," Jackson said to Warren, a man she'd only heard Jackson speak to over the phone.

The rugged man, with his long beard, and an eyebrow piercing over his left eye gave a hard nod. "You got it."

"Wait." Keagan dug in her heels. "You can't lock me away." She yanked on Jackson's arm when he looked ready to bolt.

He framed her face with his hands, softening her sense of abandonment with one of his warm smiles.

"I'm not locking you away. My room doesn't have a

deadbolt on the outside. That's why Warren will be standing outside the door. If you need something, you tell him. If you try to leave the room before I get up there, he'll tell me." He leaned forward and brought his mouth to her ear. "And if I were you, I wouldn't do that, little fox. Your tail is already going to be burning bright red when I can get these guys out of my house."

Her face burst with heat. Warren was a few steps away and wasn't paying attention, so there was at least some hope he hadn't overheard anything.

"Fine. But." She swallowed hard and tried to gather her thoughts, but these flittered away with his thumbs casually petting her jawline.

"But what?" he asked with a teasing tilt to his head.

"I want to know what's next."

His brow pulled forward in mock confusion. "I'm pretty sure I explained it already. When I'm done here, I'll come upstairs and give you a chance to beg your way out of what's coming to you. It won't work, but it will make me happy to listen to it."

She huffed a heavy breath but didn't bother trying to yank from his grip. Besides, she found his touch comforting. She'd spent the entire night pacing the bedroom playing all sorts of nightmarish ends through her mind. Whatever spanking he gave her was preferable to what could have happened had Jansen been able to go through with his plan.

"Can you at least tell me why—" It was bullshit.

She knew it, and he looked at her like the ice she was walking on was about to break beneath her feet. "Never mind."

"Good call." He winked. "Now, go. I doubt you slept at all last night, and your stomach growled a few times in the car. I'll have something brought up, but I expect you to get some rest." He brought his lips to her cheek and brushed them against her lightly. "You're going to need it for when I get up there, naughty fox," he whispered then pulled back.

He was impossible and would remain that way though she couldn't deny the appeal now that things were dying down. She had answers, there was some closure over what had happened to Katarina, but there was still one more thing to do, and she doubted Jackson would be on board with it.

KEAGAN WOKE in the late afternoon. After taking a long, hot shower, she'd climbed into Jackson's bed, but it had taken hours to relax enough to fall asleep.

"Finally awake." Jackson's dark tenor jolted her. She had thought she was still alone in the room. The blinds were drawn and no lights were lit.

The side lamp flickered on, and she made out his figure. He had pulled a chair to the bedside and was watching her sleep.

"How long were you staring at me like a stalker?" she teased, rubbing her eyes.

He laughed. "Only a few minutes. I didn't want to wake you."

"Well, I'm awake," she said and pushed the heavy quilt from her legs.

"Good," he said, and leather snapped sharply beside him.

She froze.

"My men are gone. Well, except for the three downstairs that are staying until we're sure Jansen's been dealt with." The chair scraped over the carpeting as he stood up.

"Jackson," she said with a forced chuckle. "I just woke up."

"I know. I was here." There was no joviality in his tone. "I'm glad you slept naked; it saves us time." He grabbed hold of her arm and pulled her from the bed.

Her feet hit the carpeting, but her legs hadn't been notified of the sudden movement, and her knees gave out.

He hauled her up to her feet.

"Jackson, wait!" She shoved at his chest, and he paused long enough to glare down at her in a way that sent a silent warning that she would be better obeying.

"Wait for what?" His tone dipped past that dangerous level that warned her ass it was about to feel the taste of his leather.

"I know you're mad that I left the house and went to meet with Jansen, but don't you think what happened is enough punishment?" She'd tried, it was pointless—she knew it was—but she had to at least try.

He leveled her with a serious glare. "No. I don't."

"Yeah, I didn't think you would," she said more to herself, but he must have heard her because his lips twitched at the ends.

"Do you have any idea how fucking worried I was? How dangerous what you did was? How easily Jansen could have hurt you? And I wasn't there to help. If Charlie hadn't seen you at the Flamingo Palace, how would I have known where you were?"

"Jackson—"

"The garage door was left open. I would have come home and thought you were taken or ran away, and how would I have found you," he continued, giving her a light shake.

"Jackson—"

"You would have been gone. Just gone!" He shook her harder.

"Jackson!" She reached up and touched the side of his face, feeling the roughness of his beard, the tension of his jaw, and she sensed everything inside him.

"What?" he demanded.

"I'm sorry." She stroked his beard. "You're right. I

was selfish and quick to act and wasn't thinking with my head. I was only thinking of what I wanted and not if it was the smart thing to do."

His jaw went slack.

"You have every reason to punish me. I won't fight you," she said, leaning up on her toes so she could brush her lips across his. The moment she touched his mouth, he grabbed both of her arms, pulled her to him, and as was his way, took over the kiss.

She curled her toes into the carpet, pressed her body against his, and wrapped her arms around him. His cock lengthened against her body through his slacks, but when he broke the kiss, the hard look was back in his eyes.

"Over the bed." He gave her a slight shove.

She sighed. Every word she had said was true. She wouldn't fight him. He needed to punish her as much as she needed to be punished.

As much as she could sense his anger, it wasn't the driving force here. He wouldn't harm her. He'd hurt her, and she'd feel it for a few days, but they would come out whole in the end.

Bending over the bed, she pushed up on her toes and presented her ass for him the way he'd told her to so many times before.

"Why do you take this punishment so easily?" He moved behind her. The buckle of the belt jangled as he readjusted his grip.

"Because I deserve it," she said, looking over her shoulder at him.

He stared at her, his mouth pressed tightly together. "You do. I don't want anything to happen to you." His voice was raw and full of emotion.

"You know, we never said this was a real thing, you and me. It's safe for me to go home now, so this might be your last chance to...uh..." She wiggled her ass at him with a grin on her lips.

His eyes darkened. "Are you trying to get a longer whipping?" he challenged with force.

She regretted her teasing immediately. Standing up again, she wrapped her arms around his neck and hugged him.

"I was only joking, Jackson."

He pushed her away from him and fisted her hair. "You're mine, Keagan. Not for now, not for a few days, but forever. Unless you tell me right now that's not what you want. And if it's not, you can get dressed and we'll forget this." He lifted the belt to eye level.

She'd meant to lighten the dark mood, but instead she'd scared him. She'd made him believe she wanted to leave.

"I'm not going anywhere," she vowed quietly.

He softened, his lips curled at the edge, and the little wrinkles formed around his eyes. It wasn't exactly a declaration of love in any traditional sense, but Jackson didn't need to say the words for her to know it, to feel it.

"Over the bed, little fox." The smile faded, and he released her.

She moved back into position and fisted the quilt in both hands. "Jackson?"

His hand laid on the small of her back. "What?"

"I love you, too," she breathed out just as the belt's first lash made contact.

EPILOGUE

"That son of a bitch!" Keagan slammed her laptop shut and barreled out of Jackson's office. Two months had passed since Richard Savini had taken down Jansen, but Keagan remained in Jackson's home. It seemed the exact place she was supposed to be.

"Jackson!" she yelled down the hall while she stomped toward the kitchen where he was no doubt heating up the last of the pasta from the night before. Since he still hadn't hired any staff, and she was tired of eating from takeout containers, she'd begun cooking for them.

"What's wrong?" Jackson turned from the microwave, holding a large bowl of spaghetti carbonara.

"You paid him!" She stabbed her finger in his direction.

His eyebrows darted up, and his lips parted in confusion. "I pay a lot of hims, Keagan. You'll have to be more specific, and lower your voice while you do it." He put down the bowl and leaned his hip against the counter.

She drew a steady breath, trying to calm the fire building in her chest. He had no right, none at all. It was bad enough she hadn't been able to get to Potier before Savini took it upon himself to settle the issue. She'd asked him to help her set up a meeting, and instead he'd taken care of it all by himself. Potier was found dead on the side of the road. He'd fallen asleep behind the wheel and crashed his car on the way home from work at his distillery. That was the official word.

Savini had purchased the company from Potier the week before, using the money he'd cleared from Jansen's accounts. Richard Savini had every reason to hate her simply for being born. She was living proof that his daughter had married a faithless bastard, but his relief at being able to ruin Jansen made him a generous man. He'd gifted her the brewery and left enough of Jansen's estate so that when he was found dead in the back alley of a whorehouse, she wouldn't have to worry about her future.

She'd been cut out of being able to get revenge for

her mother's death by a man who thought he was helping. She wouldn't allow Jackson to get away with it too.

"Ash. You paid Ash the two hundred thousand dollars I stole from Stanley McKinnley." She managed to keep her tone even, but her temper was riled enough she might lose her control again soon.

"Oh, that." He shrugged, like she'd just mentioned he forgot to take out the trash. "Yeah, I did that to keep him off your ass. You're welcome."

"Welcome?" She breathed. "I told you, I didn't want this. I don't want you to just swoop in and take care of things I can take care of on my own."

He nodded. "I know you don't."

"So why did you do that then? And not tell me?" She crossed her arms over her chest. Whatever answer he had, it wouldn't put out the flames.

"Honestly? I forgot."

The little tilt to his lips when he confessed worked a little to sway her irritation.

"You forgot?"

He shrugged. "Keagan, if it makes you feel better, pay me back. If not, then don't. I don't care about the money."

Why hadn't he held it over her head? All this time, he could have used it as a way to keep her bound to him, but he'd never mentioned it.

"I don't need you to take care of me like that," she

said, her body softening beneath his stare. He'd left his hair loose and he wore only a tank top with his jeans—even his feet were bare. The man looked even sexier when he was lounging around the house on a Sunday afternoon.

He crooked his finger at her. "Come here, my little fox. I have something else to tell you that is probably going to really piss you off, but you need to know."

She pinched her lips together, keeping her smart-ass retort to herself. As she approached him, his phone danced on the countertop. She stopped, letting him answer the call.

"Turner." He kept his stare directed at her. As the conversation went on, his eyes darkened. "No, don't do anything. Just keep an eye out. I'll come out to Hammelin next week."

Tension built in his neck while the conversation wrapped up.

"What's wrong?" she asked, some of the heat from her initial irritation waning at the concern written on his face.

"My brother has been spotted," he said, dropping his phone on the counter.

"Your brother?" Even with everything they'd gone through together, there was still so much to learn.

"I don't want to talk about him. It's nothing that can't wait for another day." He sighed. "Now, my little fox, you were yelling at me for something?"

She blinked at the sudden turn of subject. "I'm paying you back," she declared. There was no point in arguing with this man. Once he got an idea in his head, he was like a hound with a bone.

He reached out to her, grabbing her by the small ring on her collar that he still insisted she wear in the house, and pulled her forward. They were to go shopping soon for something a little less crude than leather and rings, but until then, she liked his mark around her neck.

"If it will make you happy, then go ahead, but there's something you should know, and you'll just have to get used to it."

"What?" Being pulled against his chest, she could feel the hardness of his body, the strength of him, and she already knew.

"I'll never stop taking care of you or trying to protect you. It's what you do for the ones you love."

She lost herself for a brief moment in his stare. Love. That's exactly where they were—in love.

"Fine." she gave in and rested her head against his chest. "But then you have to let me protect you and take care of you too."

He wrapped his arms around her and squeezed. "I'd be damn pissed if you didn't."

She smiled into his chest, basking in the warmth of his embrace and his love. She hadn't had peace in her life since the night she'd found out about Katarina's death, but finally, there in his arms, she could breathe easy, content—happy.

"Now, I'm going to eat my lunch, and you're going to go upstairs and get ready."

"Ready for what?" She pulled away from him. They didn't have plans to go anywhere, and he'd promised her to ban the guys from the house on Sundays. Now that he was more situated in the house and things were slowly getting back to normal, they were popping over more often.

"Our hunt." He winked.

Without hesitation, she padded out of the kitchen and toward their bedroom. He probably already had everything laid out for her and would expect full obedience.

And she would give it with all her heart.

After all, no matter how far she ran, the hound would always catch his fox.

THANK YOU FOR READING HOUND! I hope you loved meeting Jackson and Keagan! They'd love to meet all the people, so please spread the word- tell a friend about these books or leave a review!

Ever After continues with Siren.

My father demands I give up my dreams to follow the path he's set for me, but I want more.

And I won't settle.

In exchange for a small favor, my aunt helps get me started on a new path. My path. But I should have known life isn't that easy. One of my father's most trusted men catches up with me, and he's brought a friend.

I'm off limits, the boss' daughter, but that doesn't stop Bastian or Garrick. They're both overbearing, overprotective, and mouth-watering.

They don't approve of my aunt. Positive she's going to betray me, they won't let me out of their sight. And when I do manage to sneak away, they take turns showing me exactly what price I'll pay when I cross the line.

But I have to see this through. No matter the cost.

SIREN

CHAPTER ONE

A riella

Notes bounced and danced through the air, carrying Ariella away into the flow of the music. Her fingers gently skated across the piano keys. Her voice melted into the melody, and for a moment, she lost herself to it.

"You remind me of your mother when you're like this." Her father's deep voice cut through the sweetness of the song. Ariella pulled her fingers from the piano keys as though they burnt her fingertips. Her father's presence spoiled the air of the room.

"Father." She swung her legs around the piano

bench to face him. Henry Trident stood in the doorway of her music room. His hands relaxed at his sides, studying his youngest daughter, his graying hair swept back from his face, which his thick beard covered.

"Don't stop on my account." He stepped further into the room, glancing at the sheets on the music shelf. "Lord knows I've paid enough for all those lessons over the years." He forced a smile, but she'd become an expert on the degree of his grins. He was about to bring her bad news and was doing his best to lay pleasant groundwork before he dropped the bombshell.

"I was just playing around." She folded her hands in her lap and forced her own sweet smile for his benefit. The question she wanted to ask would have to wait. He had an agenda, and it was always best to let him go first when they spoke.

"Hmm." He made his way to the piano and struck a key. They remained silent as it finished its vibration.

"You're home early." Ariella closed the folder with her sheet music and brought it to the desk across the room, sliding it into the top drawer.

"My meeting finished early," he said. She'd never been able to find out exactly what her father did to earn all the money he brought home, the expensive cars, the enormous estate she enjoyed living on, but the secrecy of it told her it wasn't anything good. You don't shove good deeds into the shadows.

She closed the drawer and turned to face him, pressing herself against the desk. Her father had gifted her the music room for her sixteenth birthday six years ago after he'd had enough of hearing her practice her instruments in her bedroom. Her father had soundproofed the music room so she wouldn't disturb the rest of the household with her 'hobby'.

"I was meeting with Robert Faulkins," he said.

Warning shot fired.

"How is Mr. Faulkins?" She pressed her hands against the desk's sharp edge, letting it cut into her palms.

"He's fine." Henry's lips spread into a wide but thin grin. The small talk stretched his patience.

"Good." She nodded.

"Ariella." He took a deep breath, readying for the big drop. "While I was with him, we discussed your future."

Another warning shot, closer to the mark now.

"My future?" She couldn't stop the little laugh escape. "Shouldn't I have been there for such a discussion?"

"No, not for this sort of talk." He shook his head, completely ignoring the sarcasm in her tone. "His son, Chad, just finished his business on the east coast. He's back home now. He's Robert's middle son, so he won't be inheriting the family business unless something happens to Bradley, but he will take on a lot of responsibility. He will be an excellent–."

"No." She cut him off with a slash of her hand. "Don't say it, Father. Please, don't tell me you sat with Mr. Faulkins, discussing how his middle son would make a good husband for me. Don't tell me that." She raised her chin.

"Ariella." His voice hardens. "Chad *will* make a good husband. He will provide for you and all the children you'll have. It's a good match."

"I won't do it." She'd told him this more than once, and from the frown on his lips, he didn't care for it any more this time than in the past.

"You are already older than your sisters when they were married, Ariella." He reminded her. "All of their marriages were arranged, and they never complained. Not one word."

And they hadn't. Each of them had taken their marching orders and happily glided down the aisle to their futures.

"None of them wanted anything more than to get married and be spoiled the rest of their lives. They had no dreams, no aspirations. They aren't me, Father. I do have dreams. Big ones." She pushed away from the desk, becoming more animated with her speech.

"Dreams?" He said the word like he hated the taste of it. "What dreams? Singing? Playing these little instruments?" He waved his hand around the room at her variety of instruments.

"Yes, Father." She took several steps toward him. "That's exactly what I want to do. I want to make music. That's what I want to do. I'll get married, but not right now. Not yet." She took a breath. "Let me chase my dream first. Then I'll get married. To a man I choose. I swear it, Father, I will get married. And you won't have to support me. I can make money singing in clubs. Good money. I can get my own apartment, even. You won't have to support –"

"Enough!" He swiped a hand through the air, his thick, graying eyebrows pulled together. "My daughter, singing in clubs?"

"Concert halls, maybe." This topic needed to be dealt with gently, and she'd just steamrolled right into it.

"No." He dropped his hand to his side. "You are my daughter, and my daughters do not stand on stage at a club, or a concert hall, or anywhere else for that matter. You will marry. You will be a good wife, a loving mother, and that's final. I'm tired of this conversation with you, Ariella."

Her throat clenched. "You can't dictate my life," she said softly, trying to bring down the temperature of his anger. "I'm old enough to make my own decisions."

"You are old enough, yes." He brought his voice

down; his hands relaxed at his sides. "But you are *my* daughter, and it's my responsibility to be sure you are safe and taken care of."

"And that I don't embarrass you," she added before she could stop herself.

"Yes. That too." He raised an eyebrow. "I know you think I'm being unfair, but this is how it is in our family. My marriage to your mother was arranged, and we found love with each other. You will too."

Ariella stared at her father. Her mother had loved her children. She loved the lavish lifestyle Henry kept her in, but she did not love him. Not like a woman should love her husband. Ariella wanted more. She deserved more.

"Robert is having a coming home party for Chad this weekend. You will meet with him then. A casual meeting, so it's not so awkward." A warm smile spread across his lips. "When I met your mother for the first time, our parents made it more like a job interview. It was stuffy and awkward."

"Father, I don't want to do this." She willed him to understand, to consider her feelings on the matter. Didn't her happiness mean something to him?

His smile faded. "I know. But you will."

She pinched her lips together.

"Saturday is the party. I have a dinner meeting that I can't get out of, so I will meet you there. I'll have a car

ready for you at eight o'clock. Do not be late, Ariella."
He pointed a long finger at her.

"And if we don't get along? If he hates me?" She'd
make him despise her if it meant she could get her
father to forget this insanity.

"He won't hate you." He sighed. "How could he?
You're as beautiful as your mother and sharp as a tack.
To not love you would be idiocy."

He played this card so often while she grew up,
she'd become immune to it.

"Saturday," he said again. "And no more nonsense
about singing in a club." He stepped up to her and
pushed his forced smile back on. "You understand,
this is really for your best."

She curled her fingers into her palms until her
nails cut deep into her flesh.

"I know you want what's best for me." She could
concede that much without being a liar. But she also
knew he wanted what was best for him, maybe more so.

"Good." His smile warmed, and he patted her
cheek. "I'll let you get back to your piano. Your mother
would be so happy to see you playing it."

Ariella only smiled in response.

The door clicked closed after her father left.
Ariella let out a long breath. She went back to her
desk and opened the top drawer. Pulling out the music
sheets she'd stuffed inside, she looked at the contract

beneath it. She'd been offered a time slot at the Seaside Club on Saturday night. It had been her intention to speak to him about it. But she didn't have to, not once the conversation got started.

Taking a deep breath, she let the hot tear slip down her cheek untouched.

ALSO BY MEASHA STONE

EVER AFTER

Beast

Tower

Red

Hound

Siren

GIRLS OF THE ANNEX

Daddy Ever After

Obediently Ever After

DARK LACE SERIES

Club Dark Lace (Boxset)

Unzoned

Until Daddy

DARK ROMANCE STANDALONES

Valor

Kristoff

Dolly

Finding His Strength

Simmer

The Mob Boss' Pet

OWNED AND PROTECTED

Protecting His Pet

Protecting His Runaway

His Captive Pet

His Captive Kitten

Becoming His Pet

Training His Pet

MAFIA BRIDES (Staszek Family)

Taken By Him

Kept By Him

Captivated By Him

RELUCTANT BRIDES (Kaczmarek Family)

Unwilling Pawn

Reluctant Surrender

Veiled Treasure

INNOCENT BRIDES (Romanov Family)

Corrupted Innocence

Ruined Innocence

Ravaged Innocence

Surrendered Innocence

Savored Innocence

ABOUT THE AUTHOR

Measha Stone is a USA Today bestselling romance author with a deep love for romantic stories, specifically those involving the darker side of romance, all the possessive dominant heroes, and their feisty heroines. If you love a well-deserved happily ever after, you will enjoy her books.

https://meashastone.com

www.ingramcontent.com/pod-product-compliance
Lightning Source LLC
Chambersburg PA
CBHW051951240626
47153CB00005B/1711